Your Promise

◆

Camille Laurens

Translated from the French by
Adriana Hunter

Other Press | New York

Originally published in French as *Ta promesse* in 2025
by Éditions Gallimard, Paris
Copyright © Éditions Gallimard, 2025
English translation copyright © Other Press, 2026

Production editor: Yvonne E. Cárdenas
Text designer: Patrice Sheridan
This book was set in Adobe Garamond and Didot by
Alpha Design & Composition of Pittsfield, NH

Song lyrics on page 108 from "L'été indien" by Joe Dassin, written by Toto Cutugno, Vito Pallavicini, Pasquale Losito, and Sam Ward, 1975. Lyrics on pages 156 and 374 from "Mon légionnaire" by Édith Piaf, 1937. Lyrics on page 196 from "Ti amo" by Umberto Tozzi and Giancarlo Bigazzi, 1977. Lyrics on page 385 from "Tu t'en vas" by Alain Barrière and Noëlle Cordier, 1976.

1 3 5 7 9 10 8 6 4 2

All rights reserved. No part of this publication may be reproduced or transmitted in any form or by any means, electronic or mechanical, including photocopying, recording, or by any information storage and retrieval system, without written permission from Other Press LLC, except in the case of brief quotations in reviews for inclusion in a magazine, newspaper, or broadcast.
Printed in the United States of America on acid-free paper. For information write to Other Press LLC, 267 Fifth Avenue, 6th Floor, New York, NY 10016. Or visit our Web site: www.otherpress.com.

Library of Congress Cataloging-in-Publication Data
Names: Laurens, Camille author | Hunter, Adriana translator
Title: Your promise : a novel / Camille Laurens ; translated from the French by Adriana Hunter.
Other titles: Ta promesse. English
Description: New York : Other Press, 2026. | "Originally published in French as Ta promesse in 2025 by Éditions Gallimard, Paris"—Title page verso.
Identifiers: LCCN 2025042679 (print) | LCCN 2025042680 (ebook) | ISBN 9781635425734 paperback | ISBN 9781635425741 ebook
Subjects: LCGFT: Fiction | Novels
Classification: LCC PQ2672.A78365 T3713 2026 (print) | LCC PQ2672.A78365 (ebook)
LC record available at https://lccn.loc.gov/2025042679
LC ebook record available at https://lccn.loc.gov/2025042680

Publisher's Note
This is a work of fiction. Names, characters, places, and incidents either are the product of the author's imagination or are used fictitiously, and any resemblance to actual persons, living or dead, events, or locales is entirely coincidental.

Your Promise

Also by Camille Laurens

Girl

Little Dancer Aged Fourteen

Who You Think I Am

In His Arms

An artist needs to be ruthless, but a woman wants to be desired. Each woman artist needs to resolve this conflict in her own way.

—RACHEL CUSK

Prologue

◆

As soon as the car had driven off along the road, I headed back toward the house. Hugging the walls, I walked around the facade where the real estate agents had attached their FOR RENT sign, which was already starting to crack. I wanted to take it down but, out of superstition, I didn't. We'd been happy here once, could we be again? More accurately, I *thought* we'd been happy but had no recollection of it. My brain seemed to be emptied of any reality, and all that remained was a single word, the word *happiness*, which could just as easily have applied to the last two days alone.

The key that opened the back door to the kitchen, on the side with the Japanese garden, was in its usual place under the third stone. Japanese garden is generous: a square of bare earth with some scrawny bamboo and a pathway of six flat stones. Even though it doesn't get much light, it could possibly have been made into a vegetable patch—I'd had the same idea on our first visit five years earlier, but the beautiful trees and flowers on the south side of the house had made me forget it. For now, everything was dry.

I opened the shutter that I'd deliberately left unhooked when we'd closed all the exits ten minutes earlier, and then unlocked the door. Moving through the half-light, I went straight to the small writing desk in the hall, the one that his mother, who'd given it to him, called a bonheur du jour, a "happiness of the day," and whose open lid was a useful spot for keys and loose change. I'd always thought the four drawers were a trompe l'oeil—however hard anyone tugged at the gilded handles, they never opened—but earlier I'd spotted Gilles in the mirror taking something from one of them. Reflected in the mirror where I was checking that my eyebrows weren't unruly, it looked like a blister pack of medication, and he'd surreptitiously popped out a pill and swallowed it. It was mortifying to have lived in this house for years without knowing the secret to this piece of furniture; I was intrigued by it but not as much as I was by the secret within the secret. Was he hiding some illness from me? It took me a good three minutes to understand the mechanism, you really had to know it, the spring was very well hidden. Sure enough, inside there were two blister packs of capsules, but their names didn't mean anything to me, I would google it; and a piece of paper folded in four, a typed business document on letterhead that I opened, relieved that it wasn't a prescription or a love letter. I went over to the shaft of yellow light coming from the skylight. It was then that I heard someone open the gate and a car, *the* car, drove into the garage. I turned my attention back to the piece of paper. That's how it all started. And finished. It ended there, the story did. You know what happened after that. For those who attach importance to words, escritoire would have been far more appropriate than bonheur du jour. But it's not always possible to keep a secret, or to be happy for a day, it seems.

◆

It felt good writing the last page, well, one of the last pages, the beginning of the end, when Claire, my narrator, finds *proof*, by which I mean a fact that isn't open to any possible interpretation, a monolithic fact that is new but irrefutable, labeled, dated, a raw fact unacquainted with any subjectivity. This discovery brings to a close the fraught investigation to which I've subjected her life for several months, circling around crumbs, memories, testimonies, and contradictory hypotheses, without really finding either substance or meaning, still less certainty. The book needs to end like a crime novel: with the truth. Because there is a truth, with apologies to harbingers of nuance, champions of ambivalence, and adherents of universal fiction. At any given point in the full scope of a life, something is true or false, fact or fable. It might last only a moment, but it's a moment of truth. We drag our heels, approach it reluctantly, procrastinate. We don't want the truth, we want some peace. No, not peace. Peace of mind. The truth is an adventure, when what we want is just a quiet life, at any price. But a novel shouldn't sacrifice the truth, whatever that truth may be. If you're not writing to find it, then don't write. And if you don't read to get closer to it, what's the point? That's why I always start by writing the end. To give me the strength to tread the book's path. To be sure I'll go the distance and not be spineless. I will write this book because I've already finished it. I've gotten to the end of it. That's what I tell myself. I've gotten to the end of the illusion, even if it's an illusion in itself to believe I've achieved that. After all, it's the journey that counts. Never been dazzled by the truth at the end? Oh, I'd settle for a ray of light. I also have a glimpse of how to embark on the narrative, with this epigraph from Heraclitus (I don't deny myself anything): "Whoever searches for truth must be prepared for the unexpected, for it is difficult to find and, once found, disconcerting." But then, that adjective isn't right. Disconcerting? The truth? It's monstrous. It's murderous. Why wouldn't happiness want to protect itself from that? We're so much happier because of the things we *don't* know than those we do.

I need to return to the beginning now. Perhaps in everything that begins, its own end can be found, besides it's always there already. That's true of plenty of stories if you think about it. With this novel, it's a little different. I wrote the end because I couldn't get started. Not at all. Complete block, and I know why. It's because at the point where this book begins,

I'm breaking a promise. When I made the promise, ridiculously, I was convinced I would keep it. Well, I don't know about "ridiculously." When we make a promise, isn't believing in it a bare minimum? On that day seven years ago, we joked about whether someone was released from their word of honor if and when the other person went back on theirs. I maintained that they were: It was like a contract, a marriage, a tenancy agreement, one person's breach canceled out the other person's commitment. He disagreed, saying we make the commitment to ourselves—"A promise is a promise."

Let's call him Gilles. It's the first name I give my father in most of my novels but too bad, or maybe that's a good thing, people can read into it what they want in years to come—it's almost certainly not a coincidence, as my therapist used to say. Neither he nor my father is called Gilles in real life, as I'm sure you realize. Unless real life is what happens in books, and there are those who say it is. My own name isn't Claire, we're living in an imaginary world. What matters for now is that I like the sound of it, of Gilles, it gives us a sort of feminine plural version of the masculine singular pronoun *il*, coupled with that soft *g*, like the first person singular *je*; boy, girl, a hodgepodge of genders and people in just one syllable, even if what I'm really trying to do by rebaptizing him—and it's a feeble ruse—is to fraudulently keep my promise intact. As for my narrator's name and its hints at clarity, that's out of irony: The fog in which she's drowning is her own inner landscape, Claire is anything but clear. And yet, I'm searching for clarity through her. It's up to her to shed some light.

I

◆

1

It was Gilles, then, who initiated the solemn turn that our dinner by the sea suddenly took. It was summer, the sun was all pinky blues, very low on the horizon—did you know that when you see it that low, the sun has actually already set? What you see is just its reflection. The candles flickered over weighted-down white tablecloths, erasing any ugly marks—by the light of a flame, the whole world is beautiful. People were getting up to go choose their fish, tanned women in chiffon dresses, children tired of waiting or clinging to their mothers. Other kids ran about on the sand. Russian was being spoken nearby, I picked up a few words when they raised their voices. Gilles was wearing a midnight blue shirt that he'd picked to please me, I'd seen him checking himself out in the mirror before we left. I'd never known a man who paid such close attention to charming me (my husband, maybe, in the early days), and oh, how attractive I found him, plus he looked as if he knew perfectly well. That smile, for goodness' sake. We're not young but I'd like us to be pictured young, age would be a mistake here. We'd known each other for six months, and ahead of us lay eternity. The sea was mimicking love. The graveyard that it was—we'd read about this fact again in the paper that same morning—the hopes of a different life, and people set sail, and there are shipwrecks and everything, but even though we knew this, we didn't think about it. I was wearing the bracelet he'd bought me the previous day when we'd strolled around Juan-les-Pins, I had my elbows on the table and was turning it around between my fingers—it's golden with green stones. When I was a child, Juan-les-Pins was the town that my mother walked around with her lover while I was with my grandparents, and then they would go to Antibes to listen to jazz. In photos she has a huge beehive piled on her head and he has a bow tie, there's an upturned bottle in the champagne bucket, I wonder where my father was when this was going on.

The sea bass in a salt crust was very good, we weren't sure about having a dessert, and then thought yes. We looked into each other's eyes, or watched the sea, we loved and were loved. To our left, at the top of the steps down to the beach, stood a mimosa, a very young evergreen in its granite pot, with the yellow pompoms to justify its presence. We'd made love in the afternoon after swimming out far beyond the buoys and a dead-to-the-world siesta, and late that night we'd make love again, we'd be reunited in the dark. His cock in my hands, there was a precision to it, I thought about it—how dense and hard and soft it was—a scepter. He'd given it to me like someone giving their word, he wouldn't take it back. I was the queen.

"My love. What if," he wraps my hand gently in his, "what if we made each other a promise?"

"A promise? Oh, my lord..." I laugh. The ice cream has melted on the plate, we're no longer hungry. "Okay, then, go on. What do you want to promise me? Or rather, no, sorry: What do you want me to promise you?" "No, you first." "Wait, no, it was your idea! And anyway, I need time to think. *I* don't have a ready-prepared request for a vow. Whereas you look like you already know." "Yes, that's true," he says. "Well, go ahead then, I'm all ears."

He looks at me. The seaweed-green depths of his eyes.

"Promise you won't be angry?" "Is that the promise?" I laugh. "No." "So?"

He takes a deep breath.

"I'd like you to promise you'll never write about me."

◆

"I can tell you why I promised, Mrs. Niepce," I say to my attorney. "Yes, of course, I can tell you just as I told him. To my mind, it would be easy to keep the promise, very easy. Why? Because with happy people there's no story, that's why. A novel about him and me? What the heck would it have to say? The candles on tables, the blue sea, the bracelet? Seriously? Readers would lose interest after two pages. Even if I rewound to when we met, when he wasn't yet free, there was no grist for the mill. Happiness in books bores everyone, starting with me. I mean, can you think of a single book in which nothing happens except happiness? There isn't one. Happiness isn't a subject, unless it's threatened. No tension, no suspense, zero conflict? Zilch interest. People don't write about happiness. You have to write black on white, otherwise there's nothing to see. The only subject for literature is sadness. Or passion, which amounts to the same thing after a while. And from the very first day, I genuinely couldn't see how this man, this wonderful man, could ever make me suffer. The obviousness of a happy relationship—how do you write about that?"

◆

"Because I," he added, given that I hadn't replied, "I want to be in your life, not in your books."

I still said nothing. You're much better in my life, I thought to myself. What would you be doing in my books? He can't have read them all, I thought, otherwise he'd know. He'd know that love goes wrong in my books. That each book is a coffin where I bury the corpse of a relationship. That they're the chapters of an executor's inventory. Or of course, it could be precisely because he does know this, he *has* read them, and this is his way of asking for us to love each other forever, for our relationship not to end up in a book. For our relationship not to end. His way, being a reserved sort of man. I pictured a procession of the heroes from my novels, they were so unlike him. Day and night. Borderline characters, macho men, bad boys, narcissists, losers. "Love's Tomb," the press headlines often ran about my books, referencing the title of my first novel. "Passion is a labyrinth, and Claire Lancel takes pleasure in losing us in it," wrote another. "Destination Worst-Case Scenario," ran the title of one article. I'd come to be seen by my detractors as a man-hater, perhaps a perennially disappointed Bovary. "We get the relationships we deserve," one critic had even concluded. Others wondered to what extent I sabotaged my real-life relationships in order to have material for a novel—strange that people think writers don't want their lives to work. But with Gilles all that was behind me, I just knew it. At last, I wasn't taking the wrong turn. I welcomed this innocence. Honored my good luck to have met him. I wouldn't make him step over the frontier that separates the man from the character. I wouldn't nail him to the four planks of a novel, I'd keep him warm and alive in my arms, I would always sleep with him, we would stay on this side of life, he would never be put in the box.

"I promise I won't," I said.

My love, I thought. My sweet, my tender, my wonderful love.

2

"Family name, first name, age, and occupation?"

"My name's Émilie Cointre. I'm forty-five years old, married with no children. I trained as a psychosociologist and I work on developing artificial intelligence at the National Center for Scientific Research.

"I met Claire a few years ago, kind of by chance... It must have been in 2007. She had a project, a novel about robots. It was unexpected coming from her: Even though I hadn't read anything of hers at the time, I knew she mostly wrote about love. I remember she'd watched a program about sex dolls and it had made quite an impression. The footage showed the dolls being manufactured and assembled to meet customers' instructions; dozens of different faces, brunettes, blondes, redheads, Asians, Arabs, white, Black, smooth hair, curly, frizzy, short, long, dozens of pairs of breasts and buttocks in all shapes and sizes, apple-shaped, pear-shaped, spherical, teardrop, all hanging from wires in the workshop, it looked like Bluebeard's den, that was the first thing she noticed.

"She was fascinated by what the customers asked for, by the fact that they had the option to put different heads on the same body, or vice versa, depending on their fantasies. She particularly wanted to know what the dolls were made to say, what buyers ordered more frequently: Ones that talked or ones that sang, ones that cried? It wasn't really my area of expertise, but she'd been put in touch with me by a mutual friend. I made some inquiries and told her everything about the interactive dolls, then we saw each other again and became friends.

"It might seem surprising, but in order of preference, first they say, 'I love you.' Then 'I want you.' 'Take me.' 'Make me come.' 'You're hot.' And sometimes 'Daddy,' I have to admit, they ask for that quite a lot.

"At the time, Claire was still with her husband, Julien, but they were in the process of separating. He was a real womanizer, that guy, a pathological seducer, I got to experience it firsthand, she couldn't take it anymore. After that she drifted around a bit, in her relationships I mean, but she worked a lot, that was also when she made her first podcasts, and she had her daughter, Alice, to look after. She was... sad, yes, sometimes, but I wouldn't say depressed. She's never taken an antidepressant in her life, I don't think, at least not since I've known her, even though she could have: She's had plenty of tough times. But she's got something, it's not joie de vivre, no, because she has deep reserves of melancholy, it's more like a vital energy, stoicism—I don't like the word *resilience*. That's it: Claire's very stoic.

"When she introduced me to Gilles, I couldn't help remembering how she and I had met: She'd come to me about robots, which didn't end up in her books, and here she was in love with a guy who specialized in puppets! Gilles Fabian is well-known for his expertise in the field, several of his productions introduce puppets, dolls, or automatons. I thought there must be something niggling her there: mechanical or repetitive behaviors, role-played emotions, manipulation—after all, that stuff's pretty close to the subjects she explores. But I didn't say that to her, or not at the time—I try not to play the therapist too much with my friends, I don't dissect their subconscious, particularly as Claire was seeing someone, if I remember this right, she'd been in therapy since her son had died. One thing's for sure: When she met Gilles, happiness came back into her life, and probably from a long way away. Are you familiar with Spinoza's definition: 'Love is a feeling of joy accompanied by an external cause.' Well, Claire had found her external cause. Yes, that's a statement: It was so obvious! She was transformed, her feet literally didn't touch the ground.

"That must have been right at the start of 2014. A real thunderbolt, from what she told me."

◆

I decide to pick up when I see that it's Carole, but it's 9:15 p.m. and the Franprix grocery store closes at 9:30. "What are you doing, Claire?" she asks, "I'm waiting for you." I tell her I'm out in the street, just getting something to eat. To be honest, I don't really want to go, I won't know anyone, I wasn't even invited, I don't like being a hanger-on. "A hanger-on, what the hell are you talking about? They said it again just now, I can bring whomever I want. Listen, it's New Year's Eve, not some intellectual dinner! And they'd be honored to have you there." I go into Franprix. Bunches of mistletoe and holly hang from the shelves here and there. No one's kissing under them. Honored, what a load of… "No, Carole, seriously." "Anyway, you're not going to be on your own for New Year's Eve, there's no way." "It wouldn't be the first time," I say (*it will be the third, the third year*). "And I'm not dressed up, you should see me, I'm in boots and a turtleneck…" "No one gives a damn! Come as you are." I don't reply, I'm looking for something nice to eat, there isn't much, the shelves are a wasteland. "'Come as you are' is a McDonald's commercial. I'm going to buy something nice at Franprix and watch something trashy on TV, that's my secret plan for transitioning to 2014." "You don't have to be like everyone else," Carole persists, and I laugh. Carole's the exact opposite of my mother. But I still lie to her. "Oh, okay, give me the address, I'll go home to change and then meet you there." "No. You won't do it. I know you. Don't go home, come now. We're gonna dance! I already bought two bottles of bubbles, you can give them one of them. I'm at République station right at the end of the platform on line 5, headed toward Place d'Italie. I'm waiting for you." And she hangs up.

She's there
It's a private party
let's say it's December 31st
She's not wearing the right dress
she wasn't planning on coming
She's in boots and a turtleneck
with a wool skirt
The others are in sequins
black bodycon
gold sandals.

She's not expecting him.
That's something she believes in
not expecting this other person
She thinks there's
nothing anyone can do
to make themselves be loved
Which is both calming and sad
There's nothing anyone can do
of course
no dress to choose

But by the same token there's
nothing
that could be done
no miracle dress.

She wasn't meant to be there
A friend had said
Come
And she came
She'd have stayed home alone
in her apartment
opposite Père Lachaise Cemetery
She's fine with that
She likes the tombs
in daytime
Sometimes there's snow on them
and she can even see it at night.

She'd have stayed home
alone
She'd have drunk some sauternes
done that at least
for sure
or some Frontignan
her grandmother's favorite wine
back in the day
in memory
of who knows what
But there it is
the last day of the year

That's something to celebrate
with other people
She likes other people but one at a time
She's never liked other people all together
She often gets scared
But then this friend said
Come
and here she is.

She saw him first
Other guests
who arrive with him
coming through the door rowdily
He turns his head
He's seen her
he smiles at her
He smiles at her
Really at her alone?
But then there are several of her
there are three or four people
in her
One who holds back and waits to see
(she remembers he has a wife,
someone told her that once)
One who wishes
she were wearing her backless dress
even though she's facing him
One who's already lost
and wants to run away
One (and it's the same one)

who'll do everything
even if there's nothing that can be done,
everything
to be the sole object
of
that smile.

"That's Gilles Fabian," Carole tells me. "The theater director. I interviewed him last year for the *Review of Living Arts*. He's gorgeous, right? Such a smile... Shame he's not free, I'd happily make him my four o'clock. And faithful too, apparently."

He's caught up in a group near the door, he eyes me from a distance, surprised. I return his smile. Living arts, what a strange expression. Are the rest of us dead, then? I don't have time to tell Carole that we've already met, he's coming over. Carole introduces us, he says it's a pleasure, I agree, and he knows the novelist, of course. So now we have a secret. He asks me if I'm working on a book at the moment, he can't wait. "I recently visited George Sand's house," I say. "Did you know she had a small theater built there for her son?" (Even such a simple question is freighted with complexity: I said *vous*, but maybe it should have been *tu*?) Carole slips away. Yes, he knows (*of course he does, come on*), and let's switch to *tu*, yes, I'd be delighted to. "Are you a friend of Nathalie and Christian?" he asks. "No, I don't know them," I say, laughing. "Isn't it obvious that I wasn't invited?" I gesture to my wool skirt. He studies me earnestly. "You look stunning," he says.

Someone tugs at his arm, he walks away with an apologetic smile. Every time I look for him over the course of the evening, our eyes meet. He's extremely attractive. I don't remember that, not to such an extent. The light in his eyes. Gray-green river waters in sunlight. I wonder where his wife is. Shortly before midnight, he comes back and takes me to one side (*he's like me, he doesn't like crowds*), refills my glass, offers to share his helping of cake, and asks how my daughter is (*he remembers I have a daughter*), Alice, yes, that's right. We talk about our children briefly, it's tough being twenty. He asks which neighborhood I live in. "Ah, Père Lachaise!" he exclaims. "It's you and me, Paris!" And, because I must be looking perplexed, "Rastignac, he says, he issues his challenge to Paris from the heights at Père Lachaise." Someone embarks on a vigorous countdown and we smile, six, five, four, three, two, one, Happy New Year! We kiss. "I wanted to be the first to kiss you," he says, inadvertently slipping back into the formal *vous* and then correcting himself. Other people join us, everyone kisses and hugs, Happy New Year, Happy New Year, Happy New Year, Happy New Year, Happy New Year, Happy New Year. I walk away to reply to a message from Alice then pretend to have other messages, leaning against the wall and typing on my lifeless phone.

At about 3:00 a.m., Carole calls a cab. Gilles leaves with us, no he doesn't want to share our cab, he lives very nearby. Where does he live? I'd like to know, and plenty of other things, but I don't dare ask (*worst-case scenario, I have his email*). He kisses Carole just before she steps into the car, then me. "What's your 06?" he whispers this euphemistic request for my cell number in my ear with a hint of parody. "Actually, it's an 07," I reply with the same irony. I give him my number. "Would you like me to write it down?" He smiles. "I won't forget it, believe me." I flush red in the black of night, and heat fills my stomach in the icy cold. "We mustn't wait too long before seeing each other again," he adds, moving away. "No," I say, "we mustn't wait." (*He suddenly kisses me full on the mouth, bringing his hands to my temples, our teeth clunk together, then we run to his place and almost before we're inside—it's just around the corner—we fuck frantically up against a wall.*) At that exact same moment, in the early hours of January 1, 2014, I hurry into the back of a cab. Carole and I sit in silence. "Do you know Gilles's wife?" I ask after a while. "Yes," she says, "I saw them together once." "What's she like?" "She's stunning."

She does know him
though
hold fire
she's already seen him several times

It's not like she's suddenly presented
ta-da
with his teeth
on New Year's Eve
She's already met him
One time she saw him
in three-quarter profile
at the gala dinner
for some festival
in the distance
at a different table
She thought he was so
so very
that she'd rather
not be introduced
He smiled a lot
(well, there's a surprise)
so seductive
or perhaps so
much the seducer
She felt it in her chest
the beginnings of distress
She'd rather not know.

Another time
at the end of a reading she was giving
in Lille
he emerged
from the audience
and came toward her

very fast
in a hurry
As if he wanted
to get ahead of the others
"I almost cried"
he said
And she thought that, close up,
he's sensitive
and what a smile
even after
nearly crying.

That evening in Lille
She'd read from Tristan
the book
with the same name as
the child that she now has
in memory alone
She'd cited
Hélène Cixous
Two sentences
She'll never forget
"One day I lost a son. I lost him in a hyperlosing
kind of way."
It's so obvious now
this word that she invented
this word that was missing
Sometimes there aren't the right words
for things
or people

The ones
who nearly cried
for example
come to think of it
what is their failure?
Is it
that they didn't cry
or they didn't have the tears?

The next day
he'd invited her to dinner
alone
She didn't want him to find her attractive
Yes she did. She wanted him to find her attractive
but
she didn't want
to want him to find her attractive
She'd spent ages
trying on dresses
in the mirror
in the small hotel room
overlooking the city's main square
Then in the end
she'd thrown on any old thing
and spent the whole evening
talking to him
like some
regimental buddy
and she'd insisted
on paying her way

On his neck
he had
a red mark
it was
mouth-shaped.

By the door to her room
key in hand
she'd lingered
for a moment
(he had the room next door)
then she'd said
Good night
Maybe also
she remembered
that earlier
when he was waiting for her
in the lobby
she'd spotted him sitting
on a booth seat
hunched sad
a poor guy
vacant
aimless
He'd sat up with a start
when he saw her
friendly
as if he'd put a mask back on
and she
well she'd just said good evening

because what she wanted
was a bare
face
a happy
body
She went into
her hotel room
alone
and she remembered
that she'd once
written these words to another man
"There's no one and it's you."

On the afternoon of January 1st, I had a text from Gilles. The year's started like a dream, he said. He hoped we'd see each other again. Alice would be with me until the end of her vacation and I was concerned about how sad she seemed—even though she'd predicted in a Pythian voice that 2014 would be the year of big love after asking who my text was from (and why I had such a dumbass smile, although she'd tried to not say the latter out loud)—so I suggested Gilles and I meet for a drink after she left on the 6th, at my place if he didn't mind, at about six in the evening. He arrived on time, he brought flowers, I don't remember what color they were, not red, though, maybe not roses, but flowers all the same—feelings, I thought. Or manners. I offered him a glass of wine, he sat down while I looked for a vase. "Your place is very pretty," he said. "This yellow's cheerful." I put the flowers on the coffee table. When I joined him on the sofa, he took my hand carefully as if it were something fragile, and he seemed absorbed in studying my fingers for a moment. "We've been hovering around each other for a while already," he said. "Yes," I replied, "you mean in Lille?" "Yes, in Lille. Why did nothing happen?" "We could have saved time," I said, then regretted it: How coarse was I? "I didn't think you liked me." He stroked the back of my hand, keeping his eyes on mine. "You have eyes like a cat," he murmured. "My father had just died and I had a lot of issues with Alice's dad. Actually I wanted to apologize, I talked about myself too much that evening, about my problems."

I glided my hand over the bouquet. I remembered that he hadn't said much, in Lille, he'd listened to me. "Don't apologize," he said, "I liked that you confided in me."

Why doesn't he kiss me right now? Touch is worth so much more than words, my longing and the passing time are constantly at loggerheads—will I never change? Are you all familiar with the vice of wasted time, that feeling that everything plays out now, instantly, that there's nothing less reliable than tomorrow? It's often led me to make the first step, sometimes to take risks, to hustle time along. But not on this occasion. I let a sense of sincerity accumulate in me. A man who wants to talk before doing anything, what a novelty! No more two-bit fantasies, or the allegedly irrepressible impatience of desire. Accepting a tentative, unarmed meeting. Not reverting to farce. Or maybe it's full-on shyness. It's make or break, too bad: Telling the truth. Or nearly.

"I know you're with someone, Gilles. And I'm not interested (*okay, whatever*). I've worn that T-shirt a lot. I spent twenty years married to a man who never stopped cheating on me. We eventually divorced but our relationship's still very confrontational, we were still in court not that long ago. Then I explored the other side of married life, if I can put it like that, and I pretty much had nothing but affairs (*'affairs'? What the hell am I saying?*), relationships with married men, or at least they weren't free. I don't want that anymore. I'd rather not start anything, honestly. I'm done with being the fifth wheel on someone else's carriage, I want to be the carriage (*and for it to go places!*)."

We both smiled. He squeezed my hand.

"Right now, I've been alone for six months and that suits me (*three years, it'll be three years next month*). Before, my relationships were quite long but they ended pretty badly, except for the last one, which was short (*very*) and casual (*very, very*). And in answer to your question, yes, I did like you, in Lille, I like you now (*it's outrageous how much I like you*). But I don't want some one-shot wonder or a secret relationship. I'm not interested in that anymore. Actually, I've never been interested in that (*okay, whatever*)." "Really?" he asked with a hint of a smile. "But in your last book..." (*"Your last book"... "your last lover." That word* last *really hits a nerve, hiding another meaning, death lurking inside it.*) "Oh!"

I withdrew my hand with a show of annoyance. "It's a book! And not the last, I hope. Surely, I don't need to tell you about the difference between a narrator and an author!" "I know," he said gently, taking my hand again. "I'm joking. And I loved your book. You're a great writer."

I didn't pick up on this. (*I'm not looking for a reader. I'd rather have someone who can read what's in my eyes.*)

"I'm not interested in that either," he went on. "At least not with you. If I'm honest, I thought about coming back to knock on your door in Lille. But you didn't send me enough signals. And mostly because I wanted things with you to be different." "With the two of us, different means: nothing. It means: impossible." "Why?" "Because I want a man who's free. Free in what he does and says, free with his time. Free, basically! I'm not looking to settle down or get married, once was enough, or even to live with someone, I like being on my own, I write, I need it. But I want to be able to call whenever I feel like it (*without picturing you skulking in the bathroom*), go to exhibitions, the movies, for vacations, spend whole nights together...And most of all, I'm through with lying, I want, I don't know...to feel I can trust someone."

"Go-to-ex-hi-bi-tions," he murmured sweetly, as if trying to memorize the schedule. "Trust-some-one."

She's there
Blah-blah-blah
She says what she wants
as if making
a shopping list
She checks the boxes
that need filling out
Signed, sealed, and delivering herself up
Wouldn't it make
more sense
to say
what she doesn't want?
But then
she remembers
one time
the man who was with her
telling his wife
he had a file to wrap up
he'd be home late
Don't wait up
he said
And the wink
he gave her
humiliated her
the way he didn't know he was doing it
Sometimes
a lover's wife became

a sister
She was on her side
united in the humiliation
of deceit.
One evening when they were having dinner
in a restaurant
another one
had called his wife
who was abroad at the time
The wife had asked him
Where are you?
Why aren't you calling from home?
It'll cost you an arm and a leg
it's not in your contract
Call me from the landline
when you're home
And he'd fled
leaving his shrimp
on the plate.

Then the last one
the last time
she saw him
who'd asked
as he was getting dressed again
one Friday evening
What are you doing this weekend?
Not much
she'd muttered
then she asked

How about you?
And he'd looked
embarrassed
and said
You know, I feel awkward
when you ask
How about you?
because I'm with
someone
you know I am
And she'd turned to him and asked
Would you rather I said
How about the two of you?
What are you two doing
this weekend?

"You can trust me," Gilles said, pressing my hands together between his. "I don't want to hide anything from you. I'll explain where things stand with Violetta (*Violetta? Like in* The Lady of the Camellias*?*). Technically, we're no longer together, but . . ."

"Technically?" "She moved out of my place two months ago. But we just mounted a whole show together, and it's still running, so it would be complicated to separate now. And in many ways the show's an homage to her father, Matteo Lodi, the great Italian director, you must have heard of him, he mostly directed operas. Basically, it's complicated." "But you're separated?" "I told you we no longer live together."

He was talking to me like a child who was struggling to understand.

"I don't mean geographically..."

A stubborn child...

"I mean with reference to feelings, emotions (*sex*)."

He sighed, looked at me with a soft smile. The softness in his eyes, his voice, his hands—all these were new in this relationship. I luxuriated in them.

"Okay, I can see I need to tell you everything."

The truth was he was unhappy. When it started, five years earlier (*so this wasn't such a long relationship*), it was full-on passion between him and Violetta. He'd met her at a show directed by her father. He'd noticed her straightaway (*her looks, yes, obviously, she's stunning*) but she was married, she had two children, he had three, two of whom were already adults (*they have no children together*). They saw each other every now and then, as friends, they'd have coffee, he liked chatting with her. She taught classical singing, her career as a soprano had never taken off. At the time, he was also seeing someone, well, he'd been in a relationship, since his divorce actually, with an actress—Louise, and he was faithful to her. He was keen for Claire to know this, he stressed the fact: When he was with someone, he was faithful. Then one evening, not long after her father died, Violetta had literally fallen into his arms and within ten days everything was done and dusted: She'd left her marriage, he'd left Louise (*not so faithful, then*), and they'd moved in together. Violetta's elder son had stayed with his father, the younger one, Jules, was in joint custody, as was his youngest, Sophie, who was fifteen at the time. On alternate weeks they were alone, and for the other weeks they muddled through with a version of family life. But the muddle became a horrible mess because Violetta soon turned out to be a tyrant, gradually losing her temper with the whole family. "My own sons weren't allowed to stay at the apartment. If I wanted to see them, I had to meet them in a café, she couldn't stand them. Can you imagine?" I nodded at his horrified expression. But the worst part, he went on, was with his daughter, Sophie. Violetta hounded her, criticized her about her weight or her clothes, it became unbearable for the poor kid. And it was hell for him too: Violetta got hysterical every time he tried to argue a point, he even had to call for emergency medical help several times. To make a long story short, she'd found an apartment and had just moved out. "But you're still seeing each other? You haven't broken up?" "Technically, no (*technically*). I'm not like her, you know, I've grown fond of her son over the years. Mine are grown up now so I try to protect her boy, especially because he doesn't get along too well with his father. I lived alone with him when his mom was in the hospital, I'm a rock for that kid. And, like I said, she and I collaborated on my show. Let's say I'm handling her. But there's nothing going on between us, that's dead. We didn't even spend New Year's together, as you know: So you see where we stand. It meant I could meet you," he added, kissing the back of my hand. "And what about Louise, what happened to her?" "Oh, Louise is different. She cheated on me, that relationship was just waiting to end."

He looked at me. Fear. Hope.

"It's not complicated," he said eventually. "I don't want any pain. I want to be happy."

She listens
She's all ears
She drinks in his words
She eats his mouth
his beautiful mouth
with its perfect teeth
He's not unfaithful
No, she's sure of that
This isn't a man who's looking
that's obvious
This is a man who'd like
to be found
And what is and will be
his watchword
she can feel it
his catch-all mantra is:
"I don't want any pain"
even if
that's weird when
in opera

and drama
it's all about everyone's pain
even in comedies
She won't cause him pain
No
He needn't worry
With her
he'll be
happy
She's going to make him
happy
She's written those words before
about another man
in a previous book
But she doesn't remember it
She's forgotten
the first time
she told herself that.

"Just give me some time," he asked. His cell phone beeped for the third time. "I'm sorry, I need to go. My daughter's waiting for me. She's going to London on Thursday and I've hardly seen her." He stood up. I stood up. He took me in his arms and held me close, my condolences, I thought, the word drifted through my mind like a disoriented passerby. "We'll see each other again," I said—or was it a question? He stroked my hair awkwardly. "Of course." Then he left, hunched over, as if crushed by the weight of the past or the future, and I closed the door behind him. I liked that he was a father and paternal, in the same way that I felt I was, like a mirror image, a mother and maternal. But disappointment was standing right there in the hall, a worthy and familiar ghost, I conceded, still holding the door handle. The word *virile* was missing in action. "He's not very sensual," my mother offered euphemistically as she lay in ambush for my eighteen-year-old self. "He doesn't seem to know what he wants," my grandmother gave her expert opinion with her matrimonial ear to the ground from the family grave. "Grandma, it's the first time I've seen him," I replied, which was almost not a lie. "Would you prefer a hussar? You liked that Old France vibe when I was sixteen." "I liked it . . . when you were sixteen. But now it's ridiculous." I can't disagree, I thought to myself, with my eye on the peephole. He was still waiting for the elevator and was typing on his phone. No magnetism. Erotic energy below sea level. I hadn't noticed this face-to-face, but he was losing his hair. Fine. Never mind. I won't make a big deal of it. The desire I'd felt for him on New Year's Eve had dissipated, his tonsure was hard for me to take, from behind he looked like a monk in an old illumination with the vault of the heavens weighing on him. I'm passionate about men's hair, which I associate with their strength, I suppose—it's pathetic: a stupid Samson syndrome in whose shadow baldness is never a sign of great things to come. And anyway, he's too indecisive, I tell myself, succumbing to my old demons again. Too soft, too gentle. Almost shamefully sweet. But then again, I thought later as I cleared the table, then again, a man for whom a woman would leave her family, in less than two weeks leave the family she'd been living with for twenty years—why else would she do that? I projected myself into this woman, Violetta, she must be like all women who eventually up and leave, my mother, my other grandmother—why do they leave everything overnight like that, if it's not to have sex? I couldn't see it.

The following Saturday, Gilles invited me to an exhibition in the early afternoon. He knew the artist, his life and work, and explained it all to me like an educator. We met a journalist from *Arts et Spectacles* who paused for a minute to talk to him and glance at me with an intrigued expression, he must have known Violetta. Gilles didn't introduce me. Afterward, he suggested we go for a coffee or a hot chocolate, hot chocolate, yes, good idea. We were in the Opéra neighborhood and he spent a long time considering the best place for good hot chocolate, made the old way by pouring milk over melting chunks of the finest seventy percent cocoa from the equator, and stirring. We walked past about twenty streets before finding it, but he knew where he was going. He hardly touched his cup but watched me with concerned kindness while I made mine, wielding the little silver pot, the spoon, was it good, hot enough, sweet enough? He smiled, and took my hand. It was as if he didn't know what to do with me. The walls were covered with candy-pink hangings.

She's there
She couldn't give a damn
about the hot chocolate
She's so scared
of learned behaviors
informed opinions
tastes and colors
In her arms she's held
a dead child
her own child
hers
She really needs to get
that
into her head:
she couldn't give a damn about
anything that isn't
a living body
a body filled with emotion
She doesn't want
to be one of those women
who gets taken to see Basquiat
or to Angelina
for hot chocolate

as if it were only natural
one among others like maybe
an old school friend
a date from OurTime
a cousin from the Loire Valley.

She wants to be
the only one
unique
She wants to be
elected
not selected
She wants to be
loved
now
ourtime is now
ourtime is forever
Is she a Bovary?
It's easily said
Because she writes.

Afterward we said goodbye on the sidewalk, we weren't taking the same Métro train. Then I didn't hear another thing from him. The days passed. No text, no sign of life, nothing. He'd said to give him some time, fine, but what was he doing? He wasn't on social media so it was blanket-coverage absence. Radio silence. Total eclipse. Ourtime is never.

After ten days, I sent him an email:

Gilles, I'm glad I met you. But I have this feeling it was a dream. It's all so abstract. I need reality. I miss you being around.

Sending a kiss, but what can words do?

CLAIRE

Not very
TikTok tutorial
to be honest
A message not tested by
love coaches
on YouTube
She doesn't play this field
She doesn't steep
in the marinade of desire
She says it
as it is
To each
his own tactic
To each
his own her
She is a writer
But
just because
she writes
doesn't mean she's rewarded
with words
It's
because she writes
that she needs

to live
without them
She needs to be told
things
in kisses and by touch
Never in words
any bigger
than the things themselves
She doesn't shuffle around
on the periphery
She doesn't nurture
courtly love
or distant admirers
or marginal ones
She has
all of death
to help her cope without
bodies
to shut herself away
to shut her mouth
But her words
keep on talking
after death
whereas she can't make
love
under the soil.

He replied that same day, he'd been very busy but had been thinking about me the whole time although he didn't dare do anything, he didn't want to disturb me, he respected my need to be alone, didn't I tell him that myself? Meanwhile, he took pleasure in saying my name again and again on loop like a happy half-wit, would I like to come over to his place at about eight o'clock on Saturday evening, he gave me his address, he would make dinner, was there anything I didn't like, yes, I'd like to, no, nothing (*chestnuts, salsify, broccoli*).

◆

When he left Claire's apartment on January 6th, Gilles ran to the taxi stand where not a single taxi was standing—lousy neighborhood. Violetta sent him a crescendo of three consecutive texts, where was he, they were waiting for him, his lateness demonstrated yet again how little he cared about her son and her. He replied to say he was on his way, kissed Claire's hand before getting up, his daughter was waiting for him, he needed to go. He arrived bang on time for the movie—everything's fine, we can all calm down. Jules was on the sidewalk holding his mother's hand in a proprietorial way, Gilles forced himself to ruffle his hair by way of a greeting, something he'd done right from the start. Violetta had already bought the tickets and was putting the total into tricount. They went in. From the very first images, Violetta realized she'd mixed up *Stolen Kisses* with *The 400 Blows*, which would have been more suitable for an eleven-year-old boy. What do you want me to say? Gilles whispered in the dark when she pointed this out. They didn't smile when Antoine Doinel endlessly repeated Fabienne Tabard Fabienne Tabard Fabienne Tabard with every possible intonation. Then they went home—your place or mine?—to her apartment, Jules took an absurdly long time to brush his teeth, they could hear him from the living room, Gilles couldn't get used to this apartment. Eventually they went to bed and, just like in the film, they made love, dreaming of what and who, and also because it was Saturday. Before leaving in the morning, he went to the bookshelf and discreetly borrowed a Claire Lancel book that Violetta loved—she had nearly all of them and had already read some passages out loud to him. He'd only skimmed through *Tristan*, which he'd found appallingly melodramatic, but a mother mourning her child can't help but make you cry, he'd told his friend Georges on the phone.

♦

Saturday, 8:00 p.m. I went in, handing him the bottle of wine, he took me in his arms, kissed my hair, my lips. Claire, he said. I immediately lost everything, what to say, what to do, how to think. My name in his mouth, and it was game over. I got all tangled up with the bottle, if I'd drunk the whole thing on my way there I still wouldn't have been any more intoxicated in his arms, desire was stampeding like a wild horse, it's impossible to tame, it careers in every direction, you can name it and sing about it (*how to avoid losing your head*), but you can't stop it, it's invasive, it's destructive, it's tortuous and welcoming, it's voracious and wish-fulfilling, it's tyrannical and free, you feel hot, you feel scared. Lovemaking becomes the only thing to do, the only outcome to loosen the bit between your teeth—lovemaking as a way out. "Give me your coat," he said. "Shall I show you around?"

The little tour brought the horse back to its paddock, the charger became a quiet hack. The place was like a show home. He must have spent hours tidying, cleaning—maybe, it occurred to me, getting rid of every trace of Violetta. It was definitely a man's apartment, if it was a show home then it was showing visitors—in the narrowest, neatest way—what a man was, with a slightly manic edge that indicated an obsessive character coupled with single status. The living-room walls were white, the sofa immaculate, the parquet floor freshly waxed. On the shelves, well-ordered books; not one ornament, not one photo, not one vase. Just two grimacing Chinese or Balinese puppets framing an antique mirror. The heart of the room, filled with an upright piano opposite two wall-eyed club chairs, one blue, one gray, was like a stage set. A metronome stood on the piano along with headphones so that it could be played without disturbing the neighbors. On closer inspection, it said Steinway & Sons. I hate disturbing people too.

It has to be said, I wasn't expecting an apartment like that—what can he have thought of mine! I found it cold, chilling, almost snooty. It seemed to require walking on tiptoe. In all those days of silence, I'd stalked Gilles on the Internet, I'd found very little precise information about him, the few available interviews were strictly professional but by rewinding through the years, I'd come across an old discussion about the sociology of theater. In response to the first question, it was as if he'd pulled out a plug and, in a constant stream of words completely unrelated to the question, his voice shaking with a sort of contained fury, he'd said:

"My father was a dockworker, his parents were working class, communists, they lived very close to us. I spent my childhood in Marseille. I went to the conservatory in the third arrondissement, the poorest neighborhood in France, and in Europe, to this day. My family respected learning, as a lot of wage slaves did at the time, particularly commies. But I was terrible at high school so they made me do music, I started when I was six. Later I wanted to enroll in theater studies. There was a French teacher who encouraged me. I went down the puppet route because of Guignol, because of Pinocchio. They were my favorite toys as a kid. I had an uncle who was a carpenter and we called him Geppetto."

The resentment in his voice had a strange ring to it, it seemed to reverberate from somewhere backstage, to emanate from the darkness in the wings.

This ill-concealed anger appealed to me, perhaps because it was invisible in person, when he was so well-mannered. "And now I want to move to the next stage," he explained in a more recent video. "I'd like to direct an opera." "Which one?" "*Tosca*, ideally. Or *Macbeth*. In my family, opera was a middle-class thing. And for a long time I thought of it as grotesque. The first time I went to the opera, when I was twenty-five, I had to bite my lip so hard to stop myself laughing that my mouth hurt for a week. But now I think I have a lot to bring to the table."

I'd watched the videos several times, I wanted to know who he was. A class defector, I thought. But the interior look I was seeing here was more reminiscent of minimalist stage design than contemporary opera or a chic Airbnb. The books were real, though, and the musical scores annotated. A self-taught thinker, I decided. An intellectual, as we used to say at home. For a long time, I'd thought of it as a compliment, until I realized that an intellectual was someone who couldn't do anything useful with their hands, a pipe dream. But I like intelligence. Not learning or erudition, no, intelligence. People who understand what's going on. In themselves and around them. Who know how to establish links. Intelligence is the beginning of love. And in fact, a pianist, I thought, a pianist could definitely do something useful with his hands.

"It's Makassar ebony," Gilles said, stroking the piano lid. Phantoms of our faces were reflected in it. "I didn't know you played piano."

I was looking at his hands, which were slender and strong. My desire trotted over every one of his fingers. The thought that they could make music blew my mind and aroused me, I felt like a piano, a keyboard, all the keys. He smiled weakly. "I nearly devoted myself to it completely, became a concert pianist. In the end, I chose theater. But I play whenever I can." "Playing piano was my dream when I was little. But however much I asked, my father was a total music lover and he didn't want me massacring music with my scales, he wanted to listen to Arthur Rubinstein in peace. I took up dance instead." "Can you read music, though?" "No. I just studied music theory for a while in junior high, that's all." "You can take up piano even if you don't know much. I'll teach you (*I'll teach you*)." "Really? Isn't it too late?" "Of course not. If it's your dream . . ." "What I'd really like is to listen to you play. Do you play every day?" "I try to. We sometimes (*we sometimes*) give little recitals, Violetta and I. But come on, I haven't finished showing you around."

He took my hand, showed me the kitchen—colored tiles, high-tech food mixers, wine rack, transparent steamer proudly displaying some broccoli—then his study and the bathroom. "We sometimes" continued to flicker for a few seconds like a malfunctioning neon sign, while "I'll teach you" sparkled in the future. Violetta would not take over my mind, I would let Gilles manage the succession. It would probably take several weeks but I wasn't jealous: A relationship that's just beginning often contains the death throes of one that's ending. It was nothing to do with me. *I* felt as if I were at the start of something that had no end. And anyway, I thought, once we'd made love, there would be nothing but the two of us. Or no one.

We came to the bedroom. It was small. The bed, made with pin-sharp precision, filled the room. The wall opposite the only window was filled by a tall, wide mirror that made the room feel like a brothel—an austere brothel, if that oxymoron makes any sense. "I put it there to make the room bigger," Gilles explained. "It's an eighteenth-century mirror, my father paid nothing for it at a junk store." "He can't have paid nothing for it," I said, tossing this literal meaning at him to throw off the apprehension that had suddenly tightened around my chest like some inexplicable turn of the screw. I wanted to look out the window, to loosen the vise. "Come to my arms," he murmured in a different voice. I turned around. His face was tender and tense. He stroked my hair, gently undid the clip in my chignon, spreading my hair over my shoulders: "So then," he said, "you need reality?"

◆

“Oh yes, Mrs., sir, Your Honor, I think I was the first to be informed,” Georges says. “I’ve known Gilles a long time, I know everything about his life, we were coworkers when he started out at Charleville-Mézières Theater, I was stage manager. He was younger than me, but we got along from the start. Back then, twenty-five years ago, he had a strong Marseille accent, I remember, it brought some sunshine to the Ardennes! He did everything he could to lose it, I think he even had elocution lessons. I fell in love with him the moment I saw him. But wait, I’m not gay. It’s just, this guy showed up in my office with this smile, I mean what a smile! You can’t resist people like that, end of story.

“He called me right at the beginning of January 2014. He said, ‘Georges, what’s happening to me is a miracle. I’ve met this incredible woman, who matches me in every way. Intelligent, beautiful, independent. She’s a novelist. Claire Lancel. Have you heard of her?’ I hadn’t but that doesn’t mean anything. Solange, that’s my wife, had heard of her. She did some research and saw that Claire had started a podcast that was doing well, she had lots of followers, apparently. And then there were her books. Basically, we were impressed. Solange said Gilles had landed on his feet, but it was going to be complicated. I have to say he was going through hell in his relationship, we both thought it was over between them. I really liked Violetta, that wasn’t the issue, and anyway she was always very nice to us, but after everything she put him through, poor guy, we were glad he'd met someone new, a woman who measured up to him. And from the way he was talking, he'd found her." "Would you say he was more in love with her than with previous women?" "Not necessarily because he'd been very much in love with Violetta at the start. But then with his wife, the mother of his children, there was never any passion. Very unassuming, Élisabeth was, very submissive. She did everything for him and she never got over the divorce. Okay, I'll skip the short-term ones for you. No, the thing with Claire was that they never argued. In four years, Gilles never told me about a single fight, even though he told me everything, I was the only person he confided in, I think. Fine, maybe two or three times, he was a little . . . So, she was more famous than him, sometimes that bothered him, but nothing serious. Even a few weeks before . . . He was saying that they were getting married, him and Claire. He wanted to grow old with her. 'I'm happy, Georges,' he kept saying—and he could hardly believe it himself. I'd never seen him like that with any other woman. What a waste, if you think about it. And all because of me. I hate myself, I really hate myself. But then, it was a question of life or death."

3

"So?" Carole said a few days later. "How was it?" "Listen, it was fantastic. Really fantastic." "Mmm . . . tell me everything." "First of all, this is a man who knows where the clitoris is." "That's not something you see every day, you're right," Carole said. We laughed like a couple of hyenas.

"I was scared he'd be dull, I swear to you, when I saw his apartment, I thought we'd be keeping time with the metronome. Well, oh Lord no. It was sublime. Hardly ever had a lover like it. Slow, powerful, attentive, inventive. I don't know how to put this: listening. That's it. Listening to me, and even: at my service. And what's weird is he didn't come." "Really? Does he have a problem?" "No. I asked him and he looked surprised, he said it was out of respect, he thought it was intrusive to spill himself like that the first time. He's a big feminist, I think, an egalitarian, if you see what I mean, underneath that traditional exterior. I'm not used to it." "Egalitarian, yeah right... I'd be very surprised, bearing in mind his generation. Don't you think it's more because he likes to stay in control? You come and he doesn't, he has power over himself and power over you." "Oh, stop it, Carole!" "And he doesn't use a condom? You really think that's feminist behavior?" "Stop seeing problems everywhere. He's not at all that kind of guy..." "What I'm mainly seeing is a male. Either way, you shouldn't be too trusting..." "Don't stress," I said, draining my glass, "we'll see if he can stay in control next time..."

We each ordered a second Moscow mule. I didn't see things the way Carole did. I've known her since our teens, she's a freelance journalist, and she adopts every feminist cause, sometimes we don't see eye to eye. So, for example, to her—someone who cites Beauvoir left, right, and center—penetration is rape. We're allowed to like it, it's tolerated, but you have to compensate for the domination by making sure he's not on top of you—it's what she calls Lilith's law! It's the opposite experience for me. I don't feel like I'm being invaded when I make love. I can be completely crushed under a man's body, I'm the one doing the penetrating. Sex is my way of getting inside another person, my own discreet form of breaking and entering. His skin, the way he smells, his voice, his sweat, his breath, what he says about himself, his life: I have a stranglehold. A boy once told me, "In the expression *make love*, there are the words *make* and *love*. Girls hear the love bit and I hear the active bit, make." Well, I hear both. The action and the feeling. I don't distinguish between the two. When I *make* love, I make *love*.

She's there
After sex
She can't do anything
now
Can't close anything back up
She entered this place
just like that
entered things
the furniture
the walls
She entered
into that mouth
into that body
into those snug hollows
With tongue and fingers and hands
She performs her role
and penetrates
She eases herself
into the scene
into the story
honestly or otherwise
She's curious to know
She deliberately lets go
of propriety (what's that?)
of fear (a little)
She takes him

She holds him
She penetrates him
With the pleasure
That he gives her
And that makes her cry out
She knows
Only death can separate them
And it's far away.

All through the night
they talk to each other
they kiss each other
on the forehead
on the neck
on the lips
they kiss and fuck
She tells her story
She's in on the secret
She doesn't recant
She knows the point of
Life
She can do something useful
with her hands.

When I opened my eyes in the morning, his face was right next to mine. "I was waiting for you to wake up, my beauty," he said. Love, I thought as I rolled into his arms as if into fresh sheets. "What do you like in the morning? Tea, coffee? Would you like croissants? Eggs? Orange juice? If you want croissants, I'll get dressed and go get some for you." "I'm very basic, you know, I just like bread in the morning. With honey, if you have any." "Very basic, mmm, I see... I mostly get the feeling you don't want me to put my clothes on."

We had plenty of them, mornings like that, what am I saying, mornings... whole days! There were so many of them that they combine into a single ribbon wrapped around the early months. They tie in other events and incorporate them in the great fresco over the years, in fact it sometimes feels as if for a period of two or three years—even though, mixed in with this, there were difficult conversations, reservations, and feelings of reluctance—I didn't experience anything except for one endless happy day, like a sun-dappled picnic in the shade of a mimosa tree. A single extended day of happiness that no other day—not January 7th or November 13th, not horror or death—could dent for more than a moment, absolutely not, we were sheltered by love. We told each other about our lives as if describing a book that we'd read the day before, amazed by the similarities, the differences, and the coincidences. Well, it was mostly me. He got me to talk. I liked that he wanted to know about me. Isn't curiosity a foundation stone of love?

"You're beautiful. Your hair's so soft, it's like silk." "You're beautiful too. You have a body like a medieval knight." "You think?" "Yes. You remind me of a description of Perceval, 'broad of shoulder and slender of flank.' That's exactly you. You're my handsome knight." "I've never seen features as perfect as yours." "Now you've gone too far! You're not a teensy bit in love, are you?" "No, it's the truth." "I'm covered in sweat, sorry. How embarrassing, I'm so sorry." "Don't be, I really like it. My fountain woman, my liquid woman." "But you're the opposite. You just don't sweat! You're some kind of superhero, right?" "I do. Of course I do." "No, look. I'm all sweaty and you don't smell at all. In the crook of your neck here, I can just catch the smell of your cologne. It's Vétiver, right? That's what my father used to wear." "Do I remind you of your father, then?" "No, not at all. Apart from the fact that his name was Gilles, you don't have much in common." "Did you love him a lot?" "Oh, he was a very cold man, not very endearing. I have a few good memories, from vacations, nothing really. His mother abandoned him when he was little, she ran off with her lover. And then my mother did the same thing! I only ever saw him in varying degrees of glum, like nothing could make him happy. And a Protestant, too." "Oh yes, that's right, you're a Protestant... Austere, then. Except when you sweat..." "That wasn't fair! How about you?" "Me? Looks like I have something else in common with your father, apart from the cologne and the name: My mother dumped me too."

"How old were you?" "Seven. I lived alone with my father in this mood of nostalgia for communism and sadness about the adulterous absentee. He cried and he drank. But he was very kind to me. My mother, on the other hand... Well, you'll be able to see for yourself." "You're planning to introduce me to your mother?" "Maybe. I'm waiting to see if things are serious between us." "I can't wait." "It's not a treat, you know. Kiss me instead. My love, my beauty. Do you like it when I touch you there?"

"What do you like best about me?" "How do you mean?" "Physically." "I don't know. Everything." "But if you could change something, what would it be?" "Oh yikes, that's dangerous territory (*your hair*)." "My angioma?" "No! Totally not, I love it. It looks like a lipstick kiss, it's erotic." "Stop it..." "You just reminded me of a conversation with my ex-husband, he really wanted to know what I didn't like about him physically. In the end I told him, and he sulked for a week." "But I'm not like your ex-husband." "Okay. But I won't ask you the same question." "You could: I think you're perfect." "You see: I don't believe you. So it's pointless. Wouldn't you say my breasts are too small, for example?" "Nu-uh. Absolutely not. Your breasts are just right. I don't like big breasts, they're like cow's udders." "That's just as well because I don't have any plans to change them! You have to take me as I am." "I'll take you, I'll take the lot. Look at us in the mirror. Aren't your breasts just the most beautiful in my hands?"

"And what was it that you didn't like about your husband?" "His teeth. He had crooked teeth, not badly but because otherwise he was pretty good-looking, it spoiled the effect. Anyway, that's a criticism that can't be leveled at you." "So you like good-looking men, then?" "Not necessarily. I've been in love with very ugly men. Desire isn't to do with beauty, is it? Is it for you?" "You say that, but you didn't marry one of the ugly ones." "Well, first of all, he wasn't all that good-looking, even if he was convinced he was. More than anything, he was one big narcissist. I didn't realize that until quite late in the day. He behaved as if a camera were following him the whole time, he was always looking at himself in the mirror." "Why did you split up?" "I told you, he never stopped cheating on me but kept telling me that he loved no one but me. We got married three months after we met, without really knowing each other it turned out. But still, we were together for twenty years. He put me on a pedestal, called me his angel, but when the angel used her wings, sir was not at all pleased." "Did you fly away, my beauty?" "In a way, yes. Julien was never home. When he wasn't at the gym, he was taking photos, mainly portraits—which, incidentally, was a very useful way for him to lure 'models.' Meanwhile, I started writing soon after we were married. I hardly went out at all, just to teach some classes, the rest of the time I wrote. We lived in Lyon back then and that was how it worked, him out there, me inside. Then one day one of my books was a success, suddenly people were talking about me, I was translated, invited all over the place. Julien couldn't take it. It had become: him behind, me out front. So, impossible. I remember one time a TV crew came to film me in Lyon—they were all men—and he got so under their feet talking technical stuff with them, lenses, filters, etc., that in the end two hours had gone by, daylight was fading, we hadn't started, and I was beginning to show signs of impatience, and that's when, still peering at the equipment he was discussing with them and barely turning to look at me, he said, 'Can you make us a coffee instead of grousing?' He even managed to feature on-screen a few times, all smiles, the perfect husband, posing in front of the bookshelves, explaining to the camera that he read everything that I wrote sentence by sentence so that he could best advise me, so much so that the day after the piece aired one of my coworkers said, 'Say, Claire, I saw the show last night. I didn't know you guys were famous.' That was the day I started thinking something wasn't right. And when I eventually cheated on him (after fifteen years in my case, not after three weeks of marriage), it just became unlivable. It was a brutal divorce. But that's enough about me. You're not saying anything!" "No, go on, tell me more. Your daughter…I remember in

Lille you said she no longer sees her father?" "Yes. It's horrible. He disappeared overnight. Completely disappeared. He doesn't send any news and doesn't ask for any. Even after the Bataclan attack he didn't think to call even though Alice is an Eagles fan, she could have been there. She's very sensitive, she misses her father, but, I mean, what a shit! After the divorce he had a son with some complete nutcase who was in a big hurry to cut him off from everybody else. She was vile to Alice—a real hatchet job. Alice had a terrible time, she was as thin as a rake. Julien didn't notice a thing. And now he's jumped ship, she doesn't even have his address. I think it's disgusting for a man—a father—to leave like that without a backward glance." "Oh, mothers do it too, you know." "Yes, I know. I'm sorry, Gilles." "But I'd really like to meet her, to meet Alice. If she needs a father, I'm here..." "Oh, Gilles, that's really very touching. I'll introduce you when she comes to Paris. I'm sure she'll love you. Do you see your children much?" "I try to. I go to London when I can to see Sophie, she's getting a master's in film studies. My son Léon is a sports teacher in Bastia in Corsica. And then there's the eldest, he moved to Australia. With Violetta it was tough, it was complicated. It'll be easier now, I can feel it." "I like that you're a father, that you're that particular father. I think it's... sexy." "Sexy? Why?" "I don't know... it's concrete, it's real. I find fatherhood moving." "Concrete? Oh yes... I almost forgot: You need reality.

Here, give me your hand. Is that concrete enough for you right there?"

Gilles and I quickly became very intimate. When I say intimate, I don't just mean sexually. Of course, our bodies were in tune with each other, but it was really through talking that we built up our own lexicon, the classic lovers' language with elements of cliché and a private code, both hackneyed and completely original. And yet, in the early days I was uncomfortable with how quickly Gilles started using these words. From the very start he called me my beauty, my darling, my love, my sweetheart, and said "I love you" when we made love. He hardly ever used my name without preceding it with "my"—my Claire. "And what exactly is 'my' in grammatical terms?" Carole asked ironically when I told her. "The writer in you must know, but the woman doesn't. It's a possessive adjective. Po-sse-ssive." All this was strange for me, who found it hard even to say his name . . . and not because it was my father's name. It's been the same with all men: Using a name has felt more intimate than sex, I go about it slowly. Yes, that's odd, I know. The day when, bombarded with sweet nothings, I raised the subject with him, more to apologize for my failing than to criticize him, he looked like a chastened child caught in the wrong: "But when you love someone, shouldn't you tell them?" I felt like such a loser that day with my inhibitions compared to his straightforward approach! I gradually slipped into—and let myself slip into—the mold of this affectionate language. I accepted that our love was like everyone else's: crassly ordinary and flawlessly new. I experienced the subversive sweetness of our magic formulae, even though there was nothing extraordinary about them. They were just the ones we used. So my inaugural pronouncement, "I need reality," became our erotic open sesame, a little like "make cattleya" in Proust's work, do you see what I mean? Or like… One time, at his place, we were in the elevator, it was a tiny elevator, there was barely room for both of us. I pressed myself up against him as if I couldn't help it and asked, "Do you live around here?" Gilles loved super-quick role-play like this. Theater was more his thing, but he was dazzled by it from me, and found it a source of instant arousal. He remembered these mini-scenarios that seemed to thrill him like some unexpected find, and we replayed them in suggestive voices in every elevator and even in different places, pretending we didn't know each other. "Do you live around here?" Love talk is unique and idiotic—love is idiocy.

"My love. I've never been so happy. I feel like I've come back to life. You're just fantastic. I was wondering: What did you find surprising about me, in the beginning?" "What do you mean surprising?" "What were you not expecting when we met?" "Oh, I don't know…how sensual you are. I thought of you as cerebral, a little boring even. You sure put me straight there. How about you, what did you find surprising?" "Me? I thought you were an Amazon. When I read *Ballroom*, I thought I'd just be a number in your life. But really, you're a little darling. A total romantic. What you want is prince charming. 'They married and had lots of children.'" "On the children front, it's looking compromised!" "Ah, so you admit it: You want to get married!" "No, that's..." "But you do: you-want-to-get-married!" "That's not true. And I don't want a prince charming, I want a charming man, which is good enough in itself. And you are one. You're charm in the flesh." "In the flesh, mmm, yes, very in the flesh."

◆

"I completely understand why Claire remembers times like that," says Carole. "It's only natural, with her it's always the body she misses the most. She has this crazy relationship with sex, she thinks it solves everything, that that's where the truth lies—as if people couldn't fake it, on both sides! No. She sees fucking as the ultimate test. People fit together, they complement each other, and everything's hunky-dory. She's the high priestess of cis! She's always confused sex with a solemn communion, always taken the verb 'to know' in the biblical sense: 'Adam knew Eve,' that kind of nonsense. Someone gets into her, they get into her life. It's a little like 'Me

Tarzan, you Jane,' a necessary and adequate sort of introduction. Sex as a means of knowing another person ontologically, and she stands by that, despite the fact that it's contradicted by experience. So everything she thought she 'learned' about this man from fucking—how generous, tender, or violent he can be, how considerate and intuitive—all that instantly represented his moral character, it definitively constituted who he was. It works the other way around too: She feels that she's giving all of herself in that state of abandon, that she can be read like an open book, so to speak. It almost certainly matters more to her that a man makes love well than that he likes her books. The way she sees it, once you've deciphered the body, you've resolved most of the enigma posed by another person. From that point, she'll take them or leave them. But when she takes them, it's all-encompassing.

"Even so, I do remember there were times when, after a conversation with Gilles, or what amounted to one for them, she would collapse on the sofa with her head in her hands and say, 'He's so dumb.' Those were her very words. Or did she say 'shallow,' I can't remember. She could never talk about anything deep with him, he was superficial, the whole time. She told me that several times. Always in a humorous way—she can be very funny, when she puts her mind to it. Pretty rough and ready, even. I remember one time she pantomimed a pseudo-conversation between them, she wanted to show me an example.

She and I were having lunch together and she embarked on a discussion of women's status in India, and she punctuated every serious sentence or tragic piece of information from me with a 'Could you pass the salt, my love,' 'That scarf really suits you, darling,' and variations of 'Are you tired, my beauty? Shall I pour you a drink?' God, how we laughed! She was torn between irritation and just accepting male vacuity. Men use fewer words than we do, that's a known fact. In everyday conversations, they skim along the surface of language, discarding any nuance. Gilles was a case in point. He could talk brilliantly about Goldoni's plays or a Kleist text in the original German—he speaks at least five languages—but was perfectly incapable of analyzing a real situation or expressing feelings other than with stock phrases or fatuous comments. 'He's happy just to skitter blindly over the surface of things,' Claire used to say. I mean first of all, the guy who serves up 'I love you' the first time you fuck: red flag! But Claire made excuses for him, and the most nonsensical of them was... the very fact that he was a man. If I'd left her to her own devices, she could almost have ended up thinking his incapacity for introspection was virile! In fact, she used to say, 'Considering he's a man, they don't come any better.' A *mensch*, then! But the main thing was she forgot. This is a crazy thing about Claire: She bears no grudges. Have you heard the myth about drinking from the River Lethe and forgetting everything? Well, Claire must have fallen in as a child. You might think she forgives, but that's not it: Things are just erased. Or they're assimilated, I don't know. They're metabolized. They dissolve into the highest impression she has of human connections. But the truth that she so desperately wants to find is the exact opposite: *Aletheia*, the disclosure of truth, literally means 'not forgetting' in Greek. To get anywhere with the truth of her relationship, she'd need to remember everything."

◆

"Yes, it's true, Carole's right, I may have said it. 'He's completely shallow,' I did think that. I was often thrown by how little depth there was to him, but it's also because intimate conversations are one of the pleasures of love for me. I noticed it gradually—in the early days he worked at it, but then I saw: Gilles was incapable of expressing not only personal feelings but even cogent thoughts about life. Quite early in a conversation we'd reach the point where his reasoning became disjointed, threadbare, incoherent even. It was as if his sentences were missing the coordinating conjunctions. The thread was broken, there was no logic. Or he talked in formulaic, binary terms—good, bad; happy, unhappy—that wobbled about like a car with flat tires. He cast around for words from outside of himself. A puny puppet operated by a ventriloquist. Then the things he said didn't ring true, and when I tried to dig deeper, I felt I was talking in a void, literally. In fact, when he was with me, he avoided opportunities to really talk to me. He preferred *doing* something: ordering dinner, planning vacations, choosing a series on Netflix. Generic suggestions exempted him from having to be an individual. But my disappointment was quickly dispelled by three things. First of all, I liked this man-of-action side to him. To tell you the truth, before I met him I never went on vacations, I was incapable of taking out a subscription to anything or booking personal treats. Gilles, on the other hand, liked creature comforts and knew how to create a sense of well-being. This is also what life's about, I thought to myself, I'd forgotten. And I accepted the idea that men are buttoned up when it comes to feelings—my husband was the same! True, I found it irritating but also touching how deeply entrenched Gilles was in his directives about virility. His mother can't have shown much interest in his problems, I thought. And he never cried. Or yes, I saw him cry once. It was at the opera, *Tosca*, I'd bought the tickets for his birthday, I knew it was his favorite opera. At the end his eyes were misty. *Questo è luogo si lagrime*, he replied when I asked him about it. 'This is a place of tears.' It's what the traitor Scarpia says to Tosca. Incidentally—and I didn't pick up on this at the time—he quoted the traitor, not the betrayed woman. He was more moved by the monster than by the victim. Either way, that gives you an example of how he did things: masking all emotion by referring to something factual. In that specific instance, his reserve was touching, but at other times the avoidance became a problem. 'I don't want any pain,' that was his mantra. If I'd been totally confident about his sense of humor, I would have had it printed on a T-shirt and given it to him for Christmas. I DON'T WANT ANY PAIN. He had no other message to give to anyone else, whereas I see it as tantamount to saying 'I refuse to live'—yes, a sort of incompetence in really living.

"But most of all, most of all, pretty much every time I thought *he's totally shallow*, when, say, he'd left the room to avoid taking a conversation further, then a few minutes later, as if he'd heard my disappointment—and maybe deep down he *was* in touch with my inner monologue—he would come back in, sit at the piano without a word, and start to play. He would play my favorite pieces, which he'd often practiced on his own, for me, to please me. I completely melted as I listened. He wasn't superficial or shallow but sensitive, loving, endlessly thoughtful. He didn't actually play all that well, nothing like as well as he'd led me to believe, he corrected himself a lot, hesitated, made mistakes, but that was just it... he was trying to find the notes, in a way he was battling to translate an emotion, to be accurate and nuanced—all the things he found hard to master with language. He agreed to show his fumblings, his inadequacies even, and this humble trust moved me more than the music itself. Through that piano I could commune with him. After all, there are other things besides words, I told myself. Let's allow this man to say nothing. Just like bodies, music is a language. His heart spoke through his fingers. And you know, talking to you about it now and despite everything that's happened, I still love him, my heart's still in his hands.

"And he was so incredibly kind to me. Modest, attentive, considerate. Brilliant, too. Unbeatable, and not just in his own field. His erudition was vast and varied. He made a fuss over me, made love to me, arranged surprises for me, and trips, gave me presents. Jewelry! I wasn't used to it—my father didn't even wish me a happy birthday. I only had to say I liked lace, for example, and he would spend two hours on the Internet looking for a blouse for me, and it was so adorable how he blushed if I caught him at it. When we were apart, he would send me poems by Éluard. He inhaled Albert Camus's love letters to Maria Casarès and read extracts to me. What can I say? Our first years can basically be summed up in a single sentence, a sentence from Balzac. You know, there are things in literature that can't be expressed any better, peerless, limpid things that hit the spot. So Balzac has already said this for me, and it will help you understand. It's written in the past historic, which encompasses the melancholy of something long finished, but if I say it slowly, if I enunciate it, you won't have any more questions, I'm sure you won't, everything will be clear. It's from *The Deserted Woman*—you're smiling at the title, fine, of course you are:

"'They were as happy as we all dream of being.'

"There, that's all I want you to understand, despite what happened afterward:

"We were as happy as you all dream of being."

4

"Well, that's a lovely story, Mrs. Lancel," my attorney said, "but in that case, it's completely incomprehensible that the police found you sitting on the ground bleeding outside your house. I know that you're still in shock but you're going to have to unpick this idyll or we'll never get to the bottom of this." "I wasn't sitting on the ground, Mrs. Niepce. I was sitting on a tree stump in the garden."

My attorney looked dumbfounded, she raised her eyebrows.

"On a tree stump, fine. What difference does it make? What matters—" "On a tree stump, yes, I insist on that." "Very well. You were found sitting on a tree stump. Distraught and covered in blood. Fairy tales don't usually end like that. The investigation report has provided some information. But what about you? What can *you* say to shed light on this business? To read it a little differently right from the start. Weren't there clues, details you might remember from the very beginning? It would help us."

"Were there signs? Yes, if you really want to know, and even right from the start, but signs of what? We rarely read signs, mostly we just skim them. To decode something, we need to know it's in code. I'd definitely noticed some details I didn't like, I've mentioned some of them. I wouldn't go so far as to say warnings. Or maybe I would, because I'm always on the alert, like a hare on the lookout. I have a heart like a hare's, it gallops at the slightest sound and understands the threat in the beam of headlights. It would be impossible to kill me without me being aware of the danger, impossible, my instincts are faster than any arrow. Fear doesn't lie, and it's my sixth sense. Imagine a system of warning lights that flash at the tiniest perceptible cause for alarm and you'll know how I live among other people. At least, that's what I thought, I thought I was equipped with a supersophisticated warning system. I'm a writer, my craft, my ministry even, involves noticing everything—I don't let anything pass me by, well, I tried not to. But I also make a habit of not judging—not until I've watched, listened, observed, and understood for a long time—and once I understand, I can't judge. Writing is an exercise in love, a glorious and profound and audacious experiment in understanding other people. In fact, I told the judge the other day, 'If you really understand someone, how can you still judge them?' Mind you, she blew me away, she came right back at me, do you remember? 'If I understand something, then I know for sure that I'm wrong.' Jacques Lacan, she added. She looked pleased with her little coup, I could see the 'So there!' in her eyes. Maybe she's right: Maybe we're all wrong the whole time? We read the signs, but we don't read them right. Anyway, in my case it's never some*thing* that I want to understand, it's some*one*. I'm addicted to the human heart, or should I say ticker—what makes people tick. I can easily miss my Métro station in order to continue watching a girl put on her makeup despite the lurching train, the faces she pulls in the pocket mirror balanced on her bag, her fascinating skill, managing not to sabotage herself with mascara and she does all this while explaining to a friend, on the cell phone wedged between her ear and her shoulder, why she's going to dump Kevin or change her job. I'm a seismograph, I record everything, especially words—I write first and foremost with my ears. With a few exceptions, my curiosity is always kind, yes, kind, don't look at me like that, there's nothing obscene about the word, I'm sure it's not a word you use in court, but I don't know how else to put it. By kind I mean: I sometimes react but I come to no conclusions, or at least I don't interpret things. Afterward, in a book, it's different: I have to strip away my own kindness. But when I meet someone—meet him for real, I mean, not just in the social-media circus—I'm open to loving him. Unless he looks like a total bastard or his reputation's gone before him, and even then . . . I don't have a prosecutor's mindset. Life isn't a fairy tale, sure, you're right. And it's precisely because I know this that I didn't read too much into the wrong notes that occasionally made the symphony sound a little off—there were so few of them back then, and anyway I made my own share of bum notes, Gilles was quick to point them out to me. I believe, I've always believed, in human goodness. Maybe that's where I'm going wrong. Carole couldn't handle how indulgent I am—Carole and her zero tolerance. She still keeps telling me. In her opinion, I just don't get it at all: Love is blind. Call it denial or naivete, if you like, but I think it's something else. I don't *expect* people to treat me badly, even though I know bad things, evil things, do happen. Do you remember that human-interest story in the news—and what does it say about us that this stuff is called 'human interest'?—about the East Paris killer? When he was arrested, he described his crimes. And one of his victims, when he brought the knife to her throat after he'd tied her up, raped her, and poured himself a beer, said, and these were her last words, her eyes full of surprise, she said, 'What are you doing? Are you killing me?' Evil always comes as a surprise. Always. Even after years. We just don't believe in it. I believe, I've always believed, in love, if that's what you want to get me to say—are you going to claim it was passion?"

"When I opened my eyes that first morning, his face was right next to mine, he was watching me, with the fixed stare of a prison guard, literally devouring me with his eyes, eyes full of scary adoration." "Scary?" "Yes. He looked like a madman. It was just a fraction of a second, I caught him out when I opened my eyes, but that moment belonged to him, I didn't linger on it. He asked me what I liked for breakfast, brought a lovely tray with Limoges porcelain, it was all very refined. I was hungry and I felt good, even if I didn't want him to raise the window blinds too far because I didn't want him to see me in daylight. But I also felt loved, and that's a miraculous feeling, it was as if with this stranger—because that's what he still was, even if you're no longer really strangers when you're naked—it was as if to him, the bags under my eyes, the wrinkles, pasty face, morning breath, none of that stuff mattered, and that's actually what he said as he opened the blinds all the way up in spite of my protests, 'I want to see you, my beauty,' he said when I put my hand over my face, as if I were blinded by that feeble January light. It's different for a woman. (Carole would kill me if she could hear me.) I was the kind of woman who would get up at dawn to put more concealer under my eyes. But he gave me this new feeling that I would be loved for myself, that I could lower my guard. Indulgence, what a relief!

"He settled onto his pillow next to me, I buttered a piece of bread, and he asked me in this breathless voice, like he'd taken a run-up to it: 'So, then, who's the man in the photo?' I took the bread back out of my mouth. 'What? Which photo? Which man?' 'The man in the photo at your place?' Bafflement. 'You know, the photo on the shelves by the window, in a metal frame.' 'The photo on the shelves by the window,' I repeated dumbly. Then I pictured it. 'It's Gary Cooper!' I exclaimed. 'From around the time of *For Whom the Bell Tolls*. I cut it out of a magazine. You didn't recognize him? What did you think?' I was having fun. He wasn't. 'Are you going to tell me that you're just a fan? There must be another reason . . .' 'Yes, you're right,' I said, surprised. 'He reminds me of someone. The sadness, the melancholy.' He didn't ask me who. 'You like men being sad,' he said. 'No, I don't like men being sad, it's not the same.' 'Well, I'm not sad, ever. I don't know what melancholy is, I like being happy.' There was a note of defiance in his voice. I laughed glibly, without thinking. 'Well, that can work too,' I said before popping the bread into my mouth.

"The thing that stood out the most, if I have to remember all this, was his jealousy. He never liked me going out without him, even with other women—he often criticized my women friends, over trivial things, while claiming to be a feminist. One time he wanted to know how many men had mattered to me—a classic trap!—and I pretended to work it out in my head, uncurling my fingers one after the other to count, looking overwhelmed by how many there were, until he stopped me, but his smile was forced. 'Have you ever had a relationship with a woman?' he asked next. 'No, never. I like women's company but I'm not attracted to them. And you? Have you ever slept with a man?' 'No. Same as you: Men go for me, but I don't go for them. The thought of physical contact is disgusting.'

"I didn't like that he used that word, *disgusting*, it's too strong to say about someone's body.

"He was also nervous when I was involved in literary events. It didn't help telling him that ninety percent of the audience were women readers, he would reply, 'So that leaves ten percent who are men,' making it sound like he was joking. 'Yes,' I would say. 'Husbands who came along with their wives. And you'd be welcome, you know.' He never came. But he did find forms of retaliation.

"So one day, for example, when we'd known each other three or four weeks, I'd just arrived at his place after a discussion at a multimedia library, he poured us both a drink then said, 'Something weird happened to me earlier.'

"He'd gone to a furniture store to replace a carpet that Violetta had taken with her. The color he wanted wasn't available in the store so he left his contact details with the sales assistant. And now this evening, just before closing time, he received a text from this very young woman suggesting they go out for a drink. 'If you don't believe me, take a look.' And he handed me his phone.

"'Hello sir. I will let you know as soon as the carpet that you liked is back in stock. It's currently not available. But I am. I think you're handsome and charming. If you'd like to buy me a drink, call me, you have my number. Élodie.'

"My seismograph thought the message was unusually worded and punctuated, but I didn't react. 'Well?' Gilles said, watching me closely. He was trying to read me, his eagerness was palpable. 'Are you surprised someone likes me?' 'Not at all,' I replied. 'I know all about your powers of seduction, as it happens. I'm more interested in this as a woman. All these young girls looking for sugar daddies, it's sad.' 'You think the world revolves around money... Maybe the girl's just genuine. She liked the look of me, period.'

"We almost had our first fight that day. In a way he was hoping we would. He wanted to make me jealous. I thought his tactics were stupid, sycophantic, but touching, too: He'd read *Ballroom* and, like so many readers, whatever he said, he'd identified me with the narrator, with her passionate love of men. He didn't like that plural, *men* not one man, he wanted to be the only one. I accepted this, I was the same, I would have hated it if he'd written a book about *women*. To be honest with you, I was glad he specialized in puppets, they're a lot less dangerous than actresses. I've done some acting, I know desire runs the show." "So his jealousy didn't bother you? Nor the fact that he wanted to kindle yours?" "I can always explain everything with love—or the absence of love. Is that wrong of me, Mrs. Niepce? For you, in your line of work... are there other explanations? From your experiences, would you say we have other excuses?

"So the fight came to nothing, on that day and a few others in the early years. I wouldn't say I didn't pay any attention to it, no, but I either laughed about it or made out I was perfectly impervious to it. Pretended it was nothing, that's what I did. Sailing over possible snags. Not spoiling our wonderful, loving harmony. My tolerance was as bottomless as my trust. How would people ever live together if they didn't let some things go?

"'And what did you say to her?' I asked him playfully as I scrolled on his cell phone. 'Nothing, obviously,' he replied, offended, taking back his phone. 'It must happen to you a lot as a well-known writer, having readers come on to you. Do *you* reply to them?' 'No, never. And I'm not all that well-known, you know.' 'It never happens to you or you never reply?' 'It sometimes happens, private messages on Facebook or Instagram, but I don't reply.'

"And if it did happen, I wouldn't tell you, I thought to myself. I would spare you the jealousy.

"He brought it up again every now and then, testing my resistance. The first time that he went to Tbilisi for two weeks for work, he mentioned Natacha, his interpreter, he even sent me a selfie with her, she was very young. 'Oh, don't be jealous, my love,' he said when I was worried. 'I'm just happy I can tell you about my day. But I like that you're jealous,' he added a little later. 'It means you love me. It makes me happy.' And after that it became a game between us. Every time I saw him with a woman—a policewoman he was asking for directions, the caretaker in his building bringing him a parcel, his ninety-something neighbor—I would ask suspiciously, 'Are you sure she's not a little in love with you?' And we laughed. I wasn't really jealous, I was pretending. I never once searched his cell phone or his computer, or checked where he was. I was so sure of his love! But he needed my anxiety and if I didn't show enough of it, he would clam up. He often said, 'I love you more than you love me.' I ended up feeling bad about it. I was overflowing with love, literally, but I didn't show it, not as much as he did. The thing is, I'd never been so adored—yes, adored, beyond love. It was such an exquisite feeling, a sense that I was all-powerful, not that I abused it, I don't think, and it never made me lose my head. I didn't completely abandon myself to it. A part of me knows that things come to an end and we shouldn't give our whole heart. That's why I'm alive to tell you this.

"Another thing I didn't like was the way he talked about the women he'd lived with. Weirdly, he didn't try to make me jealous about them. Maybe he could tell that I don't attach that much importance to the past. Which isn't actually true. As I'm talking to you now, I feel the exact opposite. When I meet someone I like, I want to know everything about him. It's just that I don't think of his past relationships as any different than his childhood. I listen to descriptions of them with the same intensity. But how could there be rivalry between me and people or things from the past? In a pinch, the past serves as a lesson: We won't make the same mistakes. Gilles seemed to share this point of view. So, for example, he asked me a lot of questions about Julien, my ex-husband. I didn't get the feeling he was jealous of him, although on one of the rare occasions that he came to my apartment, I caught him looking in fascination at the photo of Julien that Alice kept in her bedroom. He liked it when I talked about Julien, he even encouraged me to. I have to say that the conflict with Julien was still raw, especially for Alice, and Gilles discreetly played the role of a godsend, a sort of anti-Julien who would help both of us forget past hurts. I was bowled over by this modest aspiration to make us happy. He wanted to compensate for the hard times. 'I'm not like your ex-husband,' he often said to reassure me. Meanwhile, I was so in love with him that I pitied the women who'd lost him. He once told me that one of the recurring reasons for fights with Violetta was that she'd wanted to have a child with him and he didn't. He already had three children, she had two, and anyway at his age, he didn't want to go through that whole program again, the diapers, the feedings, the sleepless nights—particularly as with Élisabeth, the mother of his children, he was the one who did everything, thank you very much, he'd done enough already. He said this in such a furious voice, anyone would think Violetta had wanted to harm him in some way. 'But Gilles,' I said—very soothingly, I remember, to calm him—'it's only natural for a woman to want to have a child with a man she loves. I mean, if I still could, I'd want to have one with you: a mini you, I'd love that.' 'But she used emotional blackmail, she threatened suicide! She ended up in the emergency room twice! The ambulance came for her, she cried, everyone gave me these terrible looks like it was my fault. A real bitch!' 'She loved you, Gilles.' He looked at me intently, all his loathing suddenly dissipated: He was discovering something he'd never considered—that it had just been a sign of love that he hadn't wanted to receive or to give. I understood Violetta, I felt close to her. She was almost certainly crazy, he was right—or maybe we always want just one more child? I myself secretly regretted the child I wouldn't have. Then again, I admired Gilles. He'd left a younger woman who could still have children, for someone his age—my age. It's so often the other way around that I was grateful to him for this. I was impressed that he renounced the false youth that so many men try to find late in life. The injustice of his resentment toward Violetta was erased by the maturity he showed in loving me. 'Anyway,' Gilles added, 'I saw her ex-husband at the hospital when he was visiting her with the children, and he admitted that Violetta used to have these outbursts with him too. I thought that was nice of him, he didn't have to tell me. But, you see, he wanted to tell me: It wasn't my fault if she went off the rails.'"

"Mr. Dugain, Georges Dugain, says that you and Gilles never fought. What can you say about that? Apart from little flare-ups of jealousy, were there other sources of conflict? Initiated by him or by you? You said earlier that he sometimes looked for a fight. Could you be more specific? Am I being annoying? You're bound to get questions about this, you know. I'm only preparing you." "Of course, Mrs. Niepce. It's just that, seen from today's perspective, these questions seem laughable. But Georges is right, we never fought. At least, the way I saw it, no pointless subject was worth wasting time on, so I often gave in, because I didn't care or I wanted to save the hassle. I'm not interested in anything that relates to opinions—which is why I don't go out. I hate social niceties, dinners in town, small talk, that whole dead language, it makes me anxious. I'm sure you'll say that now that we have the Internet, we're spoiled for choice with opinions! What happened next demonstrated that and, even though I've stopped looking, I'm guessing the frenzy has escalated. But that was just it: I was trying to protect myself from a vacuum. On the other hand, Gilles's anger was often in inverse proportion to the triviality of the topic. He would cling to the most meaningless subjects, it would come out of nowhere, the conversation would get bumpy, explosive in some instances. I sometimes suspected he did it on purpose, yes, like he needed to create tension between us, to put happiness to the test. These tests didn't work with me, I defused everything, knowing this would lead to destruction, and therefore fear. It's like the needle swiveling frantically on an internal dial, warning of a threat that needs to be averted as soon as possible.

"But I do remember two occasions when I argued a little, just to see how far things would go. They'll give you an idea of the territory. So, one time, we found our local grocery store was closed, and he started singing the praises of stores in the States that are open day and night, even on Sundays. Just picture the scene! We were walking through the Parc Montsouris and he was getting more and more angry about French storekeepers who insist on their little breaks, 'just like teachers, in fact,' he added, glancing sideways at me. He knew I'd been a teacher before 'devoting myself to my writing' as they say. But I didn't take that as a slight to me, or I pretended not to notice. 'What about you with your theater work?' I asked mischievously. 'You always have a day off on Mondays.' 'It's not the same at all,' he snarled. '*I* am an artist.' 'Maybe, but ordinary people have a right to rest too.' And I started defending workers on the receiving end of capitalism's unbridled consumerism, citing my great-grandmother who'd worked in her perfumery in Rouen until she was more than eighty, except on Sundays when she went to church. He countered by supporting people who, precisely because they worked all week, had a right to do their shopping on Sundays in a secular society. Basically, it was completely absurd, we were both right, but his catalog of examples went on and on, he was so insistent and over-the-top that the whole thing scared me by the end. I can't bear wasted time, I find it overwhelming, violent. I've been to dinners where all the talking made me want to die. Speaking but not saying anything is like an injury. Battles of opinion finish me off completely. It's almost like he knew, he was playing on that. Either way, we stayed angry with each other until the next day because of that bland conversation. That time, yes, I thought he was a total moron, I admit it. But in a nice way, if you see what I mean, like a one-off aberration, not who he was. Do you know the passage in Deleuze's *Abécédaire* when he celebrates the touch of madness in a person as what gives them their charm and even what makes us love them? What he actually says, wait, I'll tell you this from memory. He says: 'If you do not know the small root or small seed of madness in a person, you cannot love them. We are all a little mad, and I am afraid, or I am very glad, that the touch of madness in a person is the very source of their charm.' Well, that was what it was like for me: I liked his hint of craziness, without really knowing if it appealed to me or frightened me—I didn't want to dig too deep. If I'd opted for fear, I would have left and nothing would have happened. But his anger was an enigma, and his charm was endlessly powerful. The strangest part is that when I raised the subject again the following year, he vehemently denied it, retorting rather contemptuously that he didn't give a damn what people did with their Sundays!

"Another time, after the *Charlie Hebdo* attack, we were talking about our teens and I was mourning the loss of my idols, none of whom he'd heard of. 'You didn't have a normal childhood,' I told him. 'In those days I read Cabu and trawled around parties with garage music.' Oh Lord, what had I said! He just took off all on his own, working himself into a state without me saying a single word. No, he definitely wasn't like everyone else, not like the dopes who got blind drunk and smoked joints in gangs at the end of the day during high school. He preferred Mozart and Chopin, he had every right to, after all! 'You preferred Chopin to shopping,' I ventured unsuccessfully. It was getting more heated. Yes, his childhood had been different, so what? He was proud of it. Where were they now, all those little assholes who made fun of him when he went to his music lessons after school? 'But, Gilles, Gilles, wait,' I kept saying, never managing to break in. It was quite something. This disproportionate rage, the unjustified feeling that he was being accused and his wild aggression in retaliation—I noticed all that several times. He would eventually calm down when I reassured him that I loved and admired him, but he would stay withdrawn for a long time, with the stubborn distrust of a misunderstood victim." "*Do* you admire him?" "No, to be honest, no. I use that word because I often got the feeling it was needed—with my husband, of course, it was the only thing that kept *him* going, but probably with the others too, with other men, I mean. Most of them. They need to be admired, it's almost obscene. Even beneath apparent modesty, if you dig a little, there's this furious longing to be admired. Flattered, too, that's often enough for them—they don't distinguish between the two. Women aren't like that, or not so often, they're on closer terms with the truth, in other words with failure. Accepting your own weakness is a very feminine strength, one that few men have and none of them envies us. And anyway, I don't just admire spontaneously. All that glisters is not gold, as my grandmother used to say. And it's not just Gilles—even Proust or Bach, I wouldn't say I admire them." "What would you say, then?" "I love them."

"Now that I think about it, when he was like that, Gilles seemed like a misfit, as if he'd come from a parallel universe and didn't have the codes for our world. So yes, if I try to remember the early days of our relationship, I can think of little upsets, some bullying. I put it down to his jealousy—nothing too serious—and to the childhood he'd had. I thought he'd been brought up in a rather petty-minded atmosphere where there wasn't much emotional generosity, and that was confirmed when I met his mother. She loved gossip, you know, bitching about people, commenting on their quirks. He'd inherited some of this kind of pettiness, and it was the only kind I ever saw in him. For example, once we were past the first few months, he would sometimes make fun of a physical flaw—no, not make fun, actually, that's not right: He would *notice* it. I would be talking—it often happened when we disagreed, having a minor argument, always started by him—and he would suddenly stare at a particular part of my face, becoming absorbed by it as if he'd stopped listening, so I would break off and ask, 'What is it?' 'Nothing,' he replied, then I would press him and he would pronounce in a matter-of-fact voice: 'Your eyebrows are unkempt' or 'You have a hair on your chin.' But I always used the same policy, replying breezily, 'Yes, I know, I'm Robert Badinter's secret child'—which didn't stop me from being extra vigilant about my eyebrows from then on. I mostly thought it was his way of bringing our conversation to an end, when he felt he didn't have the upper hand. I got used to this weakness. When I was a girl, there was a boy in the schoolyard who always poked fun at me when I walked by, he said I was ugly, I had big feet, or mousy hair, and he later admitted that he was in love with me, hopelessly in love, he claimed, but with no hope of ever being worthy of me, and I never forgot this type of madness in boys: being absolutely vile when they love someone.

"What you must understand, Mrs. Niepce, is that none of this weighed heavy in the balance of everyday life, which was so loaded with happiness. I didn't idealize him, no, I don't think so, but, with the exception of these few details I've just described, he *was* ideal. When I was little, I always used to have the same dream—well, until the arrival of the first nightmares. I dreamed that I lived in a magic house where I could have everything I wanted, and when I'd used it up or eaten it (an ice cream, a dress, a toy), it was replaced, so I never wanted for anything. I was happy but never weary of it. Gilles had built this magic house for me, a circle around me, and he was its center, its area, and its circumference all at the same time. It was so new for me! I can go back to my childhood or my marriage, I can picture my father or my husband, no one had ever treated me like that. Sure, Julien put me on a pedestal, but it was to distance me from everything and, ultimately, to ignore me. With Gilles it was the opposite, whether it was his presents, his texts, the never-ending phone calls, the *I love you*s, his invitations, his plans, the way he looked at me, the things he did, Gilles was so attentive, yes, that's it, I can't think of a better way to summarize our connection, right from the start: He paid such caring attention to me. I mattered. I was past halfway through my life and I'd only just come across such sweetness. Sweetness and intensity. The joy of being in this world with a soulmate."

She's there
She's drinking tea
coffee
The cup is next to
the book she's reading
He came over to bring it to her
stroked her arm
kissed
the top of her head
She's languid
at the touch of his lips
He walked away again
He's in the next room
She's a thousand years old
her desire is eternal
It travels through walls
like the smell of mimosa

or a melody
She works
she's peaceful
She knows that at some point
this calm
will start to race
like her heart
when she's been running
Desire thuds
she can feel it circulating
discreet blood
without which nothing stays
alive
She wants
evening to fall
Later
she will perhaps
have drunk something other
than tea
She will have said
Cheers
with smiling eyes
Desire will have escalated
in the things around her
the curtains, their folds, the cup
with its blue watermark, the glass
with its imprint of lips
She will glide her hand
under that shirt
Skin under her fingers

under her hand
the grain of that skin
the crook of that shoulder
her arm resting along the edge
of that belt
The movement she will make
to undo it
she can't think of it
without a little jolt of pain
a feeling of dread
that one day it will be dead
that eternity is a deception
all in her head
Now these slow maneuvers in bed
need to stop
nipples pinched
between fingers
vulva peeled open
by a mouth
It needs to end
He must put it into her
deeply
he must drive inside
And she must come alive
at last
she must die
be dead
to the death
with all hands on board

and this soulmate in her head
she must take the bait.

♦

"I remember meeting them at the movie theater," says Émilie. "We were going to see Pasolini's *The Gospel According to St. Matthew.* They were beautiful, there was a sort of glow in their faces, they must have just made love, that's what I thought at the time, I was envious particularly as I was single in those days. The previous screening hadn't finished and we waited outside in a line that kept getting longer. Eventually, the doors opened, people started moving along, and Gilles suddenly started yelling, 'Don't touch me!' He turned around and his face was twisted with rage, he was talking to a woman who must have nudged him in the back. It was such an outlandish scene, everyone was transfixed. I remember the look of panic on Claire's face. The woman took a step back and apologized, Gilles found it hard to regain a semblance of composure, and Claire did what she always does: She defused the situation. She put her arms around Gilles. We were just passing a poster of the movie with a close-up of Christ. *Noli me tangere,* she said and the three of us laughed. But, you see, with hindsight, I think it's worth really listening to those words, they say literally what he meant: I don't want to be touched, I don't want to feel emotions, I don't want to feel anything. Don't touch me.

"I don't know what had happened between him and Claire just before that—too much emotion perhaps, a sense of threat. Lots of men are afraid of being moved, they want to stay in control. What I thought at the time was that they were alike, the two of them, but it produced the opposite effects: They had different ways of protecting themselves from a shared fear. When something was wrong, Gilles flew into a temper and took it out on someone, whereas Claire played everything down. Often by laughing. She's someone who laughs a lot—who used to laugh a lot. She laughs things off. And actually, that's how she uses humor in her books. I can see exactly what they would have been like as children, the two of them. He would deny pain with anger, and she would with cheerfulness. With simulated composure. In some ways, it was more of an act for her, so it was harder to bear. If you constantly stifle anger, you're always smoothing things out, well, when laughter can no longer do the trick, it explodes. That's how I see it."

◆

"So yes, Mrs. Niepce, I was happy, what they call happy. Gilles was also very much there for my daughter, right from the start. His involvement meant a lot to me. Alice needed a father as much as I needed a man.

"The first time, the three of us had arranged to meet for lunch at a Chinese restaurant. Alice was passing through Paris, she was heading off that same evening to Lyon where she was studying at the National School of Fine Arts. It must have been March or April, it was a little early in the relationship, I'd never introduced Alice to anyone before, for all the right reasons, but I wanted them to meet, and they both agreed straightaway. Maybe it was a kind of test I set for him without really framing it as such in my own mind: Even though my daughter was twenty and no longer lived with me, I wanted to know if she would like him. And similarly, Gilles had already told his children about me. 'Wow!' his son had said, glad he'd be able to go back to the apartment now that it was stripped of his stepmother. 'Phew!' said his daughter who'd had enough of being slapped by Violetta. 'You mean she hit her?' I squeaked. 'Yes. I didn't tell you?' Gilles replied. 'That was the point of no return for me. That was when I properly decided to leave Violetta. No one touches my children! And when I told my friends about it, everyone agreed with me, even the ones who really liked her.' 'Of course,' I said. 'That's unforgivable.'

"The first lunch went really well, although the conversation was just factual—they were both reserved, it wasn't going to be a time for confidences. I was sitting on the banquette with Alice, and Gilles was facing us. He asked her about what she'd done in life, about her studies, what she wanted to do. 'Your mother tells me that…' She replied with her usual reserve but I could tell that she responded to his kindness, his attention. I have to say, the way he listened to her was extraordinary—I was sitting opposite him, I could see—it was, yes, almost a caricature, the way a mime artist would have listened: kindly eyes, hands clasped, his head tilted slightly to the right, and at regular intervals he gave a little nod or murmured approvingly, anyone would have thought he was about to give us his blessing. At the end of the meal, when he said goodbye to us on the sidewalk, he looked happy but exhausted. 'I really like him,' said Alice, 'he's very kind.' Personally, I thought he'd been a little odd, like he was hamming up the role of the perfect stepfather, but Alice had an explanation. 'It's a habit with actors,' she said. 'He can't settle for just listening, he needs to *show* that he's listening. But I like him, he's cool. And you look gorgeous together!'

"Over time, she confided in him with more intimate things. She told me about it but I wasn't there. She needed to talk to him one-to-one to tell him about her father, because he—Gilles—was a good father, who loved his children…and maybe her too, a little, like a daughter of his own? She hoped so. He also confided in her, she told me, he talked about his childhood, his mother who'd walked out on him—he still saw her, though, even if he couldn't handle her for very long—and about his father who'd died during a bout of delirium tremens, toward the end he no longer even recognized Gilles. They wound up laughing about the problems of having parents. 'But your mother's wonderful, right?' he'd said with a hint of a question. Alice had said yes. 'Well, not always,' she added when she told me about the conversation."

"The following year, it was Easter 2015, we went away to the Peloponnese with Alice and a friend of hers. We rented a car and the four of us drove around from beaches to archaeological sites. It was great fun. I'd warned the girls that Gilles couldn't stand noise and liked only classical music. As we set out one day, he streamed the playlist from his phone, and they started singing along at the top of their lungs to Madonna, Prince, Amy Winehouse—"Love Is a Losing Game," and recent songs that I didn't know, Alice named them for me, and she and Gilles laughed at my ignorance. 'With Mom, besides Bach and Barbara, there's no one,' she said. I couldn't believe it. Had he put that playlist together for them with this trip in mind, to make her happy? What a darling, I thought. Isn't he overdoing it? I didn't think. Another time, the girls started talking about their piercings, Alice said she'd had the first one done when she was fifteen, behind my back and to her father's fury. And then there was Gilles getting out his phone to show them pictures of himself with two piercings in one ear and biker's rings on every finger, which sat about as well with him as Kurt Cobain with Couperin. 'Super classy!' the girls cooed. 'When was that?' I asked, stunned. The photo looked recent. 'Six, maybe seven years ago. Then I took them out,' he said, not offering any further details. 'The holes healed up.' 'Shame, they really suited you,' Alice said.

"She was right, even I found the juxtaposition very sexy. Later that evening, when I was alone with him, I laughed about it: I'd have loved a bad boy with pierced ears to play Couperin for me stripped to the waist, I'd have watched his skull rings glide over the keyboard forever. 'Would you like me to have the piercings done again?' he asked. 'If you want me to, I will.' I shook my head, then he said, 'A nose piercing, then? Or somewhere else...' he added, poker faced. I laughed. 'Do I get to choose where?' But so much willingness bothered me, I couldn't think about it without feeling uncomfortable. It was like he was completely open to another person's wishes, prepared to change just to please them, and what *he* wanted didn't even feature. Originality but with variable geometry, in a way. A chameleon personality, a movable 'me.' Personally, I would have felt I was taking advantage. You don't have to do anything special to make me love you, I thought to myself. I didn't say it."

◆

"Well, I do remember one time," said Carole. "It must have been about six, eight months after they met, Gilles threw a party—I don't know what for . . . No, I do, he'd won a prize from this arts organization called the SACD. All the guests were friends of his, except for me—Claire must have insisted that I was invited. She's actually very shy, very stressed by having lots of people around, she often quotes that line from Georges Brassens, you know, 'When there's more than four of us, we're a bunch of assholes.' The only thing she's interested in is love, I think, she saves herself for love. For friendship, in a pinch. Sometimes.

"Either way, I thought the party was odd. There were about twenty-five guests, it was the first time Gilles was seen socially with Claire, and he didn't introduce her to anyone! I even heard someone ask him how Violetta was doing, he sidestepped that one. The thing is no one knew they were together, him and Claire, and he didn't do anything to make it clear. He didn't come over to her once with a show of affection, a sign of intimacy. The only time he got her talking to some other guests—I remember it because I thought it was crass—was when she and I were talking and, without any sort of apology, Gilles just said, 'Come on, someone wants to ask you something,' and he led her by the arm toward a sneery-looking couple who asked her straight out how many copies of her books she sold. With no introduction or preamble, nothing. And she answered sweetly, as if she couldn't see what was a blatant lack of respect! And how about her podcasts, were they doing well? How much did they bring in? Gilles had already gone off schmoozing other guests, mostly women, in fact. His son was there, a sort of carbon copy of his dad, the same smile on his lips, they both hovered next to the most attractive women for a long time. Flirting, that's the word that popped into my head, they were flirting. There was a complicity between them, and it didn't give a good impression. Claire didn't even notice it, she seemed to make a point of honor of being discreet.

"I've never talked to her about it because she always thinks I'm just intolerant, but I have very uncomfortable memories of it. I think the worst bit was when she came into the room with two salmon pies that she'd made at her place and there was nothing else to eat. A few people had brought bottles of wine, that was all. It wasn't miserliness because Gilles could be very generous to Claire. No, it was worse: He'd just forgotten to buy anything for his guests to eat. Our mindset has a duty to think of others first. A reflex altruism that women are very familiar with, am I right? With him, zilch: It was his party, he was the person being celebrated, he hadn't thought about anyone but himself!"

5

"On the subject of the magic house in your dreams, tell me about the house." "The house?" "Yes. The house where the incidents took place. Did you buy it together? When? Why?"

♦

"We were in a restaurant near Nice, it was our first vacation together in the summer of 2014, by the sea. Gilles was wearing a white shirt that brought out the dark emerald of his eyes and I was in a lilac-colored dress that he'd given me that same morning—he'd bought it without me, having seen it in a shop-window when he went to get the bread. It looked fabulous on me, he'd said when I tried it on, and it really did fall beautifully. I was stunned that a man could choose a dress for a woman without getting it wrong, without her trying it on. 'I know your body,' he'd said simply. I'd pressed myself up to him and I felt him harden against my stomach, I'd followed the contours of his swelling cock through the fabric with my fingers. Stroking his penis made my head spin, sometimes I thought I might pass out, my desire ate into my consciousness. But the fact that he always responded to it gave me complete confidence.

"At the next table some people were speaking a strange foreign language, Hungarian, Finnish? Gilles asked what countries I'd traveled to and where else I'd like to go. I pulled a face. I actually traveled a lot for my books, I was often invited abroad when my work was translated, so I'd been to Brazil, Vietnam, Russia, China, and almost all over Europe, but I'd never had time to see anything, I didn't call it traveling. In fact, when—

"'With me,' Gilles interrupted. 'I meant where would you like to travel with me?' 'With you, wherever you like,' I said. '*We can go where you want, when you want*,' I sang, it's from that song by Joe Dassin. He frowned at me, I'd forgotten he loathed pop music. 'How about you, where would you like to go?' I asked.

"He'd traveled quite a lot, he liked Japan, India, Mexico, but he'd also sometimes been away for puppet festivals or workshops. He'd been to Bali and Canada, the United States of course. He wanted to get to know North America better, the continent of freedom.

"I listened to him with half an ear. (*'The continent of freedom'? Didn't he sing the praises of communism to me a week earlier?*) I was toying with changing the subject. Deep down, I've always hated travel, or at least traveling as a tourist. I like spending time somewhere. My dream is to live there, explore all of it. Places are like people: It takes time to get to know them. When we travel, we come across this breadth of people and places that we can only understand lengthwise. Only seeing them long term gives us access. Otherwise, what? Two or three snapshots, a few experiences... 'To be honest, I don't really like traveling,' I ventured. 'I agree with Beckett in I can't remember which play: I'm stupid, but not stupid enough to enjoy traveling.'

"Gilles shut right down—just like that, a firewall went up, eyes like metal. I'd upset him, how stupid of me! Darkening a smile like his next to a sunset like that? It takes a special kind of dumb. I backtracked. 'My father loved traveling, whenever he had two free weeks, he'd be off—without us, obviously. Sometimes he'd bring us back a little present. I remember he brought home jewel scarabs for us from Mexico—alive. I was horrified, I've always had a phobia of insects. But he didn't seem to know that.'

"Gilles was still shut down, stubborn, almost hostile; he wasn't interested in what I was saying and he showed it by pointedly watching the waitress flitting between the tables.

"'What I mean is that, for me, the experience of travel can be summarized as a small, badly chosen gift and a couple of anecdotes. Maybe if my father had taken me with him, it would have been different, I don't know. Anyway, I prefer places where you spend some time. With you, I'd go anywhere because... (*because* you're *my journey, I don't give a damn about the scenery, the most beautiful country is wherever you are*). But my own personal dream is to own a house... I mean not just somewhere to visit but somewhere to stay and come back to, a place to grow attached to, where you leave a part of yourself. Not somewhere you're just passing through, but more where you can let things accumulate—books, clothes, memories, a place where time passes (*where you yourself pass*). Do you see what I mean?'

"Gilles's face was transformed a second time. He smiled at me, calming the alarm signal that had lit up on my mental dashboard, my fear of coming across as bourgeois, old, and a homebody all in one go. 'You want a house?' He had this look in his eyes like a man who's just grasped something vital about someone important—or the other way around. I nodded yes, biting my lip, falsely apologetic. 'Well, I mean, someday... when I have some money.' 'What sort of house, my Claire?' he asked, taking my hand. 'I don't know. Like the houses around here. I love the sun, the light you get in the south, the strong shape it gives everything.' 'In France, then?' 'Not necessarily. Every time I visit another country, I find places I'd like to live. I'm not very realistic: a palace in Venice, a Palladian villa in Tuscany, a haunted Scottish castle . . . I've even daydreamed about renting Victor Hugo's house on the island of Guernsey! I just need to be able to project myself into a place, drinking a cappuccino on a piazza or treading the same paths as one of my great men—or women! Trouville or Tarquinia would also suit me very well. But if I think about it seriously, I have a specific reason for preferring France: the language. I need to understand the language.' 'Don't you speak English?' he asked, amused, a tad condescending, I thought. 'Yes, I do. Just about. Well, I read it, no problem, and I understand it if it's not too fast, but I get very inhibited as soon as I have to speak it. The words don't come to me when I need them. And I hate that feeling of not being able to say exactly what I want to say, being reduced to a sort of deficient means of expression. It stresses me. But I actually love English.' 'What is it? Are you scared of getting sick abroad and not being able to explain your symptoms?' I laughed. 'No, no, it's not just that! That's so funny!' 'Well then, explain,' he said irritably. 'In what circumstances do people get stressed because they can't make themselves understood?' 'Erm, I don't know . . . all the time. Every time you talk to someone except for asking the way or what time the last bus leaves . . . When you can't go into details about your ideas, your feelings, it messes with your head, surely?'

"He curled a skeptical lip. 'That's definitely a writer talking when you say stuff like that. Shall I pour you more wine, my darling?' I laughed out loud. 'You don't need to be a writer to like it when language goes beyond minimal communication—seriously! The minute people are limited in what they can say, they feel uncomfortable. Right? Is this man of the theater not interested in nuance?' 'Oh well…' Gilles said evasively. 'Either way, nothing stresses me. I don't even know what you're talking about. This Sancerre is very good, isn't it? But let's go back to your dream house. What's it like? Like Lucie's?'

"At the time we were staying in a house in Menton loaned to us by his cousin Lucie. Well, I say loaned, rented would be more accurate because at the end of the trip I was surprised to find I had to withdraw six hundred euros from an ATM to settle half the rent, it wasn't expensive for a week in July, Gilles said, slightly embarrassed, I didn't say anything, I didn't like talking money with Gilles, it seems to have been a touchy subject with Violetta, and I wanted to be completely financially independent, which I always had been—I prided myself that I hadn't been economically reliant on a man since the age of nineteen—but sometimes he dragged me into spending that I had trouble covering. He seemed to be mysteriously free of any concerns on that front and, although I felt awkward, I sometimes let him take me out to restaurants that were too expensive for me.

"'No, it's a little old school. And anyway, it's a villa. I'd like a handsome house built of stone with an old fireplace, thick walls, and most of all a garden!' 'A garden? Duly noted.' 'Basically, my dream's very simple: That's it.'

"I waved a hand toward the mimosa brightening the steps in its stoneware pot.

"'I'd like a house here, in the South of France, with some mimosas. I adore mimosas. That bright yellow, it's such a miracle! Such a powerful life force! There's a Félix Vallotton painting *Mimosas in Bloom at Cagnes*, you just have to look at it and it fills you with joy. The street, the buildings, everything is lit up. So in real life, can you imagine! Waking every morning and seeing that ball of fluffiness, smelling that strange, unique fragrance. Color and fragrance—there, that's happiness. It doesn't last in a vase, but on the tree... pure joy!' 'Aha! Now I know why your living-room walls are yellow,' Gilles said in a disconsolate voice. 'Yes! It puts me in a good mood in the morning! Don't you like it?' 'Let's say that Provence in Paris is a little trashy.' 'Oh...' 'I'm teasing you, come on. You're allowed to have bad taste.' 'Okay, oleanders if you prefer.' 'Pink walls, that's not great either. All right, where do you want this house of yours?' 'I want it... In my dreams it's by the sea, or not far from it, you can get there on foot. Or it has a pool at least, so that the children and later their children want to come there. And some land, with trees, a mimosa, as we've seen, and a vegetable plot.' 'Okay fine. Are you planning to plant cabbages?' 'I've always wanted a manual hobby, something that's a rest from writing. I like the idea of watering, watching things grow, harvesting at the right time. It's not that different from writing a novel when it comes down to it.' 'No. Either way, you end up making soup.' 'Excuse me? Are you saying my writing is soup? What a bastard!' but I was laughing too, I didn't believe a word of it. Gilles smiled, pleased with himself. 'I'm joking,' he said eventually, his face unreadable. 'You know how much I admire you. But now where were we? How do you picture this house where you can write and simmer your soups? Describe it for me.' I waved a hand at the countryside in front of us, settled back into my chair, closed my eyes, and described everything that came into my head, everything I would do in this magic house. (*Wasn't there a kids' song about living in a magic house?*) I concluded by saying, 'With you, obviously,' and leaned toward him to kiss his neck. He looked at me softly, took my hand, sat in silence for a while, and then said in an emotional voice, 'What if we bought it, this house of yours, my love? For real.' I must have looked amazed because he added lightly, 'If you told me you had dreams of the countryside, I wouldn't have gone along with it. But the sea, the Mediterranean, I'll go for that. Not too far from a town, I'll go for that.' 'Marseille?' I suggested. 'Back to some roots...Rocky inlets, the smell of rosemary, rabbit droppings (*all delivered with a Marseille accent*).' I thought we were still playing. Gilles swept his hand backward and forward in front of his face, annoyed. 'No, not Marseille, it's too rough. Nearer here. Or over toward Montpellier. But Nice would be the pick of the bunch.' 'Yes, but Nice must cost a fortune.' 'Yes, but you'd be happy.' 'Yes, but I don't have the dough.' 'Yes, but we'd be happy.' 'Yes, but we already are.'

"We laughed together. We kissed across the table. We watched the sea in silence. 'The solution,' he went on, 'would be for you to sell your apartment.' I stared at him wide-eyed, ding-dong went my warning bell. 'But...? How would that work? The idea isn't to live in the house all year round. I need to be in Paris, too.' 'Writers can write anywhere, can't they?' 'I need to be in Paris,' I said again. I could feel anxiety weaving its straitjacket around my chest. 'I have friends, I go to shows, I see people for my podcasts. And Alice has a room at my apartment, I can't throw everything out.' Gilles stroked my arm. 'I understand, my love. So I have a suggestion for you, and it won't cost your pretty arms and your pretty legs. You sell your apartment, you keep part of the money to buy a little pied-a-terre in Paris for Alice, if you really want to, and with the rest we go fifty-fifty on buying a house, and when we're not there, we live together in Paris, at my place, my apartment. Sophie will come over sometimes but she'll be flying the nest soon like the others. Our girls are grown up, my darling, we need to think about ourselves.'

"I didn't react straightaway. Time was accelerating so wildly that I couldn't think. This was shaping up into something so life-changing! My mind was having trouble taking it on board. Living with someone again . . . I hadn't had any experience of that since my divorce. I'd gotten into the habit of complete freedom, I got up when I wanted to, I wrote at night if I felt like it, I ate at any time of the day or night. But it was Gilles who was suggesting this life to me. We'd been in his cousin's house for only five days and I was already giddy with the happiness of waking beside him every morning, I loved his sleeping body, I loved his body when it moved, his smile—so much—and the way he read discreetly next to me on the terrace when I was writing, or when we peeled vegetables together in the kitchen, I loved watching him undress, unbuttoning his shirt, staying bare chested for a moment, taking his time because he knew I was waiting for him. There wasn't a piano, but we watched TV series in the evenings, sitting shoulder to shoulder and eating ice cream—we could do these things every day, and then make love. Love whenever I wanted it, whenever he wanted it . . . 'I thought you liked things concrete,' he said. 'This is concrete. We're too old now for just dreaming, wouldn't you say?' 'I haven't even finished paying off my bank loan. I have at least another fifteen years of it,' I said in the end. Gilles didn't reply. He was looking at me, as cool as a cucumber, while I wrangled between longing and blind panic. 'But do *you* have enough money for the fifty-fifty?' I asked him. 'Does theater pay *that* well?' He smiled. A while back, he'd bought and then sold several places in Paris at the right time, with substantial capital gains, he had savings, life insurance policies for his children. And yes, theater directing made pretty good money, particularly in opera, even when the critics stuck their noses in (he'd struggled to recover from the lukewarm reception of his last production for the Opera House in Brest). Besides, someday he would inherit from his mother who was very comfortably off thanks to her second marriage to a childless obstetrician. 'And you will too,' he said. 'I will what?' 'You'll also inherit from your mother sometime. That'll erase your father's stinginess.' I didn't pick up on this. He was counting—and that's exactly the word—he was counting on his mother's death; not me. 'And perhaps someday, you and I, we'll . . . My Claire,' he said. 'I can't imagine life without you now.'

"Our sea bass in a salt crust came, and the waitress filled our glasses. That's how we decided to buy the house. Someone inside me was laughing at myself. The me who writes, most likely, the one who reads. That particular me clearly remembered the rose-tinted photo-romances that her grandmother had loved and the Paul Géraldy poems that her great-grandmother used to devour. But, even though I was tangled up with that version of me, there was only one thing I wanted: to be in those photos and in those poems. I would strike the pose wearing a candy-pink dress in a chocolate-box setting drenched in yellow sunshine. Love takes you to places. It sets you down somewhere you would never go alone, even if it is a photo-romance in your grandmother's hands. All that was missing was a trip to Venice, I thought jokingly—six months later I would be letting my hand trail in the wake of a gondola with Gilles's arm around my waist. I even took a photo of a large mimosa beside a canal there. To be honest, when Gilles took selfies of us near the Bridge of Sighs with glasses of limoncello in our hands, I instinctively wiped the irony from my face. It had been my undoing up until then, I thought: irony shored up with doubt, satire, a habit for intellectualizing conventions, the effort of not being like everyone else, a horror of herd mentality. Now what I needed to do was live in the moment of this love, and take Gilles as my model for finding the joy in a word, a photo, a gift, a moment—in all simplicity. He would be my happiness teacher."

"Did you not think of doing it the other way around? Him coming to live at your place in Paris, and him buying the house on his own by selling his apartment or with the money he'd set aside?" "No. He didn't like my apartment, anyway, the neighborhood wasn't for him. He only went there three times, including the first time. And it was always disastrous. The first time he slept at my place, I woke in the middle of the night and found him huddled on the living-room sofa, looking totally lost, wrapped up in a blanket like a baby in swaddling. My neighbors were having a party and the noise woke him, he said. Mostly he looked scared, like a little boy who's been forced to sleep all on his own in an unfamiliar room. I put my arms around him like a mother and rocked him. The next day he explained that he really didn't like noise. The second night he spent at my place, after we'd made love, we heard people fucking like animals on the floor above. It went on and on. I would have laughed about it but Gilles was horrified. 'It's porn,' he said. 'It's a porn film.' 'Don't be ridiculous!' I replied. But maybe he was right because my neighbor was a solitary, paranoid guy, not the sort you'd associate with torrid performances, he could easily have wanted to make us pay for the disturbance. 'I'm more of a feminist than you are,' Gilles accused me, 'I despise pornography. Men who watch porn, yuk. Don't you find it shocking?' The truth is I never watch porn, but I was irritated by his conformism—the sort of ready-to-wear thinking that I'd already noticed in him. 'Oh, you know me,' I said, 'there are doubts about my morality: I doubt other people's morals.' But to finish up about my apartment, the fact is I quickly gathered that Gilles needed to be on his territory, at home, in his neighborhood. Which is strange from someone who likes traveling, wouldn't you say? But like I said, I loved everything about him, even his contradictions.

"So it was always me who went to his place. It didn't bother me, in fact I liked it. When I love someone, I like being in their world, I don't try to lure them into mine. For example, in the early days, I actually didn't like his apartment either—too cold, too tidy, all those straight lines, a really bourgeois neighborhood, the opposite of mine—but then later I loved going there. It was bigger and lighter with better heating and soundproofing than mine. Before I lived there completely, I spent a lot of time there, including when he was away for work—at his place I was with him, it was almost like being in his arms. Nothing in the world would have made me ask him to change anything: It was him. Even with the house, when we bought it, he was the one who mostly furnished it." "So you were a visitor in some ways? Never properly at home?" "When you love someone, you're always slightly a visitor, aren't you? What I mean is: You're careful. You don't settle into love, nothing must ever be completely familiar. As soon as you feel at home when you're with your lover, it's screwed.

"On the other hand, Gilles gave me the keys to his place very early on. In fact, it was a turning point in how much I trusted him from the start, even though it was in difficult circumstances. A man who gives you his keys is letting you into his life, he has nothing to hide." "Unless he has a secret drawer. How about you? Do you have anything to hide?" "Yes, I do, in a way. I need a place to myself. A place to write. I never gave him my keys, actually I've never given them to any man, nor my passwords and access codes, I need somewhere that's mine. But like I said, he never really came to my place." "So how did it work in Paris, once you were at his apartment?" "Oh! Gilles was wonderful, at the time. He organized a little corner of his bedroom for me. That was where I wrote, and he worked in his study." "What about at the house?" "A house is bigger. We had the space." "You mentioned difficult circumstances. What do you mean?" "One afternoon, when we'd known each other for maybe a month or two, we were in bed at his place in Paris, listening to *Tosca*, and someone buzzed the intercom. Gilles didn't answer it. His face was strained, like there was some threat, his whole body was on the alert. A few minutes later there was another ring, at the door to the apartment this time. Then someone was fumbling at the lock and that's when Gilles jumped out of bed and put his pants on. 'Wait here,' he said. 'Don't move.' I couldn't hear much. A woman's voice, plaintive sounding and soon bundled back down the stairs—Violetta? Gilles dodged my questions—'Is she still in love with you?'—but the next day he bought a new barrel for the lock and changed it right in front of me, revealing unsuspected talents as a fixer-upper, and he gave me a key. A sprinkling of white sawdust stayed on the doormat for a long time."

◆

A few days earlier, Gilles had acted on an impulse after a marriage counseling session where he'd really got it in the neck—that's what he told Georges on the phone. In front of the final judgment–style therapist, a tearful Violetta had heaped him with recriminations: He neglected her, he unfairly blamed her for the failure of the show they'd put on together about her father, and even blamed her for the chilly reception his production of *Don Giovanni* had received, it was being compared to Matteo Lodi's 1976 production (with the press insinuating he would only ever be a studious disciple of Lodi's). Even so, she was still banking on the end of their time living together to rekindle the flame. "We can do it," she'd said as they left the session, "love will triumph." He couldn't take any more. He'd thought that physical separation would set him free, but now she was turning him into an on-again, off-again relationship. Luckily, there was Claire. As soon as he and Violetta went their separate ways on the sidewalk, he'd gone to his local city hall and asked for the form to terminate a contract of civil union, which he filled in, signed, and sent to the interested party. He'd calculated that the postal service was so slow that she wouldn't receive it before the next week, and had then dreamed up a business trip away from Paris and invited Claire to spend the night at his apartment. But the postman had been overzealous, and Violetta had shown up, shaking and aggrieved, to ask Gilles for explanations. When he opened the door to her—she clutching her key, which couldn't unlock the door because he'd deliberately left his in the lock on the inside—when he'd opened the door stripped to the waist at five o'clock in the afternoon with *Tosca* blasting around the apartment, "*Torturate l'anima. Sì, l'anima mi torturate*," she'd burst into tears—did she have any other options in her repertoire? He'd driven her back out onto the landing and asked her to return her key, which she'd refused to do between sobs. She wanted them to talk (talking, always talking) about the contract of civil union, about his cowardice—it was nothing more or less than a repudiation—about his lack of respect, but he'd shut the door on her because, well, did she show any respect? He didn't talk to manipulative bitches like her, he concluded as he described the scene to Georges. "I didn't think it was exactly classy of him," said Georges, "but hey, I get it."

♦

"It was Gilles who handled looking for a house. I couldn't do it, it would have taken too much time away from writing. Honoring my promise not to write about him, I'd started a novel inspired by my father's life. I really enjoyed it and discovered that a ban doesn't necessarily cause frustration. The tour of the 'not Matteo Lodi' show was over, Gilles wasn't working on anything else, and most of all he wanted a perfect house—perfection was something he was prepared to devote himself to. I joked about it with my therapist, we gently poked fun at his obsessive little neurosis." "So, you were seeing a therapist at the time? Why was that?" "I started therapy after losing my baby. He died at three weeks as a result of a medical error. It was what I'd call survival treatment, you know, like there are survival blankets. I needed to be wrapped up in words and meaning to warm me after the effect of his death. When my grief subsided a little, I kept going, I'd come to like looking in-depth at things and people, and myself. I started reading the core texts, I drew strength and understanding from them the way you sometimes can from friendships, I became passionate about Freud, Lacan, Melanie Klein—they bandaged my pain just as well as Émilie and Carole did. I think it would be hard for a writer to be dismissive about psychoanalysis, trying to find the truth through language is their common territory. When Gilles and I met, he was very skeptical about it, 'all these people who think they can get out of a fix by talking about Mommy and Daddy, I just don't believe in it,' he didn't feel implicated, or at least not at the time because, he said, he didn't experience anxiety, it was totally alien to him and he felt sorry for unhappy people who, like me, spent time and money on tending (if you could call it that) their little problems. He loathed the past and claimed that he was all 'onward and upward.' I didn't try to argue my case. Besides, my therapist retired soon afterward and her leaving coincided with when all the positivity of love was confirmed. 'We're happy,' I told her in my last session. Looking back, it's weird using that 'we' to bring an end to twenty years of 'I.' But at the time I was euphoric. And Gilles seemed very happy that I was stopping. He probably didn't want me talking about him any more than he wanted me writing about him." "Tell me, then, did you meet his *mommy and daddy*?" "His father died a long time ago, and if I have this right, he was an alcoholic. Despite the fact that he spent his whole childhood with him, Gilles talked about his death without a shred of emotion, even with some nastiness: It was as if he resented him for being dead. He portrayed his father's death as his father throwing a wrench in his own gears at just the wrong time! And an alcoholic is someone with no self-control, no will: utterly shameful in his view. His mother was the opposite: He criticized her for having too much of a good time. An incredible woman, I have to say. Strong, self-assured. With no hint of remorse about her son, or not to all outward appearances. Proud of him but also quick to have a go at him about trifling things. He couldn't stand her, but I don't know whether she realized that. I remember the first time I met her, we'd just sat around the table for a meal and she studied Gilles and said, almost to herself, 'That's the bit I got absolutely right with him—his teeth.' Holy cow, I thought, and I didn't dare smile after that. Another time she'd seen Gilles arrive along the street from her window and when he came in, she called to him in a voice that was both mocking and factual, 'Hey, you're getting a hell of a tonsure!' Gilles was furious about it for three days. 'A tonsure! What a bitch!' It was disturbing because he seemed to be accusing her of lying when she was just being blunt. And there were always disproportionate slights with reference to the mother she'd been, insulting a ghost. Anyway, no criticism of Gilles could ever be well-founded, however objective it was. As far as he was concerned, finding fault with him amounted to wanting to cause him harm. Having said that, if *I'd* abandoned my son when he was seven years old, I'd avoid making digs about his baldness. She was mostly kind to me—no, kind isn't the word: courteous. She was courteous. I stayed on my guard every time I saw her (she still lived in Marseille) because Gilles had told me that when she heard we were an item, she'd said, 'You'll just be a number, my poor boy!' I thought it was odd that he attributed her with a criticism about me that he'd claimed to have formulated himself, as if a pronouncement could have several sources indiscriminately, especially as his mother wasn't thought to know anything about me at all and hadn't read anything I'd written. The thing that really made an impression on me was what she told me about her son, as if in confidence—and with hindsight I can see how significant it was. We were in her kitchen, I was helping her peel vegetables, and she said, 'The problem with Gilles, as you've probably noticed, Claire, is that he has no empathy.' At the time, I laughed inwardly. On the one hand, Gilles pampered me—a darling—and on the other, if there was anyone who lacked empathy, she was the one. People criticize what they see in the mirror presented by other people, in other words themselves—that's what I thought. I've had time to think it over since then." "Let's get back to the house." "The house, yes. For months, Gilles scoured real estate agencies, surfed the Net, and did virtual visits. If I'm honest, I didn't really believe in it—the dream house existed only in dreams. And then he found it. Maybe you've seen photos—are there any in the file? Oh, I wish you could see it for real! Will there be a reconstruction of events? Then you'll understand why I kept calling it the magic house, even though it's not the same anymore, inevitably. The first site visit was on February 14, 2015—so symbolic. Valentine's Day but also the anniversary of my son Tristan's death. He died a long time ago, but you know what they say: 'Suffering moves on. Having suffered never does.' Which is why we never did anything special for Valentine's Day. And also because it's so commercialized. 'Who needs a date to say they love someone, to say they're in pain?' Gilles would ask indignantly.

"We went down by car. He drove the whole way from Paris to Hyères. Not very feminist, let's agree on that, and dangerous, but I don't know why, I was scared to take the wheel with him as a passenger, I felt incompetent, I was scared he'd think I was a bad driver or, worse, that he'd be frightened. It was stupid because I love driving and I've never had the tiniest accident. Oh well. Shortly before Hyères he asked me to close my eyes. We kept going for another minute or so, then he parked and cut the engine. 'Open your eyes,' he said.

"The mimosa tree was huge, dazzling, happy—can you describe a tree like that? It was a happy tree. A few branches were stirring in the breeze, others bowed down over the road from the other side of the fence that surrounded the house. It was the pride and joy of that neighborhood, the Realtor told us a little later, people made the trip specially to come and admire it like some saint who's prayed to every day—and also, although she didn't say this, to try to pick a fragrant sprig to take home with them. I remember throwing my arms around Gilles's neck and kissing and kissing him, I was hopelessly grateful. He was smiling. My dream man, my dream house: He made everything come true.

"After that the process took a long time, we had to put together an offer, talk to banks—all things I hate. Financial affairs are a black hole where time and energy go to die. I really had to push myself, shelving the novel I was writing. I was sorry to leave my apartment and I had to put a lot of stuff into storage because the studio that I'd bought in a hurry was tiny and Gilles didn't like the rest enough to furnish our house with it. I say 'our house' but at the end of the day I could pay only a small third of it, the main contribution came from Gilles." "So you were actually 'a visitor' wherever you went: in Paris and in Hyères. You were in his homes." "In a way. But they were also the places where we loved each other. They were our homes.

"We moved in during the fall of 2015 and from that point our life felt like an idyll. We shared our time between Paris and Hyères, spending long weekends and sometimes a whole month at the house and—" "Always together?" "Often. Well . . . we both had work trips, so not always. It felt significant that we'd been there only a few weeks when Gilles first mentioned the UNESCO project: He wanted to put forward his candidacy, those were his words, for a substantial UNESCO program aimed at preserving our global human heritage. He had plans to submit a dossier on safeguarding puppet-theater work around the world. It had been an ambition of his for a long time, first mooted at the time of the Ontario Festival where he'd made contact with the Canadian minister of culture. He knew he could count on that partnership to back his project, the department of popular arts was prepared to support him. He also had backup in Japan to protect Bunraku, in Turkey, Africa . . . It would be a lengthy procedure, of course, there would be a series of hearings and substantial rivals with equally valid cultural projects, but the prestige and the budget would be up to the task, and he believed in himself, luck was on his side, and he was pumped about developing his international ambitions by radiating out from Toronto as his starting point." "How did you take the news?" "Initially, I was shocked, more than that, even: I simply couldn't understand the logic or the chronology of events. 'Radiating out from Toronto' when we'd just bought a house and moved in together? 'You look upset,' Gilles said. 'Don't you want me to realize my own dream when I've just realized yours?' What could I say? Of course I wanted him to. I wanted him to be happy. I couldn't see myself asking him to give up on his ambition, particularly as I was aware of the beginnings of bitterness in him, the kind that can happen at our age, a sense of an absence of recognition, as if there's always something missing from the picture. Mind you, I personally don't see things like that, I know that whatever's missing will always be missing. I also had the feeling that he needed my admiration and did everything he could to keep it alive. Secretly, I admit, and I'm not proud of this, I hoped he wouldn't get the position. There were more than sixty applicants. When I think of everything that his failure would have avoided! But I supported him all the way, I played against my own camp. In some ways I felt indebted. Plus, I told myself that freedom comes before everything else. Being fulfilled. Nothing must stand in the way of what someone wants."

♦

"Oh yes," says Georges, "I gave Gilles hell, believe me. Applying for an international project when he'd finally found the love of his life and settled in the south, his dream part of the country, it made no sense! He always wanted more, he always dreamed bigger, aimed higher. I warned him but it made no difference. He said Claire would follow him to the ends of the earth. I'm older, I have more experience. I was worried that if he tried to have everything, he'd lose everything. It's a universal law: jack-of-all-trades, master of none. If I'm totally honest, I saw it as a terrible sign when the mimosa was struck by lightning. In both of their descriptions of events, that tree was such a symbol of their love: something luminous that made them happy. It took a direct hit in a thunderstorm. Gilles had to cut it down with a very heavy heart. I remember how they were at the time, they were floored. Claire cried helplessly by the tree stump, then she produced photos of the tree and showed them to me one by one like they'd lost a member of the family, sobbing as she commented on them. Gilles didn't know how to comfort her. The whole neighborhood was in mourning, and I thought: Ouch! I saw it as a sign of fate. And what happened next didn't prove me wrong."

6

"I wanted to ask you, Mrs. Niepce... Do you have any news?" "News, Mrs. Lancel?" "Yes, news of Gilles." "Mr. Fabian is still in a coma. Sadly, I don't know more than that. Our case hangs on that news, as I'm sure you're aware. You'll be the first to be informed." "Thank you." "You don't seem very affected. Theoretically, he's out of danger but he could have died. Did you know that? How does it make you feel? Any regrets? Any remorse?" "No." "You're unmoved by what happens to him?" "No. I'm sad. But his silence is good for me. It was all too..." "Let's pick up where we stopped last time, if you're happy to." "Yes, Mrs. Niepce. I'm listening." "I'm the one listening to you. We'd got to Toronto. Did you go to Toronto with Mr. Fabian?" "Yes, before he was selected. He went there to fine-tune one of his flagship projects: ice puppets. A Canadian academic who was on a long posting in another country had loaned him his apartment. I joined him there at least twice for a month or more. He was mostly there in winter to test the devices, it was very complicated technically." "Technically?" "Ice puppets are large sculptures that are frozen in molds, then they're articulated with wire or worn by actors onstage. It's quite a tricky technique, particularly with wires. The smallest movement can break a joint, you have to calculate the weight of the ice, the best attaching point, the angle of each movement. They're absolutely magnificent things, even when they break—especially when they break, if you ask me. Because what's so beautiful about the show is how fragile it all is: It's the epitome of an ephemeral production. The puppets melt over the course of the performance. Depending on their size and the density of the ice, the features blur and the outline liquefies more or less quickly, the tragedy or comedy of the situation is expressed in the degree to which the characters are erased—but it's always slightly tragic. It's the opposite of what happens in the natural world, because in this instance living things are made of ice, and thawing marks the onset of death. You have to choose texts that suit these specific parameters: the end of a relationship, the death of a loved one, grief—Duras, Beckett—or social dramas, the vacuity of social niceties, people falling apart because of their own vanity, ciphers. When he first told me about it, I suggested Gilles write his own texts, adapt dialogues to fit these very unusual productions. But at the time he just didn't want to hear it. 'I'm not a writer,' he kept saying every time I mentioned that option. I admit that I considered doing it myself, I found the thought of writing for that sort of theater inspiring, I was full of ideas and really wanted to work with him. But he didn't ask me to. And actually, I was always scared of treading on his toes. To put it more accurately, I sensed that it would have been a threat to him. So for example, one time he asked me if I knew anyone who was very familiar with Philip Roth's work—he was putting together a workshop on *Sabbath's Theater* where the main character is a puppeteer. I gave him contact details for Pauline Sorman, who's *the* Roth specialist, a Frenchwoman who teaches at Harvard, she and I did our literature foundation course together back in the day. He wrote to her, they got along, he went to see her in Boston. And do you know, he didn't tell me, didn't suggest I go with him, even though I was in Toronto at the time. I found out much later, when I happened to bump into Pauline on the boulevard Saint-Michel in Paris. 'Oh, so you know Gilles Fabian?' she exclaimed, looking embarrassed. He hadn't even told her that it was me who'd put him in touch with her!" "And didn't you think that was strange—abnormal even? As if he were sort of denying your existence?" "Yes and no. I'd learned the ropes in the last two years with my husband, I thought I knew everything there was to know about male egos battered by their partner's success. Women of my generation were brought up to be careful not to assert their power. Ever since I was very little, I've learned to make myself very little. If a woman's head pops above the parapet, it gets cut off. And I thought he wanted to maintain his professional autonomy, which I completely understood." "Were you happy in Toronto?" "Like I said, I was happy wherever he was. And I'm happy anywhere that I can write. And here's another fact: When he went off to Boston for two days without me, I had two days to myself to write. By writing, I mean using my time with no constraints at all, with no one watching, even lovingly; staying in my pajamas, not noticing the daylight fading, reading my work back out loud, listening to a song, spending an hour daydreaming by the window without having to justify it. In fact, I spent hours by the window in Toronto—a huge expanse of glass like they have over there. The apartment was on the fifteenth floor of a skyscraper that must have had forty stories. At first, I was blown away by the view of the city, and so was he actually, I remember the first time I went out to see him, I'd hardly put my suitcase down before Gilles wanted to make love in front of that magnificent view, 'I've been dreaming of this,' he whispered in my ear. It was nighttime. I had both my hands pressed up to the glass and I can remember seeing his reflection—he looked ecstatic, predatory, imperial, and sexual pleasure probably played a far smaller part in that than a majestic sense of towering over the city and the future. Like he was saying, 'It's just you and me,

New World,' if you see what I mean. A sort of latter-day Rastignac. That's what I thought but I didn't say anything—if I have any discretion, it's in that area: I have a lot of respect for fantasies." "It's also reminiscent of the Michael Fassbender movie *Shame*. Have you seen it?" "No. What made you think of it?" "The scene you've described, having sex up in a skyscraper, the huge window overlooking the city. The movie's about a sex addict who's incapable of loving anyone, even his own sister, who dies by suicide. You read between the lines that something happened when they were children, but you don't know what. Anyway, it was just an association of ideas, nothing more. Forgive me." "Another thing I want to say about that apartment in Toronto is that there was a building under construction directly opposite. On the night I've described, it hadn't yet reached our level, but it was going up very quickly and the second time I visited Gilles, it was up to the thirteenth floor, there would soon be no view left. Gilles hated that building site, it was going to block his horizon, not to mention the noise during the day, despite the triple glazing. But I was fascinated by the construction work. I even pulled my desk nearer the window so that I could follow its progress. I watched the cranes swivel, materials being moved around, men in hard hats gesticulating to direct maneuvers and taking receipt of loads. The workmen could see me too, by the end they would wave hello and smile—because of them, I decided not to stay in my pajamas. I sat at my laptop right by the window and played the role of a writer in the same way that, watched by me, you could say that they played the role of construction workers, as if we were performing in the movie of our lives by living it. One of those unpindownable connections was established between us. I loved our complicity. 'Do you know,' I told Gilles when he caught me gazing out one day, 'I feel I'm getting to know Toronto better than if I schlepped all around it and went into its monuments and museums, went to the aquarium or the zoo like you keep encouraging me to. It may be dumb (he nodded in agreement) but here at this window, I'm participating in the city's energy, I'm working in it, integral to it, but if I wandered around, I'd just be a tourist.' Gilles raised a baffled eyebrow. 'And another thing,' I added, 'I see it as a sort of metaphor for my work as a writer: The composition of this structure, the balance that needs to be struck, the distribution of different loads, the need for every part of it to hold together when the scaffolding's taken down—all that's far more important than tinkering with paint colors and door handles.' 'It's true, you do like a bit of concrete reality,' Gilles said, putting his hands on my backside. I could tell he wanted to make love there, by the window, where the workmen could see us, that he wanted to take away my connection with them, this unsexualized connection, but I managed to lure him to the bedroom. His goddamn jealousy, I thought, although there was something sicker about it than that, I could sense it but hadn't formulated it as such in my mind—it's only now that I know there was something."

"What happened after that, at the house?" "The thing that saved me, I believed at the time, but actually the thing that did me in was that house. Gilles was in Toronto doing a lot of work on ice puppets, we spoke on the phone for at least an hour every day, his absence was painful, but it was a bearable sort of pain, the pain of desire rather than loneliness. My body languished in his absence but in my mind and my heart, he was right there with me. My love gave him so much space inside me that he kind of lived in tune with the timing of my life. So, for example, when I went to bed, he went to sleep with me. I put his existence to sleep while I slept. I wasn't unaware of a disconnect because of the time difference, but I didn't feel any emotional disconnect—we lived together, it was as simple as that, and his presence in me was more potent than his absence anywhere else. I never thought about what he was up to when it was my nighttime. I concentrated on my writing perfectly serenely while also counting the days. Love can give you such strength! And then out of nowhere he told me he was coming home, he missed me too much! I danced for joy in the garden that day, I put my arms around the trunk of my mimosa—my poor mimosa. 'Tomorrow I'll hold you in my arms, my love,' he wrote. 'I'm going to smother you with kisses,' I replied. 'I'd be happy to die at your hands,' he concluded. Okay, it's probably best not to remember those specific words..." "Indeed. At that point, in the house, would you say that you were inseparable?" "We became like that by force of circumstances: Always together, and so in tune—it was practically osmosis! But not in a neurotic sense. No, I never got that feeling. As I just said, I wasn't dependent on him, if that's what you want to know. Even isolated in that town where I didn't know anyone but him, I felt happy. I made podcasts, got on with my writing. To my mind, love is the opposite of being inseparable, it means knowing how to be alone together. And I experienced that exact type of harmony in the house, even if that seems strange." "Well, yes, I'd recommend you don't state that fact so ecstatically. I'm not sure I understand your strategy, Mrs. Lancel. I'm your attorney, you can tell me everything. Your case is serious, do you understand that? The last we heard, Gilles Fabian is still in a coma. As far as everyone is concerned, even if we go to great lengths to prove otherwise, he is the victim, so don't add to that by painting him as the dream partner. Please." "You can call me Claire. I don't have a strategy, Mrs. Niepce, that's precisely the problem, I've never had one, I've lived from day to day because I had faith in the future. That's what I'm trying to describe for you: the chronology of—" "I know it, Claire, I know the chronology, I have the police report here in front of me and I was with you in police custody, if you remember." "The chronology of events, sure. But what about the chronology of emotions, the sequence of feelings? You need to put yourself in my shoes for real, in real time. Otherwise you'll be just like everyone else, you won't understand, you won't be able to defend me. And, you see, it all came together there, at the house." "Okay." "Gilles came to join me at the house, straight from Toronto, and it was such a pleasure snuggling together in that special place. He subscribed to a gym app to keep in shape because it was still too cold to swim. We did the exercises together every morning, and fell about laughing when I collapsed after three push-ups. Still, I was glad to build up some muscle because a choreographer had asked if I'd like to collaborate on a show and the rehearsals were starting soon. At my age, there was plenty of work to do, but I've always liked that kind of challenge. We went shopping together and bought delicious things to eat, we went for walks around the area, he played piano, in the evenings we drank wine and watched series, we rented movies or listened to music." "Were you not writing?" "Yes, I was. I'd finished *A Father*, and my publishers had pushed back its publication date to make way for a more high-profile author, but I didn't give a damn. I had that feeling of being blessed, a sense of having achieved something even though, sure, it wasn't exactly what I'd had in mind (and that's something that never happens—I made a podcast about it, if you're interested, it's still available online despite what... it's called: *Be a Woman*), but finishing a book is always an accomplishment. It meant I could devote myself completely to my podcasts, which were now booming thanks to some new partnerships. I spent a lot of time on them, and I was also thinking about the texts that I needed to write for the dance show. It was a happy time, with so many possibilities, and I would have been floating on a cloud if Gilles hadn't gone on and on about wanting to apply for UNESCO's international program. When he told me that he was coming home from Toronto, I thought he was giving up on all that. But he talked about it every day. As well as a detailed résumé, his application had to include an extended essay of at least twenty thousand words to elaborate on his project. Registration for the competition—and it *was* a competition—was closing six months later. There would obviously be some really heavyweight candidates, and he didn't know how to stand out so that he could win. Win? I was shocked that he didn't spend more time discussing it with me, this ambition would affect our shared future, but I didn't dare point this out for fear of looking unappreciative. I wanted to be the perfect woman. Don't be selfish, I told myself. After all, he was right: We weren't old enough to get in a rut. The important thing was being together, here and now, then somewhere else if need be. 'Why don't you write about your life with puppets, right from the start?' I asked.

'Not just standard-issue memoir but a piece of proper literary narrative nonfiction. Your story.' 'I'm not a writer,' he grumbled. He always said that in a slightly doubtful way, as if waiting to be contradicted. And that's what I did. 'Not being a writer doesn't mean anything. And it's not true, anyway. I've read the texts you write for your programs, and the one on *Don Giovanni*, for example, was beautiful.' 'And I'm not like you,' he grumbled on, 'I'm not interested in myself. Talk about myself? Ugh, never!'

"I didn't pursue it, I respected his reticence. During the day he worked in his study, cramming like a student on his application, and I was in the little bedroom overlooking the garden, feeding my social-media platform, basically. My partnership with the Sonia Rykiel Foundation had given me so much more drive, agnès b. was talking about getting me to run podcast workshops for young artists. I was going to start earning money, which made me so happy because, contrary to popular belief, very few authors live off their writing. When I'd decided to stop teaching years earlier, it was like jumping with no safety net, and one success didn't necessarily mean the future was secure. And I'd had some pretty hard times, alone with my daughter, so I was pleased with the direction my career had been taking in the last few years: two theater adaptations, one for the big screen, translations, a new book, and also my podcasts. I was really on the way up, on every front. As the epigraph for one of my novels, I wrote: 'The future's never turned out very well for me.' Well, life was busy writing the perfect rebuttal." "Was Gilles Fabian happy about your success at the time?" "He wasn't very expansive but yes, he seemed to be. When my editor called to say they were delaying publication of *A Father*, Gilles wanted me to put up a fight. 'If I were you, I'd be angry. You should drop them.' I was a little offended but I was so happy that nothing else mattered. When my podcast reached fifty thousand subscribers and *Le Monde* singled me out as the 'first successful literary podcast,' we celebrated with champagne. 'To my great writer,' Gilles said. And later, when *A Father* was published, he kept asking me how the sales were going. But then, at about the same time, at the César Awards, the director who'd adapted *Farewell*—one of my novels—called me onto the stage, and Gilles seemed upset, but I didn't really notice until we got back to his apartment. He belittled the prizes, went on about how superficial that world was, compared Isabelle Huppert to an ectoplasm, then criticized me for not mentioning him in my thank-yous. 'It's what people do,' he told me. 'Everyone thanked their loved ones except you. Are you ashamed of me?' I apologized: I wasn't expecting it, I was caught out. But deep down, I couldn't see why I would have thanked him. I hadn't written the screenplay or made the movie, which was put together before I even met Gilles, anyway. In the end, it was all forgotten by the next day and we didn't talk about it again. I was careful to hide the photos that appeared in *Voici* and *Gala* so he didn't see them. To prove my feelings were genuine and I *was* proud, I posted a selfie of us arm in arm and tagged him on Facebook—he'd finally set up a profile at my instigation.

"To get back to our trip to Hyères, even though I'd never brought up the subject again, it was Gilles who eventually decided to take my advice about UNESCO. 'I'm going to write this book, you know,' he announced out of nowhere, as he headed into his study one day. 'A real book. My book.' He was excited and determined all at the same time. I won't pretend I was thrilled. I felt this sort of paradoxical fear: I was afraid that he would fail (after all, maybe he really *wasn't* a writer and his ostentatious announcement worried me) but also afraid that he'd succeed and his total success would send him off to the four corners of the world. But his project was soon a source of so much joy. Because he didn't know where to start, we ended up talking every day, every night, and every evening. We talked as we'd never talked before. I asked him about his childhood, his toys, the games he played, I asked about how he first discovered puppets, quizzing him for details. It was hard. He had a lot of trouble remembering, at first he had hardly anything to say. As if his early years hadn't left any imprint on him, or didn't matter. I realized that he balked at diving into it all because it meant being confronted with his parents and with himself in an unbearable light.

He resisted remembering. I admit that I had to push him out of his entrenched position. I may have been wrong to do that but I don't think I was. *Holding the Strings* is a very beautiful book, even if I do remember everything that it triggered. And as for the title... the irony is spot-on, it seems. I don't regret pushing him down this road where, he later admitted, he didn't want to go. I didn't push him, actually, I went down it with him. Like a sort of midwife. That was when he came the closest to the things he's constantly tried to avoid. He rekindled emotions that had been shelved, buried but not dead, he faced up to fear and shame. Whatever people think of writing about yourself, it's a beautiful undertaking—or ordeal. No need for regrets. Besides, at the time he was very happy about it and really thanked me.

"Meanwhile, I learned a lot about him, and each new revelation increased the love I felt for him. I was with him every step of the way in his slow recall process. With his uncle Jean who made him a Pinocchio that was almost as big as he was. With his father who often took him to the puppet theater, before adolescence came between them. His father was the first puppet to melt away, he drowned himself in alcohol—'a puddle,' Gilles called him one time, maybe he meant 'a muddle' but I could never forget the word 'puddle.'

"Of course, none of these stories features in his book, he decided to silence a lot of stuff that I personally thought would be wonderful to say. I didn't contribute in any way, it was his book. When he started writing, he would give me what he'd printed out every evening to read. I was moved right from the start. I was seeing proof of how secretly sensitive he was, I was touched by his modesty. I hate that word in literature but I loved it as a reality in him. His humility, the way he waited for my judgment meant I was involved in every one of his sentences. And I was very respectful in my comments. So for example, he had a way of hiding behind theoretical ideas or technical explanations that were obviously important to the project but that reduced the emotional impact. Although I managed several times to get him to express them more fully, he never crossed the pain barrier. Nope, he never could do that. There's a line from Pavese: 'We stop being young when we realize there is no point in speaking about pain.' That wasn't even the issue for Gilles. He just didn't want to express his pain. It didn't exist and never had existed. Not the abandonment, the loneliness, the fear, none of it. He'd never suffered and never would. 'I don't want any pain,' he always said. 'Period.' My job was to break down what I felt was a concrete block of manliness with what I hoped to bring to the table for him—a more feminine approach to life. I wanted him to open up, or to allow glimpses at least. It was pretty simplistic categorization, I admit, probably with a dash of pop psychology, but that's how I saw us: a man and a woman. Everything I wanted was in that pairing—our pairing. Every tiny concession he made to me in writing his book—'I get it,' he would say, 'you're right'—just bowled me over. He was working so hard to write that book, it was such a huge and obvious effort, and I thought he was doing it for me, to please me, to join me in the place I was in, to be loved. I loved him."

The prison guard showed up, visiting hours were over. My attorney said goodbye, "See you on Tuesday, Claire," she said. "I'm working to get you out, don't you worry." I went back to my cell, I wasn't doing too badly in there, although I would have preferred to be alone. My cellmate was suspected of killing her mother, which she denied, she kept saying, "She's the one who killed me," and I didn't know whether she was mentally ill or telling the absolute truth—most likely both: Aren't the insane closer to the truth? There wasn't just physical death, I knew only too well. Her name was Agnès, she was nineteen, and she had a stammer. She'd never met her father or been with a boy, she'd lived her whole life with her mother. And what was I there for? I was accused of attempted murder, but I'd simply been defending myself, that was a legitimate plea. I'd be out soon, I didn't plan on rotting in the Hyères county jail. Agnès believed me, or maybe she didn't give a damn. Every evening she asked me to tell her something about my life, but only happy times, nice stories. On the first evening I told her about the mimosa tree, I described its little balls of fluff, the color and downy feel like a chick. She'd never seen mimosa, even at a florist, she said, she'd never seen a chick either, or the sea, and it was in the hope of seeing the sea that she'd escaped on the first train that came by. She'd been arrested in Hyères, but lived 730 kilometers away in Bourges. I was kind of anesthetized by the tranquilizers I'd been given by the doctor who'd deemed me fit for detention, and at the time the memory of that felled mimosa tree felt like my worst loss. I'd also lost the words to resuscitate it: I realized that you can't describe a fragrance, at least not the fragrance of mimosa—you can't say it's lemony or woody or anything, it's unique in the same way as a moment of happiness is, it's indescribable. But what Agnès really wanted was to know about my life, and despite the age difference, she asked me if I'd made love, what it was like, kissing someone, how it felt, was it true that it gave you butterflies in your stomach? She also wanted me to tell her about my childhood and my parents. What about her? Oh, she'd rather not—if she talked about herself too much, her mother used to punish her, grinding her face into her plate of food. I told her I was a writer and my latest book was called *A Father*, I'd give her a copy if I was allowed to have books. She'd prefer it if I read to her, she wasn't great at reading, she got the letters mixed up. I didn't stay long at the county jail, but I had time to read a few pages to her. Her concentration was extraordinary—she couldn't maintain it for more than fifteen minutes but for those fifteen minutes it was magical. It was both painful and ecstatic, there was a kind of sanctity that every writer dreams of seeing on people's faces, as if their text were sacred and inclined readers to prayer. That's something Gilles didn't understand when I mentioned that I don't really like traveling. This was what I should have explained to him, I thought when I saw Agnès's expression. What Deleuze calls "motionless intensities." "I don't need to move," he writes, "when I listen to music or read a book that I find beautiful or when I'm thinking... That's far better than any journey—those are inner landscapes." I thought that could be the title of one of my books someday, if I could still write. *My Inner Landscapes*. Books, music, paintings. My motionless intensities. And I would add trees. Yes, I would add mimosa.

A FATHER, CHAPTER 3

One night I was woken by music coming from the living room. I opened the bedroom door a little way, softly so as not to wake my sister, and slipped out. My father was sitting on the sofa with his head tipped back and his eyes closed. Next to him was the sleeve of a record. On it was a picture of a man dressed in black, sitting at a piano, and in big golden letters along the top was the name Arthur Rubinstein. Dad looked as sad as the music, he must have been thinking about his mom. It was a Schumann sonata. I didn't know who that was, he never put anything on for my sister and me to listen to, but kept music for himself, at night. A floorboard creaked, he saw me, and I came to sit next to him. "Are you okay, Dad?" I asked, not daring to touch him—I wanted to, but he didn't want it, I could tell, he wasn't pleased that I was there. "Of course, everything's fine. Go back to bed, it's late." "But are you not going to bed?" "Soon. I'm waiting until the end of the record." He closed his eyes again and I did the same. There were so many emotions coming from that piano, sad emotions but they made you feel good. An envious longing to learn to play weighed on my heart—it was such a gift! Just then, the front door made a scraping noise. My mother put down her bag, she hung up her coat. "What are you doing here?" she asked, surprised. Her hair was all ruffled. "We were listening to piano music," I said.

7

My attorney sat down and took my file from her briefcase along with a copy of *A Father*, which she handed to me with a surly expression. She looked like someone who read novels only if they were about samurais. Surely, attorneys needed a dash of empathy for their clients when defending them? Maybe not, at the end of the day. Maybe it was better to keep some distance.

"We were talking about Gilles's project, you were helping him write his memoir. What happened during that period?" "When Gilles was writing, I did my podcasts, I wrote pieces about artists that I liked, mostly writers, dead or contemporary, then I'd record the texts very carefully, sometimes with music in the background—it's a really exciting creative process, where you're on your own but also connected. I told Gilles about it and got him to listen when he had the time. One evening when he seemed keen to be the one giving me advice, he asked why I always wrote in praise of people, never criticism. 'After all, there are women who do terrible stuff. Being a feminist doesn't mean being blind or biased,' he said. 'This stuff of yours is good but it drones on. You should be punchier or you'll get stuck in a rut. Fashions change quickly, there are more and more up-and-coming young women, you know, they'll take over from you.' I was reluctant at first, then tempted. After all, I had that ironic side to me. Why not use it? My podcast was called *Be a Woman*, which implied a sense of courage and dignity, of honorable power—people always say, 'Be a man,' have you noticed that? Never 'Be a woman.' I had masses of positive examples to put forward, of course I did, there's no shortage of great female figures, but I told myself that a counterpoint would serve the cause all the better. And I thought of some articles by Virginia Woolf, my idol, I adored her acerbic wit (forgetting that her irony targeted men). 'Okay,' I said to Gilles. 'But I'll need something really disgusting, not gratuitous criticism, just to play the part…' And that's when he mentioned Laetitia Valy. I hadn't heard of her even though she was well-known in the theater world. She's a storyteller who gathers traditional oral tales from different regions and adapts them into shows. So far so unremarkable, except that she reworks the source material in her own style. But her last production, which Gilles had seen at a festival of popular culture and then showed me on video, was definitely problematic.

This time she'd collated traditional African tales and adapted them for the stage and performed them herself. To be honest, the performance was unwatchable. This blond Parisienne with translucent skin wearing a haute couture version of a bubu and with a video of an African village in the background narrating legends and descriptions of women's lives that she'd transcribed in a pseudo-vernacular. It was offensive! She even put on an African accent sometimes and it made the audience laugh. And all under the pretext of communicating the authenticity of a matriarchal tradition that she was distorting and caricaturing, bringing out the naivety but none of the tenderness, the cunning but none of the grinding poverty, the fun but none of the depth. As well as being absurdly paternalistic and racist, it was unbelievably kitsch, and I made that point forcefully in a vitriolic podcast. Gilles was over the moon. I thought it was a good move for me, now that it was done, and I was grateful to him for getting me to express a different part of myself, my capacity for outrage. We encouraged each other to go to our limits." "Were you not expecting what happened next?" "At first nothing unpleasant happened. Just reactions on the platform, almost all of them favorable. At the time, it was 2017, there was less talk of cultural appropriation than there is now, but I'd raised a prickly subject and the question was now out there: Did we have a right—or actually, no: We had the right to but *should we, could we allow ourselves* to talk for someone else, to express ourselves *from* their point of view, even with the best intentions in the world? I had comments and encouragement from Africa, the United States, people thanked me, gave their own accounts. Then I devoted my next piece to a quote from Toni Morrison and moved on to something else." "Were you completely cut off from the world?" "More or less. Gilles was busting a gut to finish his memoir. He went to Paris for a few days two or three times, and for the presentation when he ended up on the UNESCO short list. I stayed behind on my own, chilled. Meanwhile, I was invited onto a France Inter show, I had to choose a song I liked—the presenter had read some of my work and knew how important songs were in my novels—then give a live commentary about it. I accepted but when I told Gilles about the invitation, he was angry, one of his mysterious outbursts . . . it was like he felt I was deliberately provoking him: How was he going to look to his friends—him the music lover, the director of *Don Giovanni*, the huge fan of *Tosca*—if his partner swooned in public over flash-in-the-pan Muzak? I stood my ground initially, arguing that there were some really beautiful songs, then I gave up, which is what I always did: My submissiveness calmed him and it cost me so little. I'm not saying that I didn't think he was being unfair and overly touchy about the image that he wanted to give of us, of himself, but I wanted to please him and some part of me was touched that he thought of us as a couple. I'd become 'his partner,' even though he hadn't changed his status from single on Facebook. I despised myself for being so tacky and kept quiet about wanting to 'officialize,' as his mother called it. Having a lot of subscribers doesn't mean you should splurge yourself all over social media. The opposite, in fact. And we were such a close-knit couple in real life that it didn't really matter how it was portrayed socially. I wanted to be 'the best version of myself,' as personal-development coaches all encourage us to be (it can't be helped, those words get inside your head), not an idiotically romantic starry-eyed girl who longed to remarry and say 'Claire Fabian' out loud to hear the sound of her new identity. As time went by, Gilles himself seemed more and more in tune with my appetite for isolation, avoiding social niceties and contemptuous about appearances. One day he saw that a theater director, an old fellow student from the Conservatoire in Marseille, had been given the Legion of Honor. He couldn't believe it. If people knew who this guy was! What a travesty! 'Well, I, good sir, have been honored by the Ministry of Culture as a Chevalier of the Order of Arts and Letters,' I told him playfully. 'And you boast about it!' he snapped back. 'I don't want any part in that rigmarole.' 'Well, you know... what matters is not being taken in by it. Sometimes it's more pretentious to refuse.' 'Either way,' he said, 'if you ever accept the Legion of Honor... I'll leave you.' 'Aw, don't you like legionnaires?' I teased and he gave me a furious scowl. *Don't leave me!* I wanted to bawl in a quavering voice, like Jacques Brel. But I now knew I should avoid conflict, often at the expense of my innate creativity. I kissed him instead. 'Roger that,' I said. Piaf's *He was slender and so fine . . . that legionnaire of mine*, I did *not* croon.

"Still, we did eventually go back to Paris together. Gilles had finished his memoir and sent it to the UNESCO commission. I'd been moping aimlessly for a while because I couldn't write anymore: A cracked vase on my desk had suddenly shattered, pouring water over my laptop. This instant impotence had all the more impact on me because the incident had no effect on Gilles at all, as if he were already off somewhere else. Not only was the laptop wrecked but I'd lost several pieces I'd been writing—I'd loaned Gilles my external hard drive and had no backup. So I wanted to get back to Paris to ask a professional what could be salvaged. Also, *A Father* had been published and I needed to do some promotional work. And lastly, I was starting to miss my friends, even if I didn't say so."

"Did you have mutual friends? Did you go out together?" "No, not much. If we were invited to friends or associates of his, he often said no or canceled at the last minute, saying he'd rather be alone with me, which meant I met very few of them. And, like I said, he didn't really like mine. Once when I took him to a birthday party, he just couldn't handle it, I had to pretend I felt sick to explain our exit. When I asked him about it, he said that watching me wiggling my hips to Claude François songs with a bunch of morons was more than he could take. 'Admit it, it's kind of ridiculous,' he said, imitating a shimmy, and I felt stupid—I like dancing. But I think he mostly felt uncomfortable because he didn't know anyone and no one knew who he was. He had this need to be on familiar territory, otherwise he wilted." "Did he sulk for long in these instances?" "No. So that time, for example, in the elevator on the way back to his place, he looked me in the eyes and said a husky, 'Do you live around here?' We hardly made it through the door before we were having wild sex, well, that's what I remember." "Was he ever violent?" "Physically? No. Never. He was gentleness incarnate." "Even during sex?" "Hmm... that's different. But I've already told you, I don't feel dominated during sex, even if that's what it looks like from the outside. I don't see it like that." "In real terms, did he ever hurt you?" "If he ever did, I honestly don't remember it. No, I don't think so. I suffered in other ways." "I thought he had, and—" "But not then! Later." "I'm sorry to press the point but, um, did he never strangle you during sex, or force you to do things?" "No. Sorry. I know it would make things easier for me but..." "I'm not asking you to lie, Mrs. Lancel." "No, that was just it. Gilles was gentle and loving, that's the worst thing about it." "Okay. So everything was fine, you were both happy. And…" "And we went to Rouen together. He wanted to meet my mother. 'Is he going to ask me for your hand?' she teased. He charmed everyone, my mother, my nephews, my sister, everyone adored him. My daughter was also there, she came up specially from Lyon. But then when Mom found out that he'd won the UNESCO competition, she said, 'Oh dear, that's not good.' 'Why do you say that?' I asked. 'I don't know: the traveling, the distance, you'll be apart…he'll meet someone else.' I told Gilles about it that same evening, to make him laugh. 'That's typical of my mother, you know,' I added. 'She always thinks women are destined to be abandoned, never the other way around.' 'I don't understand,' he said. 'Yes, you do. She could have said, the traveling, the distance… *You'll* meet someone else. But, oh no. It's always that way around. Women are made to suffer—well, other women are.' Gilles seemed to be thinking it over in silence, he didn't say anything. I kissed the crook of his neck, right where I love how soft his skin is under his port-wine birthmark. Maybe he was thinking about the opposite scenario, how his mother had made them suffer—him and his dad. I remember there was a density to his silence."

"So he won the UNESCO competition. How did the two of you manage things then?" "He was walking on air. I went to the announcement ceremony with him, I'd never seen him so happy, he sailed from one compliment to the next with a glass of champagne in his hand. There were several ambassadors there, lots of senior officials, he treated them all to that smile that I'd come to think was bestowed on me alone and that, in those circumstances, felt slightly false or a social necessity, if you like, which I found disturbing. When an official or a sponsor came and congratulated him, he just bubbled over. I couldn't wait for the thing to end, I didn't like seeing him like that, so dependent on other people's attention." "Did Gilles introduce you to people at the reception?" "Yes. He said, 'my partner.'" "Not Claire Lancel? Did anyone recognize you?" "Yes, one or two people asked me if I was Claire Lancel (but someone else congratulated me for my 'novel about samurais' so, you know, my fame's relative). I was worried it would annoy Gilles. Anyway, I made sure I was discreet. It was only natural: It was his moment of glory, not mine. In fact, I'd invited my agent, Rob Simmons, because on the back of his success, Gilles wanted to publish his memoir and had asked me to introduce him to Rob. They got along—how could anyone not get along with Rob; he's just wonderful—and they arranged to meet. Gilles was overjoyed." "Did he set off on a trip right away?" "Almost right away. He met with my agent first, by then all he could talk about was the project. 'Rob loves my book, he thinks I'm a real author,' he said after their meeting. 'You see!' I said, hugging him, a little upset that he put more store by someone else's endorsement than mine. After that he went back to Tbilisi to meet Gabriadzé, a famous puppet artist, and then straight on to Toronto. I was meant to join him there, he'd said he would buy my ticket, I was struggling a little, financially. And then the thing happened." "Tell me about it." "First there was a post on my page—a follower was outraged that I'd come down on Laetitia Valy so hard. 'Girl, who the hell do you think you are?' she said. 'Before accusing other people of cultural appropriation, you should look in the mirror—that's all you do in your books, gaze at your own navel and appropriate other people's lives.' A few trolls immediately reposted this, saying I was a total waste of space, then others waded in, claiming I was getting rich off artists who were so much better than I was, I was pathetic and old, past it, a middle-class cow, lousy, a bitch. Of course, I deleted or reported abusive posts immediately but that fanned the flames: Social media picked up the torch and ran with it, I was shouted down on Instagram, pulled apart on Twitter, hounded on Facebook.

"The smear campaign would probably have died down pretty quickly if Laetitia Valy herself hadn't commented online, condemning the 'disgraceful' way she'd been victimized. On the one hand, she explained that she'd taken inspiration for the show from a Blaise Cendrars book titled *Little Black Stories for Little White Children*, and on the other hand—more tellingly—that she herself had distant Black heritage. So she was legitimate while I was 'jealous' and 'petty,' unless I thought I was better than her and Blaise Cendrars? 'Her podcast is called *Be a Woman*, well listen up, here's my advice: Don't be a woman like her!' was her parting recommendation to my subscribers.

"Then the press started talking about it, 'the writer Claire Lancel is abusing her position on social media,' 'even literary podcasts are lousy.' I was soon stripped of my status as a writer—'these influencers have no ethics,' 'a content creator creating a vacuum'—I was linked to the women who'd recently been slated for placing fraudulent products from their base in Dubai! In all the screenshots posted online, I looked like someone wanted by the police.

"It didn't matter how much I apologized—I didn't know that Laetitia Valy had Black blood, nothing about her appearance suggested that she did—while still reminding people that my criticism, which was subjective anyway, was mostly about how kitsch and artificial the show was from an aesthetic point of view, whatever I said the controversy just snowballed. Carole posted a tweet about Cendrars's title, which was problematic to say the least, but it was no good. In the space of a few days, I lost more than half of my subscribers, the online harassment got worse, then people that I had plans to work with started asking me questions—my criticism was sadly lacking in a sense of duty to the sisterhood, they were sorry to say. I called Gilles every day, overwhelmed by this storm of hate that I didn't know how to stop, I was lost, begging for advice." "How did he react? Was he by your side in this?" "If you can say that of someone thousands of kilometers away. He reassured me, at least at first, but I could tell he was very much *somewhere else*. 'You're right, I am somewhere else, my love,' he replied when I pointed this out to him. 'Come join me.' He told me to get a ticket (there was no more talk of him sending me one, I didn't dare remind him of that, I thought he might have money problems of his own). But he asked me to join him at exactly the time when I was meant to be meeting people to safeguard the future of my partnerships. I wanted to rehabilitate my reputation—my honor. 'I can't leave Paris at the moment, I'll come later.' I hoped that he would feel my distress and offer to come home, but instead he descended into this icy rage: I didn't keep my word, I'd promised I would join him, I only ever thought of myself and my own interests. Shouldn't I have thought a bit about the consequences before doing my podcast on Laetitia Valy? Couldn't I see that I was jeopardizing him with my bullshit? 'But Gilles,' I stammered, 'Gilles, you know perfectly well that…' I was tripping over my words, I couldn't seem to find my way through his accusations, I was dumbstruck. The word *bullshit* overrode my ability to think, it was like hearsay, an imported word that didn't add anything of import, a word I could hardly believe he'd uttered: That word alone opened up a chasm. Gilles was still going with his litany. Had I thought about him for just one second? Thanks to my brilliant idea of posting us together on Facebook, everyone knew he was my partner. How did that make him look? People were commenting to him about my stupid podcast all the way over in Ontario. And now I didn't want to come join him, the great writer Claire Lancel didn't need a little puppeteer, she'd rather give interviews to the press. 'Gilles,' I said eventually, 'you're being unfair. Remember what happened, I hadn't heard of Laetitia Valy, if you hadn't mentioned her to me I would never—' 'Oh, there it is!' he interrupted me. 'There it is, it's going to be my fault, I knew it. That's what you're telling everyone, isn't it?' 'I'm not telling anyone anything, Gilles, I…' Someone rang the doorbell at his place and he broke off to open the door, I heard him speaking English in the distance. 'That was the cleaner,' he said when he came back. 'Oh, so you finally hired a cleaner!' I fumbled. 'That was a good idea.' Then, out of nowhere, he softened. 'I'm sorry for flying off the handle, my love. I'm not criticizing you, you know. I love you, I admire you. I'm reacting selfishly because I just want you here with me. I understand that you need to defend yourself against these assholes. I'm with you, my love. Hang tough. Your audience won't abandon you, you're the best.' 'Thank you, Gilles darling,' I said. 'I'll be out there as soon as possible—in a couple of weeks, I hope.'" "Did you join him?" "No. I never went back to Toronto. When I wanted to fly out it was not that long until Christmas and he said he was coming home for the holidays. I couldn't wait to see him after those terrible weeks. No explanations got through to anyone, the hate just kept coming, and the comments were getting crazy. 'Bullshit,' 'spiteful,' 'competitive': I didn't recognize myself in the things people were saying about me. I no longer dared to go out. It felt like even my local baker was eyeing me disapprovingly."

"How were things when your partner came home?" "He arrived back just before Christmas. I'd polished all the furniture at his place because he'd gotten increasingly manic and—" "At *his* place? Don't you mean your place? The both of yours?" "No, at his place, in Paris." "But you lived there at this point, didn't you?" "Yes. We'd decided to spend Christmas Eve in Paris with our children and then the two of us would go down to Hyères until mid-January.

"When Gilles arrived back, I could tell straightaway that something wasn't right. He kissed me and I cuddled up to him, he stroked my back, my ass, 'You need reality,' he said, but everything about him, the way he moved, his voice, how accessible his body felt to me, the slight resistance in his chest, everything had changed. My alarm bells went off but there's often this feeling of disconnect when people have been apart for a long time. Your body has to readapt to the other person, it's so strong that a well-established scenario can end up feeling fake.

In fact, he'd sort of forgotten the scenario itself: When we rushed to make love in his bedroom, well, I mean the bedroom, he penetrated me in a position that's very painful for me—I'd had a catastrophic delivery in the past, I'd torn, been stitched back together, and had bad scarring. Basically, there's a position that I find impossible, and Gilles knew this perfectly well. I'd even told him that, when I got divorced, my husband had raised the subject of this restriction in front of the family law judge as proof of my uncooperativeness, calling the judge as a witness to this sexual grievance and never for one moment doubting their masculine solidarity. Well, Gilles had forgotten, that's what he said when I cried out in pain, he fell over himself with apologies, I'm sorry, forgive me, but I think—I know—that it was intentional, he wanted to hurt me. I know this because when I sat up, I could see us both in the mirror and I saw the look in his eyes. It was just for a second, but there was hostility in that second." "So he has hurt you before..." "Yes, I'd forgotten that incident. Afterward, he busied around, unpacking his bag and meticulously putting away the contents, then he made some phone calls, answered emails, all without so much as a glance at me or a word of apology. We hadn't seen each other for weeks, I had been and was still embroiled in a punishing media storm and he wasn't talking to me. I was caught in my own trap: I'd always thought that making love solved everything, that this communion allowed two bodies to understand each other beyond words, making normal communication redundant. Well, he certainly seemed to think so too!

"After a long pause, I went over to him, I almost had to block his attempt to dodge me. 'What's going on, Gilles?' I asked, taking his shoulders and trying to make eye contact. 'What's wrong?' He looked at me. The chilling shallows in his eyes. 'As if you don't know,' he said. 'But I really don't know. What have I done?' 'You're fucking up my reputation, you're destroying a whole life's work, that's all.' I fought back tears. 'Gilles, I don't understand. Nothing's been destroyed. You haven't lost anything. You work for UNESCO, everyone listens to you and values you, you told me so yourself. Basically, everything's good. I'm the one who . . .' 'Everything's good. Yes, of course! You can't see beyond yourself, my poor Claire. You're so self-centered.' He wanted to leave the room, but I stood in his way. 'If I can't see anything, then explain it to me. I need to understand, I'm lost. Gilles,' I begged. 'I have no reason to be angry with you.' 'But you just said . . . just now, you said *As if you don't know*. What is it that I should see, or know? Tell me. Talk to me.' 'Listen, Claire,' he said, breaking away, 'there's nothing. I love you, I want you, I admire you, and I respect you.' And he sat down at the piano.

"I let him play, first of all because I was in a state of nervous exhaustion, and also because I hoped the music would have the same effect as sex—a feeling of relaxation, an appreciable openness, some peace. I was in agonies while he played but I was so sure of our love that I had no fears for the future. Our fundamental love, if I can put it like that, our foundations were so strong! He didn't play Couperin's *Les Barricades mystérieuses*, even though it would have been the obvious choice: Everything was suddenly inexplicably locked down. But my hope was rooted in the past like a tree. I was forgetting that a tree could become a lifeless stump.

"'Gilles. My darling. Thank you for playing. Talk to me,' I said as soon as he'd closed the cover on the piano. 'I have no reason to be angry with you,' he said again after a nasty silence. 'But here's the thing. I'm not great. It's temporary, don't worry about it. I've made an appointment with a shrink, for next Monday, I'll sort out this problem very quickly.' 'What problem, Gilles? At least tell me what the problem is.' 'That's exactly why I'm going to see a shrink. I'm doing it for me, for us. You told me that therapy saved your life, right? So you should be glad I'm doing it now, despite my reservations. Because you know how I feel about it.' 'Well, that's just it: What's the point of seeing a therapist if you don't have at least a minimum of faith in it? And it's a long-term undertaking, you won't fix the *problem* in three sessions.' 'Mrs. Freud has spoken! Do I have your permission not to follow your example? You see I don't plan to blather on about Mommy and Daddy for twenty years, I have other things to do with my life. I'm not hoping to reinvent the wheel, just straighten out some minor discrepancies between us. Don't get involved, please.'

"I didn't say anything, even though I found it hard not to be involved in something that had an impact on me. He was talking about us like an out-of-tune piano, so I hoped there would be a miraculous tuner. He came back satisfied after his first appointment with his therapist. 'She seemed very happy that I made another appointment,' he said. 'She obviously finds me interesting.'

"We spent Christmas with my daughter, Alice, and Gilles's younger two, Léon and Sophie—the eldest didn't come back from Australia, I've never met him. There was a strange atmosphere, cold but not exactly unpleasant. I should say that Alice had just been dumped without even a text—ghosted, she called it—by her girlfriend, a lovely humanities student that she'd met in Lyon who'd changed overnight after being spotted in the street by a modeling agency, she'd become unbearable and then invisible. It hurt me too, seeing her turned into something disposable. Léon was also recovering from a recent breakup, but he'd brought along a very pretty brunette and the next day Gilles couldn't stop singing her praises—'So graceful, so feminine! She's way better than the last one!' he whispered to me in the kitchen. And all evening he congratulated and celebrated his children, maintaining a polite but distant kindness toward Alice, and a sort of urbane amiability toward me, as if Alice and I were just there visiting his family. We exchanged gifts—his son acted mysterious, telling Gilles he would give him his later. I gave him a present we'd been discussing for a long time, a high-end Italian coffee machine, and I was surprised to see him put it in his bag, as if he wanted to send out every possible signal that he lived *somewhere else*." "Somewhere else, and not with you?" "Yes. But when I commented on this, he saw it as another sign of my selfishness. 'You give me a coffee machine, but it's actually for you.' He gave me a silk blouse that I put on right away—'You can exchange it if it doesn't suit you'—it really suited me, like everything that Gilles picked out for me, but I found the receipt in the bottom of the package: He'd bought two of the same blouse, in different sizes. The other one was for his mother, he admitted openly, apparently not realizing how tactless this was. In fact, the next day he went to see her in Marseille; he went without me for the first time in a long while. I usually helped him put up with her—'After what's happened, she doesn't really want to see you, you know. But I know her, it'll settle down.' In talking about her, he was talking about himself. I didn't have the strength to pick up on this or to ask yet again: 'What is this thing that happened? What happened?' I felt so emotionally battered, I was in pain, I wanted to see my daughter, and to be alone. And crucially we were meant to be meeting at the house in Hyères to spend the end of the year there, just the two of us. I was expecting a lot from that time together."

♦

"I remember the state Claire was in," Émilie says. "I went to Hyères for a day shortly after the New Year, she'd pretty much begged me to go. Gilles was friendly, as usual, but very...how can I put this? Very detached. And Claire was absolutely in pieces, her smile wasn't fooling anyone. She and I went for a walk along the seafront. She told me—and she started crying almost immediately—she told me that she didn't understand what was happening at all, Gilles had completely changed. She didn't recognize him. She said it felt, these were her exact words, 'like being with a different man.' But he was also complaining that *she'd* changed, she said. He accused her of being insensitive about his pain: He wasn't just bruised and humiliated, his life was at stake. Why didn't she acknowledge that he needed time to 'get back on his feet,' to restore his image. 'But what image?' she wailed. 'Get back on his feet after what? It's like he's assigning my problems to himself!' 'His image of himself?' I suggested tentatively. 'Maybe he feels powerless because he can't help you. Weak. He's described everywhere as your partner when he too is an artist. It belittles him—' 'But in whose eyes?' Claire interrupted tearfully. 'I love him just as much as before. And he *is* my partner. It's not an insult, surely?' 'Of course not, but in a way, it has an effect on his virility. Do you still make love?' 'Yes!' Claire howled. 'Every day! That's the worst thing. He's vile all day, says horrible things to me, looks at me like I'm rotten fish—seriously. He's hiding this while you're here, but his contempt is bottomless, I don't know where it's coming from. Then in the evening when he comes to join me in bed, where I'm usually crying, he takes me in his arms and whispers in my ear, *My love, have faith in us, it'll be fine, I love you, give me some time*, then he starts fondling me, he gets these incredible erections, even harder than usual, he penetrates me and makes me come, I come like crazy—but I'm mostly coming out of relief, in fact I'm setting aside my heartache in my pleasure and I'm reunited with it right afterward like a dog waiting outside the door. And he comes too. He gets a hard-on and he comes, so can you explain how it has an effect on his virility?'

"The pain was driving her nuts, she wailed and rubbed her face with her hands compulsively like she was trying to erase it. 'Claire, listen to his pain,' I told her. 'He needs to exist without you, that's all. He idealized you and now he's disappointed. It'll pass, don't wo—' 'Disappointed? Disappointed about what? What did I do? He should tell me, at least! And even if I have disappointed him, is it serious enough to deserve this much punishment? I feel like I'm being punished but I don't know why. It's horrible, Émilie. I want to die.' 'Calm down, Claire,'

I said, putting an arm over her shoulders. 'He's going through a rough patch—the two of you are going through a rough patch—but he loves you, that man loves you, Claire, he'll come back. He's started therapy so he's looking for a solution. Don't be so uncompromising. Love is complicated, you don't need me to tell you that.' "

◆

"Your friend Émilie Cointre, whom I've interviewed, describes you as very angry when Gilles Fabian suggested you take a break from your relationship. Could you not cope with him needing time to think?"

At first, I was speechless. I just couldn't believe that Émilie would have betrayed me like that. The judge was an abrupt, austere woman with a face like a Protestant, she reminded me of my father when I was a child. Her face was neither well-meaning nor hostile, which I found reassuring, I thought she just wanted everything to be clear, as I did.

"Gilles never suggested we should take a break, he didn't put it like that. And I wasn't angry, I was unhappy. I'd like it if we could stop confusing different feelings. We can't always use the wrong words for what we're going through, still less what other people are going through." "So you were unhappy," said the judge. "Yes, from Christmas onward I suffered nonstop, there was no letup. Every day was the same, Gilles worked, made phone calls, laughed on the phone, whistled to himself in his study... For someone who apparently needed to 'get back on his feet' he didn't seem to be tormented in any way. Except when he looked at me—well, if you can call it that: His eyes looked through me without seeing me, his face darkened, full of contempt, I felt like a fly squashed on a window or a windshield at the end of a trip: repulsive but also transparent. When I begged him to talk to me, all I got was robotic reassurances that he loved me—belied by everything about him, except at night—and promises for the future that the present seemed dead set on disproving. But I clung to my memories and to what Émilie had said, that this rough patch would pass, even if I couldn't see how. I was almost relieved when Gilles flew back out a week earlier than planned, claiming he had a stopover in New York to meet some people from the legendary Bread and Puppet Theater that he really hoped he could revive from its ashes. He had another appointment with his therapist just before leaving Paris and he seemed very pleased with the session, he emerged with this aura—I'm not sure how to put this—an aura of importance. He probably needed to feel important... not realizing how important he was to me. That's what I noticed, from the depths of my dazed state. But I hoped that it really would help us because, almost as soon as he landed, he sent me a gushing text saying how much he missed me already—'furiously.' The fury of love, I thought. And the other side of this coin, hate.

Some lines from Racine came to mind. Meanwhile, I missed his kindness and the security it gave me. That feeling had evaporated—totally and incomprehensibly. I had nothing to rely on anymore, I'd become a tightrope walker, and I didn't have a balance pole." "Did you go out to join him in Toronto?" "No, never. He kept putting it off: In November he'd said 'Come in December.' In December, January. In January, February. Either way, I did have plans to go because—through Mark, a friend of Gilles's who'd loaned him his apartment there—the University of Toronto had invited me to run a writing workshop for their Romance Languages Department: three months on a renewable contract. I was meant to start after the spring break, in late March. But Gilles told me that it had fallen through: Confronted with the scandal surrounding my podcast, which had 'crossed the Atlantic' to the New World, 'where people were very sensitive on the question of oppressed peoples,' Mark had decided to cancel, 'in our best interests,' Gilles added snidely. Everything was conspiring to keep us apart, and I was the one it was destroying. To make a long story short, I was a pariah wherever I went. I couldn't understand what was happening to me. Gilles kept on about 'getting back on his feet' but I was the one on my knees. I—" "Did you feel like a victim—a victim of some injustice?" "No. And this is the terrible thing: I felt guilty. My public and private trial was discussed everywhere, just like it is now, except that back then I didn't know why. At least now I know why I'm here. Ha! It's hilarious, if you think about it: Maybe I orchestrated all this to know once and for all what I'm accused of doing. Anyway, in those days I was totally confused: I'd done something wrong, terrible even, according to my online haters and the look in Gilles's eyes. It was like battling through Kafka's *The Trial*. It was driving me crazy. And I had no help, my therapist had retired. Sure, I had friends, but it's not the same. And at the time, Gilles..." "Yes?" "No, nothing." "Mr. Fabian *was* seeing a therapist, is that right?" "Yes..." "Are you a little unsure of the role that Mr. Fabian's therapist played?" "One time he called me and he was so excited, like he was happy about some big news. His therapist had helped him work out what was wrong between us. Ta-da: I'd become a 'toxic mother' to him. It took very few sessions for this blindingly obvious fact to leap out at him, plus it had been exactly the same with Violetta, incredible how we repeat the same patterns! But that sort of symbiotic relationship doesn't suit him, he was suffocating, I was suffocating him, *smothering* him, I was invasive, it was all about me, always, everywhere, I was the bad mother, the deadly mother who destroyed everything while claiming to do good. Basically, I was undermining his foundations, slowly draining all his energy, sucking him dry like a vampire. It was high time we changed the dynamics of our relationship, he needed to breeeeathe.

"I was so stunned by this latest twist that I don't know where I found the strength to be ironic about it—probably from my own survival instinct. 'So you finally adopted the Mommy and Daddy system, then?' I said. I was at his place in Paris, I could see myself in the antique mirror in the bedroom and, this is hard to say, I looked like his mother. I had the same haircut, I only just realized then, a sensible bob that Gilles had talked me into—I didn't like the way I looked but I wanted him to like the way I looked. I had the same blouse as her, and we all know why. But most of all, I was the same age as her, clearly pushing eighty in the spiteful shadows in that mirror. 'There, you see, that's typical,' Gilles said. 'You're actually laughing at me.' 'I'm not laughing at you, Gilles, please, but it's just the way you put it. All of a sudden, you're exultant and you call me a toxic mother, slapping this revelation on me like an unquestionable guilty verdict, a definitive explanation. You're forgetting one little detail: I'm not your mother.' 'Condescending, yet again . . . I'm well aware that you're not my mother, as it happens. But you are to me. That's how I see you. And toxic in the extreme.' 'Well, we agree on that, then: It's how you see me. So it's your problem, not mine. It's *your* neurosis. I'm not responsible for your projected fantasies, so stop making me carry the can for our fights and deal with your actual mother with your shrink—there's a lot of work to do.'

"Although his accusation horrified me, it also—weirdly—pepped me up, I had some newfound energy, as if I'd touched down briefly in the rock bottom of my misery. Psychoanalysis felt like familiar territory to me, whereas for him... His gloating sense of accomplishment with this toxic-mother idea was exasperating, and I kicked back against his stupid smugness, something that I hadn't seen in him before. Instead of being humbled by the complexities of his psyche, he seemed to be parading his own symptoms and seeing them as a source of pride while blaming someone else—me—for their devastating effects. All the same, what I wanted more than anything was to end this conflict, which was hardening the line of my jaw: In the mirror I saw an ice puppet, frozen solid but prepared to turn to liquid—to be liquidated. 'Do you know,' I added in a melting voice, 'I also see you as my father sometimes. You said it yourself, if you remember, the two of you have a lot in common, starting with your name. Our imagoes of our parents can reappear in relationships, and the traumas that go with them, that's normal, we're all making this up as we go along, we—' 'Imagoes of parents, trauma, projected fantasies, here we go again, Sigmund's widow is back in the building! She'll explain everything. You're always calling out mansplaining, but you're just the same... Happy now? Now that you've put me back in my place, I know how much you like to do that.

Well, if you'll excuse me, I need to go, I have work to do.'

"He hung up. I sat there dazed for a while, my mind blank. I'd gone too far again, I was a fool. Always neutralize his anger—I'd forgotten that. Mollify him, bring him around. I went to my dance rehearsal with John like an automaton, the opening night was a few weeks later. It was hard right from the start—a real challenge for me, I'm about as supple as a wooden clog—but John was a born teacher, perceptive but also reserved, and he managed to relax me. He'd just been to the market, and he posted some pictures of us arm in arm on Instagram, him with a cauliflower on his head and me with some broccoli. That earned me another raft of taunts online: 'She should have put a rotten egg on her head,' 'Is she still around? Can someone cancel her?,' and other niceties like that.

"Two hours later, Gilles sent me a text: 'I love you, I want you, I admire you, and I respect you. I have faith in us.' Once again he used that sequence of four verbs like a sort of open sesame, although it was actually intended to *close* the access routes whenever the conversation got too specific or I argued against him, so that things could start again as if nothing had been said. But I so desperately needed to find the harmony we'd lost that I replied, 'Thank you, my love. I love you too.' Then I regretted it—do you thank someone for loving you? And just before I went to bed, he sent another text with the photo that John had posted: 'If you really love me, Claire, stop humiliating me and everything will be fine.'

"I was his mother again—his terrible mother."

◆

"Oh my God, give us a break with your mothers!" said Carole. "Or go home to them if you can't live without them! We can't take any more of your soul-searching. You're forgetting one thing: When you suddenly see us as your mother, it means you're little boys. It doesn't mean we're mothers, toxic or not, it means that you're sons, perpetual sons. That's what you need to deal with, either with your shrinks or some other way: the little boys still moaning inside your men's bodies. Romain Gary's lament is poisoning us: 'With maternal love, life makes us an early promise that it never keeps.' And so on and so woe-is-me forth. Women aren't here to keep your mothers' promises, can we just make that clear! 'Then we have to eat cold food for the rest of our lives.' Oh, poor little bubbas! How sad! But we're not here on this earth so that you can eat hot food your whole lives. We don't want to be stuck in the kitchen, we have bigger plans. Go cook yourself an egg. Grow up enough to reach the pan at the top of the cupboard for yourself! And anyway, your mothers didn't promise you anything. You dreamed it. They're not aware of any promises. Did anyone promise *them* anything?

"Well, if you love your mother, you just about have a point. No woman can ever measure up. Sure, you eat cold meals, but it still tastes good. The real problem is when she didn't keep the pledge that you thought she made because she was holding you in her arms. If your mother betrayed you, then every woman is bound to. That omen hounds you, it haunts you. You won't eat cold food, oh no, you'll die of hunger. No woman will ever feed you, you'll always be starving, going from breast to breast looking for the one that won't dry up and whose milk won't turn. But we're not nectar or venom, we're not your remedy or your poison. We're not your never-ending disappointment or the source of your dejection. We don't want this infernal cycle that you automatically subject us to, projecting your aging-little-boy's phantasmagorias onto each new woman you meet: First she's a perfect lover, then a mother who thwarts you, followed by a toxic mother, and finally, in your dilapidated minds, a praying mantis intent on devouring you—don't give up, run! We're not who you think we are. Break away from these wonderful promises, these false promises, and then you'll find us, I promise. We're women, not your mlovers."

♦

"It was like that for weeks, a yo-yoing of emotions made all the more unbearable because it affected every aspect of my life. For four years I'd reveled in confidence as never before—Gilles's love, the loving depths in his eyes, affection from my readers, loyalty from my subscribers—and it had forsaken me, I was floundering in the desert, it literally felt like I was swallowing sand. Nothing worked anymore, I was disintegrating in other people's hostility as if it were a corrosive chemical. Some days the silence was horrendous, reverberating with my unworthiness. That's it, I'd become unworthy, unworthy to write, or to live. I stayed at the apartment, helpless, not even daring to open my laptop, waiting for a sign of support that never came. 'I thought you liked being alone, make the most of it,' Gilles said if I complained, which I only ever did gently because I was afraid of how he would react. But this wasn't being alone, it was desolation. I'd been abandoned by the people to whom I thought I was connected. I had my friends, thank goodness, Émilie and Carole, who could still make me laugh... At the time they saved my skin, each in her own way, they stopped me from being submerged by other people's hate and Gilles's indifference, or the other way around. I wouldn't have made it without them.

"He returned to Paris at the end of January. We made love as soon as he arrived, and it was just as brutal as in December: enemies who love each other or lovers who hate each other. He was in a good mood, though, because Rob, my agent who was now also his, had found a really good publisher for his memoir, *Holding the Strings*. He just needed to do a few little rewrites before it was sent off to the printer, he said. In fact, there were countless suggested edits, mostly cuts, which meant writing new segues. Gilles found it irritating and bewildering, he wasn't used to that sort of work. I advised him to do it with his editor—which is the usual practice—but he didn't want to, he 'didn't get a good vibe from him.' On top of this, he had to go down to the Charleville-Mézières Theater for a meeting about his puppets so he begged me to help him. 'You're a great writer, my Claire, I need your eye, you're the only person I trust.'

"I know I should have refused. Émilie and Carole had told me enough times. Gilles was making me play the part of a mother again, a mother devoted to her beloved child. 'Maybe,' I replied, 'but a good mother, the sort you trust.' (All I wanted was to erase the word *toxic* from the language.) 'A good-ah mother,' Carole exclaimed triumphantly, putting on a Marseille accent. 'That's exactly it! Don't let's forget our little guy's from Marseille! But a mother all the same.' 'Well, in that case, he's sleeping with his mother,' I retorted. 'Aye, there's the rub,' said Émilie. And all my fears came home to roost again.

"I made all the corrections while he was away. We chatted briefly on the phone every evening, he hardly listened to my questions about his book, agreed with everything, and deluged me with gratitude, as if this love now worked only long distance.

When he came back from Charleville, the tension immediately bubbled up between us again, and despite how much he claimed to want me, I felt unwanted, so when I was invited to Basel for the last night of a show based on *Ballroom*, I didn't ask if he'd like to come with me. I'd already been to Switzerland several times to meet the director and for the premiere, I knew the whole theater company, and I was looking forward to the after-party—we would dance and I would forget everything else. When Gilles found out, he was offended that I was planning a trip without him: Wasn't he my partner? 'But I... I thought that you... that you didn't want to be seen, well, in public, as my partner, openly,' I stammered. 'Not at all,' he said, apparently amazed. 'I never said that. We're together, as far as I know. And anyway, in Switzerland,' he added with an ironic grimace, 'anonymity is guaranteed. I'm even wondering why you're so keen to go, what's in it for you? Look, come on, I'll come with you, I won't abandon you to the cowherds.' Besides, he decided he would use the trip to go to the Zentrum Paul Klee in Bern and have another look at the puppets, and then meet me at the show. So I asked for another invitation and to be given a double room. That night was neutral, as far as I remember.

"Before Gilles arrived in Basel, I told Luc, the director, that I didn't want to be invited onto the stage at the end of the show—I remembered the ceremony for the César Awards. It was a small sacrifice because I loved the play and the company, and after so many slights I would have enjoyed some applause. But I was walking on eggshells—and these eggs were the size of ostrich eggs, the same size as my denial—while also obscurely aware of how unfair the situation was. Deep down, I was sorry that Gilles was there, even though I saw the possibility of a definitive reconciliation in every night that lay ahead. I still believed in erotic catharsis: My deep-seated knowledge of him would be restored when we were in each other's arms.

"The performance was an ordeal. I'd forgotten how edgy the dramatization was, how crude the images, along with the dialogues that had been lifted from my book. At one point there was even a simulated sex act stripped of any romanticism, the two actors miming a rough, urgent climax. It didn't embarrass me the first time I saw it, but with Gilles there, I wanted the ground to swallow me up. Once, when I was about twelve, a fellatio scene suddenly gate-crashed a film I was watching with my father—it was the same feeling of shame, but shame about what? I avoided turning to look at Gilles, I could feel his hostility through the armrest of the chair, it was palpable, indestructible, raw. He sat as rigid as a wooden puppet, not laughing at the funny bits, balling his fists as if crushing the loving exchanges, and he clapped mechanically when the curtain came down, already starting to make for the exit. 'Didn't you like it?' I asked, finding it hard to keep up with him. 'It was so long! I thought I'd die of boredom. And I wasn't the only one judging by the people behind me.' 'Really? I didn't hear anything.' 'And the script,' he went on, 'I'd never noticed how coarse it is in places—crass and shameless. It's not your fault, or, well, let's say that the dramatization made things worse. Where's our hotel?'

"I followed him like a dog, not even going to congratulate the cast, his hostile body that had once been so loving led me away, how could I shake off a leash like that? As soon as we reached the room, he started pointedly typing on his laptop, his face a picture of lofty disdain. I watched him in disbelief for a while, staring at this antagonistic, self-satisfied, obstinate mask of his. A stranger. Worse: an enemy. How did we come to this? I waited for him to look up, to see the challenge in my eyes. But no. I no longer existed. In the end I exploded. Was this who my partner was? Was this what being together meant? Where the hell had the love gone? 'The love, Gilles!' He stopped what he was doing with a weary sigh and looked at me calmly. 'Maybe you should be asking yourself why the theater reserved a room for you in a whorehouse,' he said.

"The hotel really had once been a brothel—all its advertising relied on its spicy past. The rooms had been decorated to respect this history: The lights were diffused with draped velvet, saucy lithographs covered the walls, there was a mirror on the ceiling and no wall between the bathroom and the bedroom, even the toilet area—which included a bidet—had no door. 'It must be because I'm a whore,' I said, spitting out my words. Enough of this walking on eggshells, might as well make an omelet. He raised his eyebrows and twisted his neck as if to say: There we have it. 'Come on, Gilles, what's going on?' I asked more quietly. 'We won't get anywhere if we don't talk. What's wrong? I'm totally lost. Why are you angry with me? Don't you love me anymore? Have you met someone else? Talk to me, I'm begging you.' He took a breath in and then huffed it out in exasperation. 'What the hell! The thing with you is you just don't think of taking a good look at yourself. It has to be because of me, I have to be the baddie, the unfaithful one. Of course!' 'I'm sorry, Gilles. But you've changed so much. *I* haven't. I don't think. Or if I have, tell me. What's toxic about me? In real terms? Tell me. Give me examples. You say we need to change our relationship, but be more specific. What do I need to improve?' I was almost yelling as I asked for these instructions. He didn't reply, half reached for his earplugs. 'I thought things were going better, but actually they're not,' I added, quickly softening my voice. 'Is it because you didn't like the show?' He gave a sort of snicker. 'You and your fucking, you mean?' 'What?' 'You did sleep with that guy, right?' 'Which guy?' 'Onstage just now, we did see you sleeping with a guy?' 'Onstage we saw an actress simulating sex with an actor.

That's what we saw. And I need to explain that to a theater expert? I can't believe this!' 'I have to say the actress is wonderful. She adopted the way you hold yourself, how you move, your intonations, your hairstyle. It's like the real thing.' 'She's a very good actor, yes. But she's not me (*and I'm not your mother*).' 'In other news, it's based on one of your autobiographical novels.' 'From fifteen years ago. I'm a writer, Gilles, were you aware of that? I have a past, I—' 'Oh, I'm well aware of *that*. How could I not be?' 'I adapted it into a novel and Luc adapted it onto the stage. What's the problem?'

"He didn't answer, returned to his laptop. I almost went back to the theater to be with the others, with normal people, but I was so mentally exhausted that I gave up on the idea. I felt so ugly and empty—a waste of space. I undressed in the bathroom, trying to hide behind a pillar, which was pointless because he wasn't watching me. When I was in bed, trying to get to sleep as I fought back tears, he turned on a lamp next to his chair and the light crept under my eyelids. 'Not having another go, then?' he said, half stating, half asking. I opened my eyes. I saw myself in the mirror on the ceiling, defeated in the depths of the bed. I hadn't removed my makeup in order to maintain a semblance . . . a semblance of what? My face was ravaged with exhaustion and misery, my cheeks furrowed with shadows and lines I'd never seen before. 'Another go at what?'

I whimpered. 'What is it you want to tell me? This is torture, Gilles.' 'Nothing. I don't know. It's just sometimes you go on and on.'

"Later in the night he came and lay next to me. I had my back to him, he pressed himself up to me and put his arms around me. 'I love you,' he said as he penetrated me."

"He left the country again on February 10, having given his editor his manuscript that I'd amended—he hadn't even read it through after I'd worked on it, and in my confused state I valued this evidence of his trust. Two days earlier, Alice had come from Lyon to spend an evening with us, I think she mostly wanted to see Gilles—she missed her father and needed advice about her future, she would be finishing her fine arts studies soon. They talked a lot, I'd withdrawn to the kitchen and could hear them laughing, and when I came in with the coffee, they both turned to look at me and I saw the word *Mommy* in both of their faces, happy in Alice's case, contemptuous in his—was I going crazy? Gilles suggested that Alice rent a studio to start her career as an artist. He'd seen her drawings, she'd shown him her work using fragile materials like paper and cardboard, and he expressed genuine admiration. 'Congratulations, I really mean it! I'll give you your first commission,' he said. 'Papier-mâché puppets for a new project. Together we'll break totally new ground, I promise!' He'd been collaborating with the same artist for a long time, but had had enough, it was getting humdrum. 'Make way for the young!' he'd decided. Alice came and joined me in the kitchen. 'I *love* him,' she said. I can still see her smile.

"So he left on February 10. 'Don't worry,' he said, taking me in his arms. 'There are just some minor adjustments we need to make between us, we'll be together again soon and everything will be like before, you'll see.' 'I'm sad that you're going.' He hugged me tighter and I closed my eyes, enveloped in his cologne. 'My Claire,' he said. 'I won't suggest you come with me, even if I wanted to, I know you have your show coming up.' The first night of *Together* was scheduled for February 16. It would have been too late, anyway; it takes at least four days to get an electronic visa for Canada. On the doorstep at his apartment—no, you're right, I can't bring myself to say 'our apartment,' I never could, even before all this, and he never said it either, certainly not that day, I remember, he said, and it felt to me like a gift: 'I'm glad you're at my apartment.' So, anyway, on the doorstep, with his bag at his feet, he hugged me again. 'Have faith in the future,' he said in my ear, pressing his hands against my back. I was crying. Picture a funeral, an unmoved distant cousin, and you'll have the scene. But then the next day, straight off the plane, he sent me a message: a whole row of hearts and a viral YouTube video of an old couple dancing rock and roll.

"You're shaking, Claire. Are you cold? Would you like to stop?" "No, Mrs. Niepce, or actually, yes, maybe. We're getting to the crux, not long now till the death scene. I'll need my strength."

8

I pick up as soon as I see it's Gilles—otherwise I avoid talking to people on February 14: I don't feel like pretending to be happy on this day and no one now remembers that it's the anniversary of Tristan's death, except his father maybe, but he stopped calling me long ago. "My Claire, I wanted to call you on this special day, even though I don't have much time this morning," he says. It's very early for him in Toronto, lunchtime in Paris. His voice sounds muted. I picture him in his bedroom on the far side of the ocean. I'm the first thing he thought of when he woke, I think. "How are you doing, bearing up okay?" he asks. "Are the dance rehearsals going well? You didn't call yesterday, I waited for your call." "No, I told you we'd be working late, it was the dress rehearsal. Then we all went out for dinner together and I had far too much to drink." "You could have called me when you got back..." "I was dead beat. I went straight to bed."

(*I'm mostly trying to meet your expectations—not stifling you, so you don't feel hounded.*) "Were there lots of you?" "Everyone was there, John, the musicians, the costume designer, the production guys, and the stage management team. All such great people." (*I'm also trying to make you jealous, subtly, make you scared of losing me.*) "Well, that's great. Do you feel you've found where you belong now, you're no longer scared of looking ridiculous? Anyway, I'm thinking of you so much." "Where I belong? I don't know where I belong, I—" He interrupts me, he's very sorry, he has another call, it's Mark and he needs to take it. "Who?" "Mark. He may be leaving his job in Paris, in which case I'll need to give him back his apartment here. Nightmare! Let's speak tomorrow," he adds quickly. "But I'll be with you this evening. As for where you belong, you belong in my heart."

◆

Love doesn't make you blind, it makes you deaf. But the writer needs to surface again at some point. In love or not. Otherwise, it can't work. So many words are exchanged, so many pronouncements do battle, so much is said and is out there—wounding, tender, truthful, lying—and eventually the writer's ear pricks up. Or else, what's the point?

So it happened, it happens, even if that ear switches off again afterward—except when you're writing, you can't listen to language the whole time, it's too tiring, and too painful, especially when it's about love. Let's say that sometimes you don't want to hear anything. Well, it happened that day. On February 14, almost unwittingly—maybe because it's hard to tell yourself lies on the anniversary of a death, even if they are lies about love on that day for lovers—Claire Lancel pays attention to what's being said. The ear is a writer's lucidity. During the day, Claire worked on giving words some resonance, she recited from memory the texts she would say into the mic onstage a little later between two dance sequences; she also read the poems out loud, these are her little rituals, like a believer lighting a candle, her benevolent lucky charms, her prayers to no one. She read Baudelaire, she read the ending of Racine's *Bérénice*, she went to find "The Hollow Men" on her bookshelves, her heart constricting at the thought that she may have lost it, but no, it was there, she read it in English, happy to have this beloved language that's spoken over there on her lips again, then went on to read Louise Labé and Emily Dickinson. And then, out of nowhere, something she'd heard earlier that morning chimed in, broke into what she was reading, creasing the handsome fabric of language and derailing the score like a finger playing a wrong note on a keyboard, clunk, or someone pouring water into the piano.

"You belong in my heart."

The sentence does its work, one corner of the mind is broached, it's fissured and forced and fractured.

You belong in my heart.
You belong in my heart.

"I'll be with you this evening."

The sentence sits within a frame, it could be hung on a wall like kitsch lithographs of little Paris urchins and phony Valentine cards—*Today I love you more than yesterday and less than tomorrow.*

And: "on this special day."

And: "I'm thinking of you so much."

Special. So. So much. Special. Of you. With you. On this special day. You belong in my heart. Special. Special day. In my heart. With you this evening.

Claire Lancel has watched many marital scenes and fights at the theater and in movies—she remembers Ingmar Bergman and Pascal Rambert, and how alive the ferocity made it. Not here. This is the opposite: The ferocity is in how dead it is. The words aren't arguing anything, that's just the point. The violence of those empty words is suddenly audible in this scene about nonlife. And it stinks. Ears have a good nose: It smells of death. Language has breathed its last. Cliché is a rotting carcass.

Dead language, passion killer. The common ground being deceased words. An urge to toy with them to bring them back to life. The smooth-talking assassin. The blah-blah-blah that shoots you down, the spiel that takes you out. The hot air, the wind that life's gone with. "It's all just bullshit," Alice summarized when it became impossible for her to talk to her father. "He just talks crap."

So these empty words were scratching away at the door of her hermetically sealed subconscious. Unless it's the door to the Paris restaurant where she and Gilles regularly have dinner, on the corner of their street, and where she stops off this evening because the manageress waves to her to come in—she'd like Claire to sign her copy of her latest book (and also, although she doesn't dare say this, to ask why Claire's going home alone tonight, poor thing, on Valentine's Day). The place is already packed, and Claire's sense of unfamiliarity derives from the multitude of tables for two. The room is full of tables—all the regulation one arm's length apart—for two people, a man and a woman, although a couple of young women holding hands over their plates can just be seen at the back. This unusual layout under garlands of sequined hearts; the double rows of diners conspicuously ignoring their immediate neighbors—even though they live in the same building or work in the local shops, Claire recognizes them; the pairs of lovers pretending to be alone in the world surrounded by the hubbub of conjugated whisperings; their expressions of suppressed boredom or their muzzled smiles staring unseeing at a this'll-never-actually-happen girl in silky, scarlet lingerie behind the libido-special menu while Umberto Tozzi busts his lungs with his "Ti amo," as if no one understands any Italian except for the chorus . . . all these details make their mark on her, infiltrating a sandy sediment in her consciousness where they join the empty words that have come to settle there, "*ti amo*," empty shells that you can pick up at low tide in conversations, "*un soldo . . . in aria . . . se viene testa vuol dire che, basta*." "Lovers are alone in the world," says the manageress casting an indulgent eye over the tables, while on the retina of her other eye she multiplies the cost of the "special event" menu by the number of covers. How right she is, thinks Claire as she takes the elevator up to the apartment. So alone, yes! Which doesn't stop her singing, "*ti odio e ti amo*," that's it, the earworm's caught on, "*ti amo ti amo ti amo*," she can't help it, in Italian, whatever you do, love always feels like it's something. She scrutinizes herself in the elevator mirror, steps closer to her reflection, although it's distorted by the neon light. "Do you live around here?"

♦

On the night of February 14, I had a nightmare. I was in a sort of American desert, a bit like Cary Grant in that Hitchcock movie with the plane—a vast flat expanse with just a road through the middle of it. I was crossing the desert with my phone to my ear, concentrating on words I couldn't hear clearly, when a bus that appeared from nowhere was suddenly hurtling toward me. Its terminus was "Heart Belongsville," written in large letters on its sequined front, and Gilles was driving it—I could see his eyes bulging with hate, his hands gripping the wheel as he accelerated, passing the *Ti odio—I hate you*—bus stop to ram into me in a shrill scream that woke me in a cold sweat, gasping and terrified, *vuol dire che, basta*, sitting upright against the bedroom wall, riding shotgun and the gun had shot me—*I want to say enough is enough.*

It was four in the morning; ten o'clock at night in Toronto. In all those years, whenever Gilles was abroad or I was, I never called him in the middle of the night—his or mine—not once. My trust and an obsessive need not to be any bother always stopped me. *Stopped* isn't the word: I didn't even think of it. On that particular night, my concern about annoying him with a "maternal" intrusion might have dissuaded me, but my fear was stronger, an instinctive fear, you know, the sort of mortal dread that has to fight its way out through the crowd of ghosts.

First it just rings unanswered, then a hissing sound and it cuts out. I go to another room and call again, I'm getting to know WhatsApp. This time he picks up. I can hear a woman's laugh in the background, overlaid by loud moving about of crockery and cutlery—a table being cleared unceremoniously.

"Gilles? Are you at a restaurant?" I say, amused—and all my fear dispelled—to be passing via his ear thousands of kilometers away into the soundscape he's experiencing, moved that I've entered the intimacy of his day-to-day existence, something I'm being denied and can't wait to share again. Valentine's Day–restaurant–woman: My brain doesn't make the connection. I say "Gilles?" again cheerfully, he doesn't answer, I check my screen, it's definitely his number. In fact, I can now hear his voice, he's speaking English, breezily playful. He's not talking to me, I realize. A pocket call, I also realize—which is stupid because I'm the one calling him. A few words are exchanged, I can't quite make them out, cutlery clinks on plates, there are two of them, it's not a restaurant, the voices are in very high spirits. At last, a voice comes closer. "Should I make you a coffee, darling?" says Gilles.

She's there
She's in Toronto
She's not there
in the same way she has been
before
With walls around her
With arms around her
Touched by fingers
that leave
the piano
for her breasts
for her cheeks

She's come out of the body
she had
It's been left shaking and numbed
in Paris
She's in the
northernmost point
of love
The cold is
biting
A snowdrift forms
where her heart used to be
Nothing circulates now
through her veins
just the sound of voices
words
that turn her to ice
Her hands are
trapped
in the marble
of tombs
where time ticks by
Her head
is reduced to the
idea
of a head
(memory lingers)
The word skull
suits it better
and rattling inside it are
precarious thoughts

soon to be
moss, flies,
lichen, futility
soon to be liquidated.

There she is on a bench
The frozen words
bumbling
mumbling
A polar frost
snatches the words
from her mouth
which is a crevasse.

Her heart has been turned to stone
She has the exact date
It's Pompeii at the North Pole
She won't make it through
the winter
that's obvious
She's covered with frost
But they say
it's the most beautiful way to go
dying of cold
It's a kind of sleep
People drift off
just as they are
under the avalanche
She's already a statue

by the graveside
No flowers or gravel
Still less a wreath.

She's alone
She's so alone
when she dies
it's terrifying
She's nothing
when she dies
in the significant other
She's nothing
She no longer has any
say
But a say in what?
Her words are deadened.

And yet
She's there
in Toronto
She's been set down
on the coffee table
by the sofa
or the breakfast bar in the
American-style
kitchen perhaps
(she can hear, relatively clearly,
the sound of water, of dishes)
Unless she's

in his hand
but no, she doesn't believe that
she can't be
(doesn't want to be)
entirely
at his mercy.

She's nothing
nothing human is left of her
But she keeps going
in the form of a high-end
cell phone
an iPhone, a Samsung
way up in a high-rise
in Toronto (Canada)
the last word
—how appropriate—
in telecommunications
and it's shaped more or less
like a rectangular
ear—
they do exist.

She's reduced to
her sense of hearing
and even then
only half words
in a language
that she loves
that's betraying her

a foreign language
not one she knows well
not her mother tongue
a bad
mother
who couldn't care less
whether she's understood.

She's there
She's an inanimate object
picking up waves
(hasn't she always been?)
She also has eyes
although the camera
is off
She sees what she can grasp from words
The voices form images
of the present and the past
She's in Toronto
with them
There are three of them
in the room
even if
it doesn't look like it
She's in Toronto
by the huge window
It's a black night
The building opposite
has grown taller
There are no workmen

at this time of night
Are they celebrating
Valentine's Day
those men
who used to
wave to her?
She wishes she were
there
in stationary time
the lingering memory
of a red hard hat
a blue hammer
the bread with
cranberry jelly
she was eating
that day
to the sound of a world
growing taller
building itself.

She's in Toronto
It's cold there
too
so cold that sometimes
an ear breaks off
and falls
amputated
rigid and hard
like an iPhone

ringing
unnoticed
then answered
and forgotten.

"Should I make you a coffee, darling? You know, a good strong one from my coffee machine, not your sock juice!" Him, his voice. The coffee machine. My Christmas present. A laugh. A woman's. Quite throaty. Simpering but hearty. No, not hearty. Throaty. Husky. A smoker? Someone older? "Yes, my love," she replies. My love. A screwdriver in your chest. Where your heart should be. What are you doing? Are you killing me? Myocardial stunning. That's what's written in Tristan's autopsy report: "Death due to myocardial stunning." There's no comeback, it says what it means.

An accent in her English. A foreign accent. Not Canadian. Harsh. Not refined. Russian? Hispanic? Arabic? Crass. Coarse. Not an intellectual. Another laugh. A self-assured woman. Who's playing. Confident of her appeal. Or maybe not all that confident. Awkward. Inferior to him. Socially? Intellectually? Flattered. A flattered laugh. He pours the coffee. My coffee machine. Inaudible sentence, sugar, milk, soft murmuring. Familiar voice. Tender. Oh, so tender! Head spin. Nausea. Pinched lips, mouth zippered shut. Her chuckle. Vulgar. An older woman's voice? Not young. Fifty or more. Can't believe she's there. Waited on like a queen. Clearing the table. Starting to do the dishes. The words, Do you like it? But in English there's only one word for "you," no distinction between formal and intimate. Would you like a coffee? Maybe it was just to the cleaner. Darling. My love. A little game? Would you like a coffee, darling? Plenty of men who say darling to all women. Doesn't mean they're sleeping with them. Shall I make you a little coffee, darling? Yes. Thank you, my love. For a laugh. It has been known. Everyday smooth talking. My darling. My love. A little game. Parodying Valentine's Day. A coffee, my darling? Thank you, my love.

Laughter. Happy people. Relaxed. Inaudible sentences. Him. Darker voice. Talking about work. UNESCO. People's names. My job. Her, mmm, sound of cups, teaspoons. Family life. Talking to himself. Getting angry. Useless collaborators. Her, nothing. Doesn't care or maybe out of her depth. Crushed. The cleaner? A coworker? A neighbor? Sentences, he's monologuing, my claim, my project, my future.

Nausea. Scrutinizing. Scrutinizing everything. Suffering. Hoping. Ear resting on the sofa, on the shawl left there—the red and blue one. Ear. The ear listens and sees itself there. Set down in that distant place. Ogreish hearing. Mouth zippered to the ear. Scar. Missing the key words. Faraway, nearby, interrupted. Lost sight of. Not understanding. Can't understand a thing. Zilch. Mentally exhausted. Feverish pain. And the cold. The annihilating clairvoyance of the cold. Pull yourself together? Yell I'M HERE? A last gasp. Glaciation. The body's ultra-lucidity before decomposing.

Laughter. Young-sounding. She's young. Husky but young-sounding laughter. Music. The word music. Piano. The tuner? In the evening. It's ten-thirty in the evening. On Valentine's Day. An intern? Dangerous. Too dangerous. #MeToo.

"*Mark ne rentre pas, finalement.*" A sentence in French! "So it turns out Mark isn't coming back." A whole sentence IN FRENCH. "*Je garde l'appartement.*" "I'm keeping the apartment." That's two! Her voice, "*Oui.*" Laughter. Only word she knows in French, *oui*. Doesn't understand at all, doesn't care. Sips her coffee. Young, definitely. Him. Goes over to the window. The darkness and city lights communicated by ear. "It's good, it means you'll still be able to enjoy the view of the building under construction." In French. A sentence for me. A gift. Talking to me. Addressed to the ear resting on the sofa. Knows it's there. Talks to it. The other woman doesn't give a damn about the building under construction. *I* do. I'm who this is intended for. Helpless. Grateful. Stifled sobs. He's talking to me. Relief. It's me that he's talking to. ME. In my ear. Wants me to come back. To see the view again, the workmen. In Toronto.

Still be able to enjoy.
Your home. With you. Tells me so.

Hot and cold.
Blowing hot and cold. Blown out of proportion.

But then: He knows. That I'm there. I'm listening. If he's talking to me, then he knows I'm listening. My blood freezes again. No circulation. Amputation. Just the ear left, the ear to the ground, such lethal ground.

He did it on purpose. Picking up and not saying anything, he did that on purpose.

Spiteful. Sick. A game? A punishment? For what?

Dirty trick.

Cruel.

No respect for anything. In fact, the opposite. Reveling in disrespect.

In the pain.

Not possible. Not on purpose. Not him.

Not him.

Not possible.

Not pos-si-ble.

Yell. I'm here. Hang up?

Can't. Transfixed. I'm here. Caught up in the game. The play of mirrors. Transfixed in a corner of the triangle. Is she in on it? No. She's laughing. A dumb laugh. An innocent laugh. Young. Doesn't know about the ear. It's him. Him alone. He's not with her. He's with me. Two people in the room.

Him and me. Him there to hurt me. Deliberately. So that I know. So that I understand my pain.

Silence. Long silence. Painful. The ear clings to it. A fishhook for the tiniest noise. Swishing sound, brushing sound, sigh, mouth noises, mmm. His nose in my hair, sniffing my longing at the roots, mmm. I remember. His hands in my hair. Not my hair. Not there. Absent. Out of shot. Out of contention. A hypersensitive ear. Skinned alive. Bitten.

Drawing blood.

The hair is hers. Her hair. No more images. The ear can't see things in the voices anymore.

Kissing her? Dangerous silence. Cadaverized. Imminent death in the crook of the eardrum.

Mmm.

Tiny ossicles in the middle ear pick up a two-time rhythm.

Two-time.

Two-timing.

Two-timer.

His voice at last. Clear. Nearby. He's moved the ear. On purpose. So that I can hear better? Not so well? In his hand?

Crooning voice. His voice. Familiar. So familiar. Identified. Tender. Husky. Insinuating. Erotic. "I need something more concrete, you know."

My sentence. Spoken in English. Our sentence. Given over to the enemy. No longer mine. Me or another. Another or me. Same thing. Interchangeable. The same sentence.

Not me. Not me on the receiving end of this sentence from me.

That sentence belongs to me.

No longer belongs to me.

No longer for me.

Alone. Ousted. Dispossessed.

No more me. A witness. Sitting on the living-room sofa with my father. Waiting for the night to wear on. For the lovers to wear out.

The chalice. Down to the dregs. The last drop of blood. A blood sport.

Liar. Lies, all of it. Everything that was. All of the past dissolving in the present.

You belong in my heart.

Not in my arms.

Alone in the future.

Alone in the present.

Don't let yourself be put in a coffin. Don't.

Abandoned.

Technically.

Don't.

You belong in my heart. Special day.

The hate.

The promise.

Alone in the past. This past that you described to each other now coming to an end. The things that you experienced melting away. Memories nailed up. Crucified. Cards reshuffled. To the death. Fragments arranged another way. A kaleidoscope. But. Nothing. Is. Beautiful. A rearrangement of the body's cells. The story pitched another way. The ear can't hear it. Despite its perfect pitch. And then there are the organs and tissues, subject to this great aggregation. The cancer spreads, you can feel it move, doing the rounds of the homeowner, unbelievable. It feels at home, every molecule molding snugly to its itinerary. You track its progress along marbled veins and whitened bones. If you get cancer someday, in a year, ten years, you'll be able to date it. That line from *Bérénice*, "In a month, a year, how must we suffer too." You know when it started. Its date of birth. The beginning of the decline. The exact time.

The great segregation.

Toronto, February 14, 2019. Four o'clock the following morning Paris time.

Tristan would be twenty-five.

The cancer is twenty minutes old.

Hang up? Message him? "I'm unhappy."

But there's no unhappiness in the word *unhappy*. Words are all so dry. Left teetering on the brink of tears.

Hate.

Heartbreak.

Frozen words.

Shame. Shame drunk down to the last drop.

She can see herself: She doesn't get it at all.

There's no love in the verb to love.

Words, words.

Anger doesn't brew.
Nothing. Not an atom
of anger.
Just heartbreak.
She doesn't have
No she doesn't have
love there to help her.
His words
His promise.

The line goes dead.

She's there
at his place
in Paris
On this bed
where they
made love
even if others
orgasmed
and slept
and stayed awake
in it
She had no imagination
The mirror
on the other hand
is inhabited
Its silvering is haunted
memory crumbling
in the aluminum

When she leans in
she can see
other
reflections
a succession of them
in the four corners
of the image
In that mirror
bought for a song
she's just passing through
she can see that she is
she knows she is
she's
light-years
centuries away
from the beginning
of love.

9

It's summer. Gilles has reserved a table at an elegant restaurant where he's eaten before, with steps leading down to the beach. A mimosa in a pot is gently losing its glow in the dwindling daylight. You're wearing the dress that he chose for you, a white one that really suits you, so why do you feel awkward, out of place, how to explain the feeling? *Borrowed*—borrowed from whom? From a Marguerite Duras novel, from a 1960s film shot on the French Riviera? But your name isn't Anne-Marie Stretter or Lol V. Stein, you're not Grace Kelly or Audrey Hepburn. You're playing a part—is your acting any good?—in a setting you don't like, a play you haven't rehearsed; a light comedy with you as the middle-class wife, and equally a mindless series. It's a formulaic scene, hackneyed, trotted out all along the coast and in other places, in so many other equally beautiful locations, populated with ritzy parents and children untroubled by their wealth, whose mommy is the prettiest. You look at the diners with walk-on parts in your life, and the very idea would make them laugh because they're totally playing the lead, here and everywhere else, in every language—*you're* the secondary character, which would also make them laugh because you don't know that you are. A few couples are inhaling the evening air less ostentatiously, their heads tipped back, in heaven—and who wouldn't be, in Saint-Tropez on a warm summer evening? It's the dream. Even the waitresses are only passing through, waiting for Brad Pitt to take them away. But you wish you were somewhere else, eating a pizza any old where, at the villa would be even better, making the most of the garden at the cousin's house. Even first thing this morning when Gilles suggested a day in Saint-Trop, you wanted to say no, you were planning to write this afternoon, but you can't refuse him anything, you want him to be happy with you, and anyway you'd just made love. He's tender, besotted. You're so lucky! "What? You've never had Sénéquier's nougat?" he exclaimed, and you didn't point out that you'd never been to Saint-Tropez either. No, never been except in a photograph of your mother with her lover, you can picture the SÉNÉQUIER awning over the table where she's posing with André, an upturned bottle of champagne in their ice bucket—until today, you always thought it was in Juan-les-Pins. There were professional photographers in those days who offered their services to vacationers, not to mention the paparazzi, but your mother wasn't Bardot, even if she did have the same gingham headband. You don't know where your father was at the time. He could never have been there, in any event, it wasn't his world. But your mother had followed André—André's gazing eyes, André's smile, André's high-rolling tendencies—although, if you study the photo closely, you can tell that she feels a little lost, it's something deep in her eyes, the subtle fear of being out of place, or perhaps only in the posed side of the photo?

You and Gilles got stuck in traffic and then drove around for ages looking for a parking space. You strolled past the yachts where models in bikinis occasionally appeared from below deck; you identified La Madrague, and bought nougat from Sénéquier. You walked hand in hand, found a bit of beach that wasn't too crowded, and in the sea he held you tightly in his arms, your legs coiled together in the clear water. And now you're here with your fingers interlaced on the immaculate tablecloth—you've used your plate to hide the rouille stain you made when you were eating your bouillabaisse, it'll appear when the waitress takes the plate away. It's not yet dark and a boy is doing cartwheels on the beach, crying, "Mom, are you watching?" Gilles smiles at you, his eyes are the gray green of the sea when you move away from the shore. Can a communist's grandson really feel unambivalently happy sitting in such a setting, next to you in a white silk dress, next to the aquarium where lobsters living on borrowed time are languishing? You don't know. You imagine he can. He probably thinks he's giving you a treat that's up to your standards, and to think your father was a dentist. You find his thoughtfulness touching and painful, you should have cleared up any misunderstanding. What's he talking about now in that soft voice? Your dreams, the future. The things you remember most clearly are how soft his voice is, and his fingers shelling a lobster claw—even in this snapping action you long for them. "Would you like a taste, my love?" You tilt your mouth toward him. In your video memory, survivors in fluorescent life jackets land on a tourist beach, take a few staggering steps between the brightly colored towels, and you can smile as much as you like with a scrap of lobster meat between your teeth, but you can't shake off the image of those vacationers, their astonishment, mixed with terror as if confronted by a sea monster, and shame in some cases, though not many, your shame, shame for being there, on the right side of life but the wrong side of the story—you can't in all decency remind Gilles how much of a graveyard the sea is when he's offering you this setting to prove his love to you. There isn't any love, there are just ways to prove love, and he gives you all of them. "Do you like the Chablis, my darling?" You smile. Shame downed in one. He's wearing a midnight blue shirt from Figaret, you stroked it as you unbuttoned it a day ago, before he threw it onto the back of a chair—incredibly soft, fine fabric, and a color the ordinary brands never use. If he's acting, he's acting well, theater's his domain, after all, life is a dream, and you're gradually easing into this character whose silky costume you've donned, next to this very good-looking man whose happiness is the only objective. The waitress offers to take a photo of you with the sunset in the background, in it you're smiling as if enraptured in your virginal dress, when Gilles texts it to you in the morning, you'll think you look ugly, what were you thinking wearing white when you don't have a tan, and your smile makes your cheeks look stupidly chubby—stop smiling in photos, especially next to him, everyone can see your teeth. "I don't think so," Gilles will say.

Over dessert, he starts talking about your books, he steers them into the conversation—he says "your body of work," you loathe this expression, which he uses more than once, it ages you, and perhaps you also loathe the admiration that you think you can see in his eyes; you want to be loved. He hasn't read them all, far from it, but he finds your body of work so superior to everything else that's referred to as autofiction. You're a great author, not like some women writers—he cites a few novelists whom you like. The tiramisu is very good, so is the ice-cream cake. It's then that he has an idea: What if you made each other a vow? A vow? Yes, a vow. A solemn vow. A promise. Please don't let him swear he'll always love me, you think. Not that you don't want that: You desperately want him to always love you, in fact it's the only thing that interests you about living this life, nothing, absolutely nothing feels more important to you than the succor of love, but without words, without pronouncements, and not on anyone's head. Otherwise it's in books. Unless he's asking to marry you? That would explain the romantic dinner, the flickering candles. You would say yes. Yes outright. Yes, my love. You would forget that your husband proposed to you in more or less the same circumstances, twenty-five years earlier, but in Étretat; he ordered a "Royal" seafood platter and you didn't dare tell him that you couldn't stand oysters—you've eaten them ever since. The future didn't turn out very well for you. But Gilles is explaining what he means. The idea is that each of you chooses a promise for the other, a promise they must keep. Okay, you say. Well, keep it . . . only if the other person keeps theirs. You think this is fun, you've had too much to drink and just want to go home and be naked next to him, with the window open to the breeze. No, come on, he says seriously, almost irritably. A promise is a promise. You laugh, he's so sanctimonious. Claire Fabian. It sounds good. You've had enough of being you, you want to change your stripes, your name. You like the idea of breaking up with yourself for him. Writing and being his wife: You can definitely see yourself conducting your life like that. To the very end.

Ending it in his arms. You can see yourself dying in this man's arms. You once said in an interview: "I hope that death is a man." And that it has Gilles's smile, you add to yourself. Gilles takes your hand and strokes it.

"I'd like you to promise me..."

He's looking at you as he says it, almost studying you.

"... that you'll never write about me."

You didn't see it coming. You look down—a reflexive fixed grin; whatever you do, hide the disappointment that instantly hardens your jaw like a gum shield. Your mouth's dry. Fear sounds the alarm in your hunted-down chest. Death has the same intent boxer's eyes as he does. At first you don't say anything, he absolutely mustn't hear your shame. Is shame the right word? You're humiliated. You need to pick yourself back up.

"I thought you liked my books," you say.

He doesn't seem to understand. He's watching you, his eyes scanning, radar-like.

"So actually, you don't trust me."

He looks stunned.

"Of course, I do, my love. And I really admire you. It's completely unrelated."

He reaches for my hand.

"But it is. If you liked my books, you'd be... you wouldn't be worried, or well, you'd be glad, you'd feel proud..."

The sea is dark, its vast roar threatening you, the mimosa has melted into the shadows.

"Proud...?"

He raises an eyebrow. Isn't there a note of insolence in his voice? You choose, yes you choose, to detect only crass incomprehension—you've already noticed his lack of acuity in sensitive conversations. But you're still irked. How boorish can a man get!

"Yes. Proud. Happy that you inspire me. I don't know."

You're tired and don't feel like explaining. Anyway, you're talking to an idiot. He may be an artist, but he doesn't understand anything about your work. You could be a hairdresser and it would be the same.

"No, that's the whole point: I want to be in your life, not in your books. Do you understand?" he adds. "My love? Are you upset? Angry?"

You don't answer—at least let him see that you're not happy. After all, why hide the fact? And how? It's out of your control.

"Are you sulking?" he tries now. Kindness in his eyes. Then everything changes, a barrier comes down over his face, it's sudden, his generosity vanishes, like marbles swept up by a hand. "In that case, forget it," he says looking around the restaurant. "Let's drop the subject. I'll ask for the check."

You don't like this stranger's face, it frightens you. You pull yourself together, bring yourself back from the brink—in fact it's him you're bringing back from the brink of anger, you laugh, the two of you are happy, you're on vacation, look at the mimosa! You lean toward him and kiss him.

"Hey, come on, I'm happy to promise you that."

Your voice is bright, cheerful.

"And anyway, people don't write about happiness."

He unknits his brow, unlocks his grimace, it's extraordinary how much his face changes, you're blown away—it takes so little to make this man happy, you have that power.

"So there you are: I promise. Does that put your mind at rest?"

"My love," he says.

Goddamn it, what a smile. You smile too. Your heart's still beating fast but it doesn't show.

"How about you?" he asks.

"Me?"

"Yes you. What do you want me to promise?"

You're caught unprepared, you've no idea what you'd like to be sure of for life, apart from untold love. You say, "I don't know." The waitress is clearing the table, she has a little nose like a Pekinese and bronzed legs under her miniskirt, will you be having coffee? The candles on the table have gone out, the wax has melted on the tablecloth. What to say? What to ask for? You can't think of anything and feel useless, you're taking an exam and can't answer the question. And then you can, an idea comes to you, it pops into your head and stakes a claim as the only possible riposte to what's threatening you—what is it if it's not the eye contact between Gilles and the waitress, or the look he gives her, you can't be sure it's reciprocated, she stays all the more professional because he's not Brad Pitt, but the look in his eyes, that you catch, the furtive but keen glance, the age-old cliché of alpha males, the scar left by cut-price virility, a retina sweep from head to feet that's not aimed at the head *or* the feet, you pick up on it and decipher it: He's on her side, the waitress's side. With her enhanced breasts. And her blond thighs. You're alone, even if you'll have forgotten her in thirty seconds—an act of denial, sleight of hand. Fear goes into overdrive and wants to be soothed, right here, right now, to be lulled—you know, you know everything there is to know, you just don't know it. So you take a deep breath, the sea is noisy, you lean over to him, hoping he'll hear the word you've chosen, a specific verb and not another, not the trivial, man-in-the-street one, no, the other one, the one that needs just a look, a word, a smile:

"I . . ." you say.

Such solemnity.

". . . I'd like you to promise you'll never betray me."

◆

"I haven't betrayed you."

It's nearly the end of our telephone conversation on February 15, 2019, when I called him again. Gilles kept his promise, he wants to reiterate that. He has absolutely nothing to feel bad about. End of story, he adds.

When the line was cut the night before, I waited in vain for him to call me back, my eyes glued to my phone. Whether or not he'd done it on purpose, he must have seen—when he hung up—that I was there, that I'd heard everything. It deserved an explanation. But nothing. A silence that spoke volumes, but I refused to draw any conclusions. Waiting for him to explain. Not allowing myself to imagine what happened next. All through the night and the morning of the 15th, I truly gauged the time difference for the first time, its enigma: the mystery of two parallel sequences. Him, me. Day and night. Pain and this double distance: time and space. In the end, unable to wait any longer, I called him. Dread was crushing my rib cage. He hadn't answered my first call, sent a text: "I'm busy. Call me back in an hour." I'd called back. I called back. I'm calling back. I can't shake off the cold, my teeth are chattering.

"Hello?"

"Hello, Gilles? It's me."

It's me.

"It's Claire."

"Yeah. How are you?"

"Well, things could be better. How about you?"

"Me too. I'm having issues with the theater director, you know, Roy, I've already mentioned him, a real dick. And then there's my assistant who just doesn't understand anything, I had to go over all the calculations for the puppets. Sometimes I think, What the hell am I doing here? These people don't deserve me. Pearls before swine. Honestly."

Honestly.

"What else is going on?"

"What else is going on? It's bitterly cold here. I bought myself a lined parka from Hugo Boss yesterday, it's warm but I don't think it'll be enough. It's minus twenty degrees this morning. It must be easier going in Paris. You're lucky."

You're lucky.

"Gilles, did you do it deliberately?"

"Deliberately? Do what deliberately? What's gotten into you? This isn't the time, believe me."

"It's the time for me. Gilles. Do you really think you can avoid talking about what happened yesterday evening?"

"What did happen exactly? What's that tragic voice for?"

"Your dinner, the..."

"My dinner? What about it? I don't have to report back to you about everything I do. Or do I?"

"I heard everything. Do you know that?"

"What did you hear?"

"You were with a woman. I didn't understand all of it, the English I mean, but enough to... well, to understand. That's what you wanted, right? You did it on purpose. I didn't think you could show so little... (*love*), so little... (*respect*) consideration. I'm surprised (*thunderstruck*). And sad (*devastated*). You can't imagine."

"Oh my God, stop this! Of course I didn't do it on purpose. I'm not the bastard you'd like to think. And when it comes to consideration, I'm sorry but I don't need any lessons from you: If you had the teeniest bit of class, you'd have hung up immediately when you realized my mistake. At least, that's what I would have done..."

"If you caught me with a man on Saint Valentine's night, you'd hang up?"

"Yes. In the name of dignity. Discretion."

"Everything I don't have, then..."

"I'm not criticizing you."

"Who is it?"

"What?"

"Her. Who is she?"

"It's no one. She's the wife of an actor, she ha—"

"Are you sleeping together?"

I wish I could measure the silence to the nearest tenth of a second. When people tell the truth they don't hesitate. The facts aren't options.

"No," he says.

"Well, you sounded very intimate. 'Yes, my love,' 'darling.' Are you in love with her?"

"In love? What the hell. Definitely not in love. We have things in common, that's all. Her husband is never around, you keep abandoning me, so, you know, we've gotten close."

"Wait what? I abandon you? *I* abandon *you*?"

"Yes. All you think about these days is your own problems, and you have your dance show, do I need to point out that that's why you're not here with me?"

"For pity's sake, Gilles."

"Pity for me, yes. I feel alone and because she does too . . . the two of us thought: Come on, let's spend Valentine's Day together."

"The two of you thought: Come on, let's sleep together."

"Stop it. Don't stoop to clichés. Who cares about February 14th. It's just another day. Here in Canada, it's a celebration of friendship—you should open up a bit to other cultures, instead of seeing everything through your little France-centric spyglass. But what you really want is for me not to have any friends."

"You called her darling. My love. You even said 'our' sentence to her. I heard it really clearly: 'I need something more concrete.' And she's a friend?"

"Great accent! You've really come along."

"Oh, Gilles, this is too painful. Tell me the truth. Just the truth. I can hear it. I need to."

"You've already heard the truth loud and clear, you said so yourself. 'I need something more concrete.' Now, what does that prove, other than the fact that nothing concrete happened? It's just banter, okay, I'll admit to a bit of banter if you like. Maybe that's even why my subconscious made me make that Freudian slip when I picked up: Subconsciously, I wanted you to know, to see the danger that you've put us in, so that it doesn't become more concrete. In fact, I said your name, I don't know if you heard, when I thought I'd stopped it ringing I told her, 'It was Claire.' I was subconsciously putting your name between us."

He laughed and added, "I sure have some stuff to tell my therapist tomorrow."

"And you didn't wonder why I was calling you at four o'clock in the morning? Something serious could have happened."

"I didn't think about the time difference, no. I thought I'd call you back."

"You didn't, though."

"And did you call me after your rehearsal the day before?"

"What's the connection? I'd called you earlier in the day. And anyway, I didn't have any reason to. Whereas you... You can't deny there's a problem..."

"Listen, Claire, if you don't stop guilt-tripping me, we'll never make it. You're being toxic right now."

"So if I have this right, *my* subconscious was kind of inspired: If I hadn't called you yesterday evening, you two would have fucked."

"I didn't say that. She's married, in case you'd forgotten. And stop being so coarse, you sound like your friend Carole. Don't forget who you are."

"But who am I? Who am I, Gilles? Who am I to you?"

"What I mean is: You're a great writer. Stylish. Don't lose that, my darling."

"What's her name?"

"I have no intention of telling you her name."

"Why?"

"You can be so nasty when you put your mind to it, you'd be quite capable of wanting to harm her in some way."

"Oh, because she's not harming me in any way? And she does know my name."

"She couldn't give a damn about you and your issues, you know. She has a difficult child, a ton of problems, I help her where I can, I've taken the child off her hands two or three times to teach him some music. I'm just trying to be useful, that's all. I take an interest in other people."

"And I have a dead child. And that's the day you chose to betray me."

"Claire, for the last time: I didn't choose. And I didn't betray you. End of story."

"She didn't sound like she had tons of problems last night. Where was the child? Asleep in your bedroom?"

"Okay, that's enough. I'm going to hang up."

"Gilles, Gilles, I'm begging you. Don't hang up. Tell me something."

"You're impossible, self-absorbed and jealous. I don't even recognize you."

"I love you, Gilles. I'm trying to understand. Put yourself in my shoes for two seconds."

Silence.

"I'm totally lost."

Silence.

"Do you still love me?"

"I love you, I respect you, and I admire you. But stop this sick little game, these pathetic suspicions. Is it so hard for you to trust someone?"

◆

"Of course he did it on purpose," says Carole. "It's well hidden and no one can prove anything but it's-all-done-on-pur-pose. It's all calculated, absolutely all of it, starting with the date. Valentine's Day, the anniversary of Tristan's death, and the day before the dance show that Claire was so nervous about. He really overloaded the boat to help it sink! He's a prize asshole, end of story, as he says. The worst kind of bastard. Even the Band-Aid sentence is chopped about so it doesn't cover any wounds. No, it's actually designed to rip her flesh: 'I love you, I respect you, and I admire you.' The 'I want you' is missing, and he knows it. He knows she'll notice, and it will cause her pain. He's flaying her with every word. He casually drops his poison into all the gaps in the conversation. He's lying, he's gaslighting…it's all done to weaken her, to empty her of any—" "He's gas-what?" "It's an English word, Mrs. Niepce. It's become very common, including in courthouses. You should look it up, it could be useful. It's taken from Cukor's film *Gaslight* with Ingrid Bergman and Charles Boyer. You have to see it. Gaslighting means driving someone—usually a woman—insane by confusing them with contradictory messages. Destroying them with words. What could be worse for a writer? That's what you should argue, Mrs. Niepce: psychological violence, perverse control. And it's been happening right from the start, despite the idyllic outward appearances. Just think about the promise: He asks a writer whose entire output is based on accounts of her own life, who's known and renowned for that, he makes her swear she'll never write about him! He might as well say: Never write again. Take up macramé! And anyway, why's the promise negative? 'Promise that you won't . . .' An outright ban right in the middle of a vow! It warps the promise, undermines it, takes away its potential for a future, for a happy commitment, turns it into a restriction, a deprivation: It's a denial of who Claire is in the thing she holds most dear, her most intimate and one of her most profound reasons for being alive. That's clearly why Claire responded in the same way, with a negative: 'Promise me that you won't betray me.' She saw the betrayal right there in the promise he'd asked her to make. She'd already been betrayed at that point.

Betrayed in her heart of hearts. By that bastard. I hope he dies!"

♦

"Well, I don't believe he did it deliberately," says Émilie. "Subconsciously, yes, he probably wanted to get a message across to her. It was a classic Freudian slip, revealing something he thought he wanted to hide. But that doesn't prove anything about his actual intentions. Making him a monster doesn't resolve the mystery of this tragedy. And anyway, it was Claire who called him, at a time when he thought he had nothing to worry about. If he'd wanted to orchestrate a revelation, *he* would have chosen when. At worst, it was an impulse, nothing premeditated. As for the promise, I don't think it's as negative as Carole says. After all, it was while honoring that promise that Claire wrote perhaps her most beautiful book. *A Father*, which she wrote with Gilles by her side, illustrates the subterfuges in literature and love. On the surface it's a book about her father and Gilles doesn't feature at all because she needed to keep her promise. But if you read it carefully Gilles is really all over this portrait of a brooding man who was abandoned by his mother, and so is Claire, as a daughter and as a woman in love. Claire's promise steered her toward a new reading of her own life, even if—sadly—sublimation wasn't enough: She 'killed the father' in real life. Love is just a meeting of two subconsciouses. His mother and her father: It's two ghosts coming together. Dialogue is impossible. Suffering inevitable."

♦

"No, he didn't do it on purpose," says Georges. "I'm sure he didn't. What would have been the point? He loved Claire, he wanted to keep her. Mind you, he definitely didn't appreciate the impact of the incident. I remember when he called me to tell me about it, he sounded like a kid who'd been caught raiding the cookie jar. 'Georges, you'll never guess what happened yesterday evening...' He laughed about it like it was a great joke. When I told him a week later that Claire had called me, going crazy with the pain, he still didn't get it, he just made me promise not to call her back: I was *his* friend, he reminded me, not hers. He was totally unaware of what he'd unleashed, he was wrapped up in his own little world. He's just a blundering oaf, like most men—and I'm one of them—we avoid emotions. But then Claire wouldn't give up, she bombarded me with emotions, a real tsunami. I'm sensitive, in spite of everything, I couldn't ignore her pain."

♦

"What about you, Claire, deep down, what do you think? Were you taken in by all his talk? You didn't think your partner might be stringing you along?"

my attorney asked. "It's a little hard to follow you with such a display of gullibility." "If you find it hard to follow me, Mrs. Niepce, you might as well step down now because there are plenty more surprises to come." "Be that as it may... Why didn't you break up with him at that point?" "I did. At least, I pretended to. The important thing is breaking up in your own head. Well, I broke up on paper. My heartbreak hadn't reached its peak, it had strategies, it thought it was clever. I wrote to Gilles. How naive! I was exhausted by our conversations where we never listened to each other, but I still believed in the power of the written word, you can read something in writing over and over until you cherish it, I had faith in the beauty of my language, in the power of its truth. Basically, I still believed in myself. I even contemplated sending him a real letter, over there in Toronto, I thought the effect it had—its effectiveness—would be multiplied, symbolically, in comparison to all the emails we receive every day and hardly even read. But I wasn't brave enough—or patient enough. I should have been, it would have given me a few days' respite. Because the minute you click Send you start waiting for a reply. In the end I wrote an email. I told him how distraught I was, but rationally, if you see what I mean. That's my hallmark: looking like I can handle everything. I didn't want to scare him with too much emotion or annoy him with criticism. With every sentence, I second-guessed his reaction, fretted about his mood, anticipated his anger—to make a long story short, I morphed a message of absolute terror into a perfectly controlled piece of prose." "What did you say to him?" "That I was withdrawing. I would wait until he was in a better place himself. That I belonged, I wanted to belong, in his heart and in his life. In his arms. That I had once belonged there, I'd cherished it and hoped I would belong there again. That in the meantime I would stop writing to him and stop calling him. That I loved him.

"He replied the next day. He agreed: A pause seemed like a good idea, he needed to refocus on himself. He knew he had a problem, and his therapy was helping him identify it. He thanked me for my support. He was very aware of the dignity in my email, the beauty of my withdrawal reminded him of *Bérénice*, a talisman of a play for me—Carole managed to raise a smile from me when I read that bit out to her: '*Bérénice*, now that's interesting…' she said. 'Basically, he sees himself as the emperor! Except that Titus's dilemma is between Rome and love, not between a slut and you. That gives you an idea of his narcissism. In his mind he has an empire! He's a ruler! Titus, my ass!' After that bit, Gilles recycled his old metaphor about things that needed adjusting ('We're not machines,' Carole bellowed) but told me I didn't need to worry about it too much ('Not too much, whatever, the asshole!'), that we'd soon enjoy all the happiness of being together again ('I get the feeling he hasn't read the play to the end').

"And I was at his place, don't forget. I lived in his apartment. I watered his plants and looked after his home. In my muddled mind, it was a period of transition, I'd had the same sort of thing with my husband: Even when he was cheating on me, his priority was to not lose me. It was painful but I kept thinking that love—such a great love—couldn't vanish just like that. I was also expecting a lot from his therapy, it would give him the depth he didn't have. His therapist would guide him toward understanding everything, embracing everything. He would understand and if he understood, I was prepared to forgive. I was waiting for him to come back. To come back to himself. And come back to me."

◆

"My name's John Denver, I'm a choreographer. I'm Scottish but I've lived in France for twenty years. I clearly remember the opening night of *Together* at the Carreau du Temple on February 16th. Claire was in a *terrible* state, scary. She could hardly stay on her feet in the last few rehearsals, we nearly canceled the whole thing. She admitted she hadn't eaten for days—nothing, not a thing. I gave her some cashews, but she couldn't swallow anything. 'Except a pack of lies,' she said—she still had her sense of humor at that point. That's something I really like about you, the French, how you can still be ironic in adversity. Her voice was only just audible,

I had to reset the sound levels. She was completely switched off, yes, I can't think how else to put it, like someone had unplugged the power—her face was gray, her body shrunken, no get-up-and-go. All the things you need for dancing, in other words! She checked her phone every thirty seconds and, honestly, I think if she hadn't had a text twenty minutes before curtain, we'd have had to postpone. He—Gilles Fabian—sent her something along the lines of 'Good luck with the show' and she was transformed: He'd given her a crumb, and she fed on it. On the other hand, *I* nearly fell apart: A man who works in theater saying anything other than 'Break a leg!'—or '*Merde!*' in French—it's out-and-out provocation. But it gave Claire the strength to dance. So yes, I'd say she was completely dependent on him, yes, no doubt about it: total emotional control, that's what I saw."

◆

"I wanted to keep my promise," says Georges. "I'd promised Gilles I wouldn't speak to Claire. And when I made that promise, I meant it: You don't betray a thirty-year friendship. I didn't know Claire so well. The last time I'd seen her was the summer before their breakup, they'd come to visit us in Quiberon. I remember Gilles sulked when I showed Claire how to do archery, which is my passion. Gilles is a very jealous type, insecure deep down, which probably explains a bunch of things. But I have to say, they looked disgustingly happy that summer. When we were getting the barbecue going, he even mentioned again that he planned to marry her. Since his divorce he'd thought he'd never try that again, but this was miraculous: 'I don't know what's happening to me, Georges, I want to be married to her. She's gentle, she's tender. And she's shown me the way: I'm writing again.' They held hands, napped in each other's arms on the beach, kissed like schoolkids, Solange and I were almost embarrassed, we felt old compared to them. I'd never seen him like that, never. And Claire, she just radiated love.

"So anyway, the first time Claire called me, I didn't pick up, like a coward, but her message was so desperate it got to me. I was scared too: She said she was going crazy, she wanted to throw herself out the window. I thought it was true, although my wife thought she was laying it on a bit. It was Solange who said, 'Ask if she'd like to come see us this weekend, the weather's nice, we can go for walks, it'll do her good.'

"And she came.

"It was what? Early March?

"The day she arrived the three of us went for a walk along the beach. Claire had lost a lot of weight. That evening she took us out to a restaurant and picked at her food while she tried to worm something out of us, but it didn't work. I kept changing the subject and Solange didn't know the details.

When Claire realized this, she was furious and said, 'You're all the same.' She's not totally wrong there, we're all dickheads, men, I mean. The problem was that Solange's mother fell down the stairs at her place in Bordeaux and Solange had to leave in a hurry. And when Claire and I were alone together, she started hounding me. Questions, tears, begging. I found it harder and harder to handle, I was panicking. Plus she already knew some stuff—it's incredible what a woman's intuition can achieve when she puts her mind to it. Like for example, she'd guessed that this woman—her rival? her eyes seemed to be asking—was Gilles's neighbor and wasn't Canadian. She even thought she'd seen her once in the corridor in Toronto—a tubby little thing with peroxided hair and horse teeth, and a kid tagging along. I was impressed, even if she was bound to be wrong: Tubby and horse teeth definitely didn't match the bombshell Gilles had described to me. But, well, I didn't say that! At one point I went to the bathroom and when I came back into the living room, I could see she'd tried to look through my phone. She was ashen, shaking, a terrible sight. She begged me. So I caved. I told her everything." "Everything?" "Everything Gilles had confided in me. I did something worse than that: I showed Claire his texts—at first, I read them to her, skipping the bits that were too steamy, but she snatched the phone from me and went through all of it. I gave in to her manic hunger for the truth. I even let her listen to this woman's two voicemails." "Why?" "I wanted to help her! I'm a man, I get what an affair means. I wanted Claire to understand him, and it was so clear in the things Gilles said: He loved *her*. This other woman was nothing. A dumbass fantasy. And anyway, she was the one who pounced on him—he would never have made the first move. He'd met her in the 'elevator to seventh heaven,' as he put it in a text that raved about her 'she-devil breasts.' A she-devil with a little kid, mind you! Later he told me he felt ridiculous when he went out in the streets with them and she made him push the stroller. Another thing, and this was a big deal: She hadn't opened a book for twenty years (she owned twenty-six!), their conversations boiled down to nothing. 'Seeing as she doesn't speak French either,' he added, 'our conversations are very limited, I find it hard not being able to discuss the nuances, you see, the subtleties of emotions.' In a word, he just wanted to fuck her. Did you ever hear anything more banal? I told Claire she should do nothing, completely disappear, until Gilles realized what he risked losing for this boring casual fuck." "A boring casual fuck that had been going on for six months, though . . ." "It needed time to run its course. A young body is such an ego boost, it drives a man crazy in the early days . . . Sorry but it's true. And Gilles wanted to keep both of them. A woman in every port, a classic. If it works, then we're all happy. But he would have tired of it, definitely. If Claire had been more patient, she would have gotten her man back. In fact, that's what happened: He came back. Sadly, he just came back too late, Claire had already lost her mind." "Is that how you explain what happened? My client lost her mind?" "Yes. Or at least, that's what I would argue, if I were you. Which doesn't erase any of *his* guilt, we're clear about that, right? He behaved like a coward, a liar, an idiot. It was a stupid mistake, sure. But with Claire, it drove her crazy. With all due respect, Mrs. Niepce, women go crazy pretty quickly. It's our fault, okay. But it's your, it's their madness."

◆

"I came home from Quiberon in pieces. Humiliated. Anger kept me on my feet for a couple of days. I thought about buying red paint and daubing the walls of his apartment, I pictured it in my head like a film on loop, me with my spray can, covering everything even down to my own face in the mirror in the bedroom, him finding it like that when he arrived home—because he would come home!—his apartment butchered. I thought about flooding the piano, shredding his suits, ripping open his swanky armchairs.

"I didn't do any of that. I want to stress that point, Mrs. Niepce, because it matters to you: I didn't act on it, however angry I was. I even called the plumber when I noticed the dishwasher was leaking. I say that to explain that I'm not capable of violence. Maybe verbal, in a pinch, and even then... What I mean is: Words, books can be violent, or be seen that way. But physical aggression isn't me." "But you did hit him on the head at the house in Hyères. Violently, according to the forensics report. With all your strength. The witness confirmed it." "No. *He* threw himself at *me*. True, I was furious, devastated by what I'd found in the drawer. But if I hadn't been scared of him, I wouldn't have done anything. The witness lied: I so wish she would admit that." "That's why you're in custody, Claire. A witness can't be made to change their version of the facts. You do understand that this doesn't work in your favor?" "Yes, Mrs. Niepce. But she lied. And hid the evidence. There's no other explanation." "I believe you, Claire, I'm your attorney. But your medical examination found no signs of violence. You say that he attacked you first, but you just had some bruising on your biceps, which seems more likely to imply that Mr. Fabian tried to restrain you." "He shook me brutally, I thought he would bring his hands up to my throat. There was so much hate in his expression. He was killing me with his eyes."

"You had just returned from Quiberon. I imagine you were leaving him this time?" "I should have done it without saying anything. But I'm obsessed with the truth—'a terrorist of the truth' according to my agent. Now that I knew it, the truth, I wanted to back him into it, crucify him on it, just like it was crucifying me. For him to say it. So I wrote to him again, forcing myself to stay dignified, almost factual: I now knew why he hadn't wanted me to join him in Toronto for several months, he'd been lying to me all along, shifting the blame onto me to hide his betrayal. Because yes, he'd betrayed me. He hadn't kept his promise. I showed a lot of restraint in that email, I could have been way more vindictive, but he still couldn't take it—I think the one thing Gilles can't stand is criticism, whether or not it's well-founded. He only sees the attack in it, never the justification. He's never guilty of anything. 'It's not my fault' is his pet saying, after 'I don't want any pain.' He replied almost immediately. He'd never betrayed me, I was a bad person so I thought everyone else was like me, but they weren't: He was truthful and straightforward. Sure, he wasn't in a good place, he was aware of that, but he was trying in all humility to find out what hadn't worked between us (that pluperfect broke my heart—it's what he wanted to see in the mirror: something beyond perfect), thank goodness he had his therapist to help him dig his way out of this because he was so alone, he could see I wasn't with him at all anymore whereas he'd always, always been by my side—even on the other side of the ocean.

"I received his email at two a.m. There was too much duplicity for me, only three weeks after the nightmare of Valentine's Day. I played out the same scene, I called him. And he picked up.

"There's pleasure in the truth. You of all people must recognize that, Mrs. Niepce? That feeling when you spell out the truth even if it kills you. Except with you, maybe it's mostly the other way around: Lying must be a more effective way to defend someone. It won't work like that with me, I can assure you.

"Either way, Gilles certainly argued his case with lies, yet again and every time. I was hanging on the phone, thousands of kilometers away, worn to shreds, and I could hear the vehemence in his voice: He defended his lie as if his life depended on it. He kept up his fabrication of a noble, solitary existence with only his creative work to save him from mental collapse, from the existential suffering that I was inflicting on him when I didn't understand the situation at all. And I claimed to be a writer, pfft . . . I knew nothing about the human soul. I let him talk for a while, prompting him with questions that he answered by digging himself deeper into denial. For five minutes I manipulated him with the exquisite pleasure of despair. I was pulling the strings at last, he was the puppet! Then when his lies started heading back toward cruel accusations aimed at me—I saw evil in everything, I was mad and paranoid—I dealt my first blow. I knew I was betraying Georges even though I'd promised to keep his revelations secret, but my pain just swept everything else aside.

" 'Gilles,' I said slowly, savoring my perfectly hollow victory, 'I know everything. Georges told me everything.' A hint of anxiety broke through the irritation in Gilles's voice. 'Everything what?' 'Everything. Everything you told him, he told me.' '(*Cautious voice, trickster's intonation:*) By which you mean?' 'That you're cheating on me. And lying to me and humiliating me.' '(*Silence. Then angrily:*) What a bastard! What a total bastard! He's jealous of me, jealous of how happy we are, he always has been. He's doing everything he can to drive us apart when he has nothing, nothing, he's inventing stuff to fill the void in his own life. Don't fall into his trap, I beg you. Claire.' 'He's inventing stuff?' '(*A sigh. Silence. Then in a firm, honest-sounding voice:*) Okay, fine, I slept with her once on Valentine's Day. You already know that anyway, you're not stupid.' 'Thank you.' 'No, but what I mean is I don't give a damn about that girl, I invited her over on February 14th and never saw her again. End of story.'

"I sharpened the final blow on the cutting edge of my own pain, still maintaining a thin blade of irony.

"'It must be tricky not seeing her again. Don't you bump into her in the elevator?' 'What?' 'Gilles,' I continued. 'I've read your texts.'

"The silence tracked the progress of someone swallowing with difficulty. 'My texts? What was in my texts?' 'Well, you wrote them, I mean, just take a look. Scroll back six months.'

"There was a long pause—was he reading them? Probably not. He must have erased them like he erased everything else with his duster of cautiousness and his sponge of clean conscience. Then he went back to maligning Georges, you couldn't trust anyone these days, he'd just lost a friend of thirty years' standing, he was sad and angry.

"'Gilles, this isn't about Georges. You're losing more than a friend today. Do you even get that?' 'I'm also losing my rag.' 'And I'm losing my illusions. It's excruciating, Gilles, I can't tell you how excruciating it is.' 'So you're on his side. Of course you are. The version that says Gilles is a bastard covering up his infidelity obviously works much better . . .' 'Because there are other versions?' 'He wants to destroy me. When I think of everything I've done for him.' 'Gilles. I saw your messages. I-read-them. With the dates. The day, the time. Do you understand? It's not a version, it's the facts. We're not storyboarding a show here.' 'He's had so many affairs, Georges I mean. He's such a love rat Solange should call in Rentokil.' 'Gilles.' 'He wants to destroy me. He's toxic. I'm deleting him from my contacts right now. Ciao, you traitor!' 'You betrayed me, he betrayed you, I betrayed him. We've come full circle. You—' 'No. I didn't betray anyone. Least of all you. I've always been on your side. Always.' 'Except for my pussy. On that subject, if I read things right, you're more on the side of completely hairless pussies with no obstetric history and that can be fucked in every position.' Silence on his end. 'And with breasts, it looks like you changed cup size. You're on the side of stacked bombshells now.' 'Claire. I understand that you're angry but—' 'I'm not angry,' I said in an angry voice. 'I'm unhappy.' 'But that was just guuuuy talk. Think who it was for. Georges is the one who talks like that. Claire. I went down to his level. It's nothing serious.' 'But it was you talking, not Georges.' 'I never said anything bad about you. I've never discussed our private life with anyone. I've always respected you.' 'Well, it must have been out of respect for me that your son gave you a dildo for Christmas. What does your therapist have to say about your sexual confidences to your son?' 'Oh come on, don't drag my son into all this, that's sleazy. Children are sacred.' 'Sacred…'

"My voice went hoarse. I was by the window, there were two lamps still on in the building opposite. If I jumped out right there and then, the pain would disperse, releasing the fierce pincer grip of my shame. I remembered an expression that Alice often used: 'I've had it up to here with life,' and she waved a hand over her head. So it wasn't just a turn of phrase—that drowning feeling existed.

"'Gilles,' I said, 'I'm not asking you to tell me the truth. I'm just asking you to tell me something that's true.'

"His silence went on a long time. I could hear him weighing his words. He put them into the dish on the scales then withdrew them and tried other ones.

"'Claire,' he said eventually. 'This fall, I felt I needed to give my ego a boost, I was on a low after what you did, on the verge of burnout, and it helped. But that little dalliance never meant that you and I were splitting up.' 'Not for you. But what about me? Maybe I get to have an opinion? Maybe I don't want to stay with a liar? A man who humiliates me.' (I wanted to scream at him but it was two in the morning, I might wake the neighbors.) 'I might be a little disappointed to know that the man I love started sleeping with his neighbor at the first stumbling block, a neighbor who, incidentally, is young enough to be his daughter...' 'Oh, there you go, that is to-tal-ly out-ra-geous! My daughter now! You won't stop at anything.' 'Am I wrong? Couldn't she be your daughter?' 'Leave my children alone, please. Children are sacred.' 'Aren't you old enough to be her father, then, if you prefer? Isn't that the truth?' 'The truth! It's all you can talk about. Ah, but what truth? Yours and only yours. The one you claim to put out there in your shitty autofictions! Well, I see the truth differently, would you believe.' 'I thought you liked my books, I thought I was a great writer.' 'In your dreams. I never said that! Your essay, at a stretch. But all that me-me-me blathering, if you really want to know—seeing as you're so keen on *the truth*—is shiiiiit. You trot out all your exes, it makes me puke. And I guess I'll come in for the treatment one of these days.' 'Yes. And I have the title already if you want to know. It'll be called *Pinocchio*.' 'You have no right,' Gilles said as if factually reciting an article from the penal code. 'We'll see about that.' 'But what about your promise?' "

10

"My name is Rob Simmons, I've been Claire Lancel's agent for nearly twenty years, I handle all her publishing and audiovisual contracts. I know her well—from her books, obviously, but also personally: We're friends, although there's still a professional formality between us.

"The way I see it is that Gilles—Gilles Fabian who, through Claire, has occasionally been a client of mine—Gilles couldn't handle his partner's high profile. Which might seem strange because he knew who she was when they met; you could even say it was her *reputation* as a writer that appealed to him more than she did herself, seeing as, if I understood this right, at the time, he'd basically read nothing she'd written. I'm not saying he didn't find her attractive as a woman, but the way I see it, he fell in love first and foremost with an image, a fantasy. Everyone wants to be a writer, I see proof of that every day. In some ways, that makes me happy, the fact that literature still has such a pull, who's complaining? But with men of Gilles's age, which is the same as mine, and from his world, it's even more blatant: They have successful careers, some have even been published—you know, essays and manuals—but what's missing is being labeled a writer. These belated ambitions rarely deserve to be called a vocation. They're more like an additional step toward social achievement, a sort of media highpoint. These men don't really have an urge to write, they want to have written something.

"Gilles Fabian doesn't quite fit into that categorization in that he did demonstrate a degree of talent. Claire insisted that I meet him but if he hadn't been any good, I would have refused to represent him. His manuscript was restrained and precise. But the stakes with his writing felt more existential than socially motivated, and that's because he imitated Claire. I can state clearly: If he hadn't met her, he would never have written it—or at least not the way he did. I'm not saying she wrote it for him, not at all, or even wrote it with him, but he drew on her to write it. It's a symbiotic book, there you are, like some relationships—unless it was more parasitic than that. She was writing *A Father* at the same time, and from what I know of her writing process, I could see the energy that her romantic happiness gave her. But their experiences weren't symmetrical: Claire was still herself, the person she'd always been, while Gilles wanted to appropriate her—as if he didn't have a self of his own and was trying to work out who to be. I think he wanted to be her. Really. To take her place. Become a writer. The only one. There wasn't room for two of them in his mind." "That's a rather nebulous theory, Mr. Simmons. If we look at the facts, she's the one who wanted to eliminate him." "Because she felt existentially threatened. He wanted to suffocate what she was. It's a perfect crime and the only body is a silenced voice. That would be a legitimate defense." "Hmm..." "*He's* the potential murderer. I'm worried that Claire won't be able to show any tangible proof of this feeling that came to her in a terrifying flash, by which I mean the inescapable fact that Gilles had become her executioner. But I saw it. I don't have any proof either, but I'm sure of it." "What did you see, Mr. Simmons?" "As soon as Gilles's book was acquired by a good publisher, he started subtly running Claire down in our conversations. Then, whenever we talked on the phone, he would throw in two or three digs dressed up as jokes, things like she just kept churning out the same stuff, and if she kept going she'd end up with the Legion of Honor or alongside the stuffed shirts of the Académie Française, that sort of thing. Or he insinuated that she complained about me and had been in touch with another agent. But he changed his tone a few weeks later. One day he called me and he was furious. He said he couldn't take any more, Claire was jealous of him, was calling him a rival, and it was now obvious that she wanted to crush him. He'd suspected this several times before but it was clear now. He'd 'seen behind her mask,' he claimed.

"It didn't make any sense. Why would Claire Lancel, a renowned writer with a thirty-year career, need to be afraid of Gilles Fabian, in literature or in social circles? There was no reason. But if you put it the other way around, you have the truth: He was the one who was jealous, he felt there was rivalry between them, he wanted to destroy her as he advanced stealthily behind a mask. It's a typical sociopath's inversion. And these delusions went on after they separated. He was convinced that Claire was maligning him all over the place, trying to stymie his career as an author. He compared his stylistic qualities favorably to hers, portrayed himself as the victim of sabotage, and came to me with his 'poor me' stories. In the end he started talking about a new writing project of his—not autofiction, of course, he had higher ambitions, 'something between Kerouac and Faulkner.' I dodged that bullet: He was neither Kerouac nor Faulkner, or anyone in between!

"I don't know any details of their private life but there is one thing I know for sure: Under his mild-mannered exterior, that guy's capable of anything. He uses people like stairs to raise himself up to God knows what ambition. Then tramples on them. In fact, you should do some research: He'd already done it to his previous partner." "So you're saying that this is about artistic rivalry not jealousy of another woman? But it was when she found Viagra in a hidden drawer that Mrs. Lancel attacked Mr. Fabian." "No, I'm sure that's not right. I've read the press coverage, but I don't believe it. I knew Claire's ex-husband. He cheated on her all the time, and she knew it; I don't think a bit of Viagra in a drawer would be enough for her to fly off the handle. Mind you, she almost certainly has a psychological problem herself, she's hypersensitive, like a lot of creatives, but hey, she's the salt of the earth. Because Julien, her ex-husband, was from the same stable as Gilles. Except that, in his defense, Julien met her and married her when she was a no one, socially, she was a teacher. Then he couldn't handle her success and he, too, tried to destroy her—in her career and in life. During their divorce proceedings, he asked the family judge to bar her from having custody of their daughter on the grounds that in her latest novel she 'confessed' to swinging and that Alice featured on the next page of the book. What a moron . . . first of all, he couldn't separate the narrator from the author, or fantasy from reality. But mostly he saw the book as a kind of apartment with real people going about their lives in it. The pages were rooms with the little girl asleep in her bedroom while her mother was having a gang bang in the living room! So she was a bad mother who couldn't raise their daughter morally or even look after her on a day-today basis. It was borderline psychosis. Our attorney did a good job calling out his raving, and his claim was dismissed. But he still made off with half of everything she'd earned as a novelist—they'd been married under the community property regime. It didn't bother his conscience at all: He told anyone who would listen that she owed it to him because he'd actually written most of her material. People like that live in a falsified reality, the truth is what they decide it is.

"I said all that to show you that Claire has a weakness for that type of man. Or maybe she attracts them. Men who can't stand the fact that she writes. Can't stand her being who she is—meanwhile they're completely cashing in on who she is. I also remember a dentist (like her father, incidentally) who she was with for a while after her divorce. You'd have thought she'd be safe from competition there. Well, there was a farcical variation on the same scenario: He jumped straight into writing a memoir, and on social occasions he pontificated about an epic in verse on the subject of gingivitis while Claire just sat in silence. Feminism still has a way to go, believe me. So long as men want to grab all the glory, if the spotlight doesn't deign to shine on them, they'll go looking for it somewhere else. I know a lot of writers and I can tell you: Behind male writers there are often muses, partners, women who inspire them, mothers... behind women writers there's no one." "Did you mention your suspicions to her after you'd met Mr. Fabian?" "Not really. I wish I had. It's hard warning someone who's in love. They don't listen and end up resenting you. She had misgivings, from time to time, but her intuition was hazy, as if she couldn't believe it. She always gave him another chance. And then she'd forget the incident. I remember one time, when things were actually fine between them, she thought he was behaving strangely. Her computer crashed and she had the feeling he was glad. She described it to me over the phone like a scene from a film, it really stuck in my mind, one of those thrillers where the heroine feels uncomfortable around her husband but can't articulate why, her uneasiness can't be pinned down. Joan Fontaine in *Suspicion* or Ingrid Bergman in *Gaslight*, do you see what I mean? Maybe you're not a movie lover?" "I am, Mr. Simmons, and enough to know that the husband in *Suspicion* is innocent." "You're right. But Cary Grant played the whole film as if his character were guilty. I'd say it was the opposite with Gilles, he played innocent when he was guilty. A positive image—nothing else mattered, image was the only truth he valued. Not a true and just image. Just an image. Proof in the eyes of the world that he was someone worthwhile. A good guy." "Sadly, this isn't a film, Mr. Simmons. There's nothing to corroborate what you're saying. There's room for doubt, and so doubt there still is."

♦

I was reading to Agnès when I was called to the visiting room. It was Mrs. Niepce—who else? I'm not allowed visitors. She took out her paperwork and her little recorder.

"We were at Georges's revelations and your turbulent argument with your partner. If my calculations are right, this must have been March 2019. I imagine you didn't see each other again after such a showdown. So how do we get to November 22, 2019, the date of the incident?"

I smiled to myself. What a wonderful thing that "we" is from an attorney; it makes you feel you're not entirely alone.

"We did. See each other again, I mean." "You saw each other again?" "Yes. After our last fight on the phone, I moved almost all my stuff out of his place—there wasn't much of it, to be honest—and set up house, if you can call it that, in the little furnished studio I'd bought after I sold my apartment. I had to throw out my tenant. At the time, I couldn't see any other option than to leave, but I was devastated. My pride was the only thing that kept me going, including with my dancing. I had a drastic sense of failure, of total regression: betrayed by Gilles, hounded on social media, and now isolated in that cramped space, with no future. A suicidal fifty-something teenager, that's what I'd turned into overnight." "You could have gone to the house in Hyères, couldn't you?" "We'd rented it out a few weeks earlier because I'd spent all my royalties and no longer had enough money to live on. I hoped Gilles would help me, but he'd suggested this vacation-rentals solution 'in the meantime.' The agency handled everything on-site, they would take the rent and send me thirty percent, which was pro rata on my share of the house, and he'd said that that should be plenty because, as he'd pointed out, I was living for free at his place." "So, in fact, you suffered an appreciable loss in social position at that point. Was that painful for you?" "Yes and no. My pain was somewhere else. Apart from abandonment, I can adapt to anything." "Did you take antianxiety drugs? Antidepressants? Were you on tranquilizers at the time of the incident?" "No. I let myself sink right to the depths of my pain. I had an obscure sense of trying to find a solid base that would help me get back up, give me some desperately needed momentum." "So then, you saw each other again?" "Yes. Gilles kept up his habit of sending messages that seesawed between affection and hate. He didn't want our relationship to end, it had been a misunderstanding, he had no future with that girl, he realized that. He was still going to therapy. He asked me to let go of my anger in the name of the magical years we'd spent together. He kept talking about my anger, as if it was the only emotion he recognized. And whatever I replied, as soon as he heard from me, he would be distant again, hostile even, or silent. In the end, he came back to Paris, we agreed to meet on neutral territory at the Parc Montsouris. 'Let's try not to betray our love,' he messaged me. When I describe all this to you, I look like I can handle it, but the truth is I missed him with terrible intensity, it was physically painful like some kind of withdrawal, I'd lost eight kilos in three weeks, I was scrawny, in pieces, and when I stared dumbly in the mirror, I could see the junkie I'd become: I couldn't kick the habit—Gilles was my drug of choice. I was poisoning myself with memories and hope.

"He arrived late to our rendezvous. I saw him from quite a distance, tanned, sprightly, wearing a herringbone jacket I hadn't seen before. I thought we would kiss hello, but he pulled away. 'Listen, give me time to get here,' he said with a little laugh, 'only yesterday I was in Toronto in my partner's arms.' I know what you'll say, exactly what Carole said: I should have thwacked him there and then, in front of everyone, as hard as I could, and left. Instead, I dropped down onto the bench and cried. Great big sobs like a child, completely inconsolable. It really was *a place of tears*. I don't know how long I cried, my shoulders shuddering, maybe twenty minutes, and he sat next to me the whole time, holding my hand like it was a doorknob, not saying a word. I'll never forget the feeling: no sensitivity, no emotion, nothing communicated, nothing.

"As soon as I stopped crying, he said, 'Are you all done? Have you calmed down?' He was keen to tell me what his therapist had shown him—such an intelligent woman and it hadn't taken her long to 'crack my shell' (his fingers snapping lobster claws in Saint-Tropez): Contrary to the image that I worked so hard to portray, I was a socialite, a social climber just like his mother, with no curiosity about anything, indifferent to everything. His flaw was that he never dared to formulate what was wrong with a relationship, he'd made the same mistake with Violetta, he always tried to fix things, even the most toxic situations. But with his therapist's help, he now knew that the facts needed to be said. 'Like what, for example?' I stammered.

"He gave a sniff. Like for example, it suited me just fine to spread the story that he'd abandoned me for a younger woman when the truth lay somewhere else altogether. The truth was that, right from the start, there had been a lot wrong with our relationship, which, incidentally, didn't fully satisfy him. 'I thought you had nothing but wonderful memories?' 'Don't let's go there, Claire. There would be so, so much to say. But I don't want to hurt you. I'm not like you, I don't want to destroy anyone. We can still be friends. Your daughter wrote to me, by the way. I can just imagine what you've told her: She bombarded me with criticism. At the end of the day, I think she's mostly disappointed that she can't work with me anymore. We had a great project together, it's a shame.'

"Alice had read me his reply over the phone: He needed to step away to protect himself from my determination to sabotage him but he would always be there for her. My daughter doesn't speak bafflegab, but she knows it when she hears it. 'He's a loser, Mom,' she told me. The sadness in her voice was devastating. Yet another father to put on the scrap-heap. And a terrible mother.

"He started to get to his feet.

" 'Tell me one more thing, Gilles: What have you lost?' 'Huh?' he asked, sitting back down. 'Yes. I know what I've lost (*love, trust, joy, you at the piano, your arms: lost in a hyperlosing way*). How about you?' 'Look, if you mean the house, we—' 'No, this isn't about the house. If we split up right now, do you lose anything?'

"He gave a contemptuous pout.

" 'I'm going to admit something to you, Claire: I've never understood a word you say.'

"He stood up.

" 'By the way, did you think to bring the keys to my apartment?'

"His voice sounded threatening.

" 'No.'

"He asked me to repeat myself. He couldn't hear me.

" 'No.'

"I could feel them in my hand in the depths of my pocket—my lover's open sesame, the last link to him. I'd given my set of keys for the house in Hyères to the rental manager, I would have no place left to keep some vestige of us, which was an imaginary pronoun. I couldn't make the break; it was physically impossible—an addiction. Gripping those keys with my hand was my ticket to my next hit.

"'I can't give them back to you now, Gilles. It's all too brutal.'

"My voice failed me, just a whisper, ashamed of being a nuisance.

"'I can't.'

"At that point my phone rang. It was John, the choreographer. 'John,' I said with a sigh of relief: a knight in shining armor—perhaps the Prince of Montsouris—was galloping toward me with a cauliflower on his head to carry me off on his white charger. I walked away to talk to him and Gilles looked at me so insistently that I turned my back to him, pretending there was some secret. John managed to make me laugh a couple of times and we agreed to meet. I went back over to the bench with an exaggerated smile, yes, see you tomorrow, John. Love you. Gilles—my God, he was so predictable—wiped a look of withering disapproval off his face and it suddenly lit up with luminous charm, like a double-sided glove puppet switching around.

"'Listen,' he said, touching my wrist gently, 'keep them, the keys, I mean. In fact, I'd like that.' 'Really?' 'Of course. Nothing's closed off between us, you know that. In two days, I'm going to my mother's house, then to see my children in Corsica. Let's talk again when I get back, okay?'

"He ran a hand lightly over my cheek. I was clutching the keys in my pocket.

"'I really want to take you in my arms,' he said. 'But I don't think my therapist would like it.'

"He stood up and kissed the top of my head.

"'See you soon, my Claire. Promise me you'll put some weight back on before then, thin doesn't suit you.'

"He walked away, then came back.

"'About your promise,' he said, 'I wanted to reiterate something, so you know for sure: I never betrayed you. Ever. So, I never shared our bed with anyone, I swear it. In Toronto and in Paris, I've always respected you.'"

When I got back from the visiting room, I sat in silence next to Agnès. She was watching some true crime show on TV, her eyes popping out of her head in fascination. It was about an eighteen-year-old man—cute guy, girlfriends, middle-class family, no police record—who, in his last year of high school, killed a ten-year-old girl. He'd spotted her as they came out of their respective schools each day, and two or three times he'd followed her home to a fourth-floor apartment where she let herself in with her own set of keys. One day, armed with duct tape in his schoolbag, he'd barged through the door behind the child, bound and gagged her, run a bath, and then drowned her in it, holding her down with his foot—the sole of his shoe had left an imprint on her flowery T-shirt. When he was arrested a few months later, by which time he'd graduated from high school, he admitted the crime and, because there was no sexual motive, was unable to explain why he'd done it. On the date of the crime, he'd posted on Facebook: "I feel good today." He'd attended his trial and shown no emotion in front of the child's parents, reacting only when the prosecution's summing up recommended a life sentence. He thought the punishment unfair, he'd said in a shocked and indignant voice—and neither the shock nor the indignation was simulated for an eleventh-hour challenge, oh no, the punishment was unfair because it didn't take into account one important fact: Perhaps when her mother found the little girl, the bath was cold. But when he'd filled the tub, he'd used warm water.

♦

"Yes, I think their cruel relationship could have gone on longer," said Émilie. "We're not always spared from wanting to sustain unhappiness, and when someone's wounded, they often want to be wounded again. Love doesn't obey reason or our friends' reasoning; it has its own logic that feeds on hope and denial. There are people who can move on. Not Claire. She rakes things over with the same energy others would use to move forward. Maybe that's the problem with writers—their weakness and their strength: They can't turn the page until they've read it over and over. Claire kept backtracking; even at that stage and despite the evidence, she still sometimes blamed herself for the relationship failing. Or she tortured herself: There must be some way to make that piece of writing beautiful again. We—her friends—didn't know what else to do. Nothing made any difference. Not that we didn't try to shake her out of it, I can tell you! Carole was especially tough. 'Stop eroticizing that waste of space,' she kept saying, convinced it was physical memories that were holding Claire back, a sort of sexual stranglehold that Carole just didn't understand. 'That Pinocchio guy who thinks he's Brad Pitt. He's not Brad Pitt, he's Bad the Pits.' We could still make her laugh, thank God, but not for long.

"I remember what triggered the breakup—which, sadly, was only temporary, as you know. Claire called me, it must have been May, she was outside Gilles's apartment and her voice sounded numb. She said that, knowing he was away, she'd come to collect some crockery of her grandmother's that she'd forgotten. Mostly I think she wanted to go back there, the way people want to go back to somewhere they've been happy. See the place again, smell its smells, touch the furniture, look at herself in the mirror, try to find memories and perhaps a future. Check that it's still there. 'Nothing is closed off between us,' Gilles had told her at the park. Words matter to Claire, she gives them meaning. But with Gilles...there was too much discrepancy between what he said and what he did, he'd undermined the use of language and driven his Pinocchio nose into it right up to the hilt. Before even reaching the top of the stairs, Claire noticed metal filings on the doormat. The barrel—that's the word she used and, listening on the phone, I pictured a revolver—the barrel was all new and shiny in the familiar wooden door. She tried her key anyway, to be sure. She took the bullet right in the heart. There was a pause, then in a robotic voice she said the enigmatic words: 'I can't hear *Tosca*.'"

11

"What happened on November 22, 2019?"

"We need to go back to a few days before that. Gilles messaged me in mid-November. We hadn't been talking to each other since May—he'd tried to reestablish contact twice, on my birthday, I can't remember now, he was thinking of me, he had nothing but wonderful memories, we'd been so happy, he was sad that he no longer knew anything about my life... I didn't reply. I'd blocked him on social media, I didn't hear anything more from him. For me the days went by one by one and at night they crash-landed into a sort of cruel drip-drip effect. Rob, my agent, pulled out all the stops to find me work to pay the bills, I'd reluctantly accepted a small column in a TV magazine. I'd used him as an intermediary to tell Gilles that I wanted to recoup my share of the price we'd paid for the house in Hyères, but had no reply. My friends gave me a lot of support, encouraged me to write, asked me out.

Carole posted pictures of me smiling on Instagram to 'kick back against all those assholes.' I was really only pretending, and even then only long enough to say 'cheese.' I was just paralyzed in a cage of anxiety, freeze-framed on a single image—the image of us. I wasn't living, I was waiting to live.

"That day, November 14 or 15, he sent me an invitation to a show he'd put on with ice puppets, first in Toronto then in the Ardèche region with a small traditional theater company—he'd be glad for me to see this production because I'd been a part of it in the planning stages, his message said. Been a part of it, that was the expression he used. He also said he would be happy to see me, if I would like that. He missed me a lot. And in a PS he added that at some point, we needed to discuss where things stood with the house in Hyères.

"I went to the show, of course I went. No one could have stopped me; besides, I didn't tell anyone. Time hadn't erased my heartbreak but had obscured its causes. Everything was so jumbled in my mind, I couldn't really remember why we'd split up. This mental blur was like early-onset dementia, when you remember distant memories but forget everything from the recent past. I'm sure you know that wonderful reflection of La Rochefoucauld's, one of the most beautiful sentences in the French language, I can't resist the pleasure of quoting it: 'Which two people would have started to love each other if they saw each other for the first time as they would in years to come? But then which two people could separate if they could see each other again as they did the first time?' See each other as they did the first time... Yes, that's what I wanted. I forgot that the first time I hadn't been all that enthusiastic. I was adopting his strategy: After all, holding on to only the best memories protects us from the horrors of the worst. And I hoped he'd changed—or was himself again, the man I originally met, that wonderful man. Georges must have been right: Gilles had just let himself get carried away with a casual fuck. Not unkindly meant, despite the unkindness. When that invitation came from him, I'd been waiting for it, I'd never stopped believing it would come. What can I tell you? We want love to exist. We want it to endure.

"With these mixed feelings I took the train to Valence, then another one to Privas. Gilles had offered to pick me up in Valence, but I'd said no—I couldn't picture us together in a car, with me sitting passively, woodenly in the passenger seat, chatting about everything and anything. He was waiting for me on the platform, looking meek and anxious. Seeing him really shook me, like seeing a dead person, and in a way I was; I was seeing the man I'd lost. I've always loved ghost stories, when people come back and hearts start beating. That's what he was: a revenant. The cold was dry and piercing, and he was wearing a knit cap pulled right down to his eyes. Oh, those eyes! They communicated a shy happiness that freed me from everything without a word. We hugged.

"He gave me a front-row seat in the theater and left me there while he dealt with last-minute arrangements. The audience came in steadily, good-naturedly, people knew each other, called out their hellos. The title of the show was *At the Very Door to Life*. Gilles had put together a montage of texts by Antonin Artaud, letters to Jacques Rivière, to his mother, the groundbreaking live event he'd put on at the Théâtre du Vieux Colombier. One quote had been used as an epigraph in the program: 'I know I was born another way, through my work and not from a mother, but the MOTHER wanted to claim me and you can see the result of that in my life.' Well, well, the mother again, I thought. The uppercase mother. I was scared.

"Then these tall, emaciated ice puppets came onto the stage, they looked as if they were molded on Giacometti statues or Artaud's own face, lanky figures dancing a jig. No effort had been made to minimize the creaking of the machinery that operated them, so the voices of the actors, who were offstage, blended with these noises in a tragic musical score.

> We are a life of controlled puppets, and those who control us and pull the strings of this vile drama count on one thing above anything else: the inveterate pride of each individual. We are a world of automatons with no self-awareness or

freedoms, we are organic subconsciouses grafted onto bodies, we are bodies grafted onto nothing.

"How can I explain this? I knew these weren't Gilles's words but the whole play trumpeted his message. Here he was telling me all the things he couldn't formulate, perhaps couldn't even understand for himself. It was all there, the key to everything he and I had been through, had suffered. I sat in helpless admiration—yes, I can use that word: I admired him that evening. I admired his strategy of using art to tell the truth. Gilles was explaining who he was through another man's words, he was making his speech for the defense, asking to be understood, appealing for absolution for his silences, his cruelty, and his vanity. The puppets melted slowly, their features and limbs sagging. Their dying made you want to live. He loves me, I thought, and I sat there shaking.

And here, sir, is the whole problem, holding within us the inseparable reality and material clarity of an emotion, feeling it to the point that it would be impossible for it not to be expressed, having a wealth of words and turns of phrase that have been learned and could enter into the dance, serve the game; and just as the soul is preparing to organize its riches, its discoveries, this revelation, in that reckless moment when the thing is about to pour forth, a spiteful higher will attacks

> the soul like vitriol, attacks the accumulation of words and images, attacks the accumulation of feelings, and leaves me gasping at the very door to life.

"You can guess what happened next. No one stays at the door to life: They go in. After the show, Gilles suggested we drive straight to Hyères, 'home,' he said. There were no tenants now, were we going to sell it? We drove for three hours, not talking much, from time to time he took my hand and squeezed it. Once there, he fumbled in the dark to open the door and in the pitch-black of the corridor we kissed frenziedly. Like a kiss in the movies, quite a performance. I thought this fleetingly, the word *performance* came into my muddled mind, a performance, and then it melted into his words. 'Claire, my Claire, my love,' he kept saying, holding my face in his hands. My head was spinning, I almost didn't know where I was in the dark, and I leaned against the wall so that I didn't fall. 'I love you, you know, I've only ever loved you. I'm desperately sorry if I've caused you pain. You're the only woman I love.'

"'I'm desperately sorry if I've caused you pain.' I smiled in the darkness, with his mouth on my hair. Everything I'd been going through for months could be condensed into a hypothetical in his mind.

"We were together again. It feels terrible saying that to you, seen from today's perspective, I realize how fatuous it sounds. But then . . . making love is our only existence. Our only presence—in the world and for each other. We're together again because we're here. We're here now, you and I. Our hands between each other's legs. It's real. It's unfailing. In your arms I'm afraid of nothing, not death or absence or betrayal. In your hands nothing can happen to me, nothing but the happiness I feel now.

"We made love all night, interspersed with long whispering cuddles, like before. He asked if I'd met anyone else, and I was evasive—'Don't be all pathetic,' Carole hissed in my ear. What about him? Was it over with . . . ? 'With Marina? It's over, yes, of course. It never really started, you know. That bastard Georges got you all wound up over nothing. And I'm not going back to Toronto, anyway. My next job is in Saint Petersburg. Or Beijing. I can't decide. Would you like to go to China, my love?'

"In the morning, I was woken by *Les Barricades mystérieuses*, he was playing it on the piano in the living room. 'It needs tuning,' he said. Then he went to buy bread and some honey, he brought me a sprig of heather that he'd stolen from a window box. There was a cradling tenderness in his eyes, I didn't dream that.

"While we were eating, we had a more practical conversation. What were we going to do with the house (*we*)? Gilles knew I needed money, so he suggested either buying my share or selling, which amounted to the same thing for me in financial terms. We had plenty of time to decide, he said, looking at me softly (*we*), but to get an idea of price, he'd arranged for a Realtor to come over that afternoon, the same woman who'd sold us the house and handled the rentals. The Realtor's car had broken down and he'd arranged to pick her up at four o'clock. Afterward, he would need to get back to Privas to help the team with the next day's show, and he would drop me at the station first. But we had our lives ahead of us. 'And right now we have time to go back to bed,' he said.

"He arrived at about four-thirty with the girl from the agency who introduced herself with a firm handshake. 'Hello, ma'am. Charlotte Rossi.' She'd been promoted—on our first visit, years earlier, she'd been so shy, an impressionable trainee, a shadow. She knew the house well, its features and flaws, but the three of us looked around the whole place together. 'It definitely hasn't improved with age,' she said, looking at me for confirmation. 'Can you see the gaps in the tiles there and the signs of seepage?' The insulation was hopeless, the roots of a fig tree that had grown in a crack at the front of the house were threatening to shatter the stone, and the render was already crumbling. There were also new town plans under consideration and if they were implemented, quite a lot of traffic would be sent along our road. Not to mention the garden, which needed completely relandscaping, and the poor mimosa that was now gone. In a nutshell, its salability had, sadly, dropped appreciably and, having considered the market with her manager, she estimated the house was worth 260,000 euros at the very most—and even then, we'd need to find buyers prepared to do the work.

"I was dumbstruck: We'd bought it for more than 360,000. At first, Gilles protested vociferously, then he took me aside. We'd made a bad investment, we would both come out of this a little battered but, well, other things were more important. 'We need to get some different quotes,' I said. 'I really think that's a huge drop in value.' 'Yes, my darling, you're right,' he said. 'So we won't sign right away, then?' 'Sign what?' 'The listing agreement.' 'I wouldn't want to. And anyway, we might keep it, right?' Gilles took me in his arms, nodding.

"Then he went to talk to the Realtor. I saw him explaining things to her and she listened attentively, not moving except to glance at me occasionally. Gilles came back over to me and said she wasn't happy not to have clinched the deal, he was going to drive her back, and we would go by the station first. The three of us went to different parts of the house to close all the windows and doors. That was when I stopped by the mirror in the hall and saw Gilles open a drawer in the writing desk, take out a pill, and swallow it.

"My heart rate quickened—the super-acceleration of fear. I didn't know that drawer existed. But I didn't say anything, always afraid of putting Gilles in an awkward situation, of how he would react. So

I pretended I hadn't noticed, but left the shutter in the kitchen unlocked, determined to come back and clear up this mystery. That's also why, out on the doorstep, I told Gilles that, because the train station was in the opposite direction to the Realtor's office, I would take the bus, it would be easier. He tried to dissuade me but eventually agreed to leave me at the bus stop at the end of the road—there was a screen under the shelter saying when the next shuttle would be along. He stepped out of the car to say goodbye to me, the girl from the agency moved to my seat in the front, and they left. Then I went back to the house. It was a real struggle opening the drawer and that's where I found the medication."

"The Viagra..." "I didn't know it was Viagra! That wasn't written on it. And who gives a damn about Viagra; the important thing was the letter." "No letter was found there, Claire, I want to reiterate that. The police searched the place from top to bottom, they found nothing that meets your description. I've asked the examining magistrate to conduct an investigation to at least trace the person who wrote the document, but as you don't remember the name, it won't be easy..." "You need to question the girl from the agency! She took it, she's the only person who could have, how many times do I have to tell you? She needs to be accused of hiding evidence." "Don't shout, Claire, or the guard will come. The judge has questioned her, and I've seen her statement. Need I remind you that you tried to intimidate the witness, she even mentions death threats. Subornation of a witness is a serious offense and that's why you're in prison. Besides, it paints a picture of you as not only a violent woman but a domineering one who doesn't respect the law." "But it's not true! I went to see her at her office the day after I was held in custody to ask her to tell the truth, that's all. She immediately started crying and called me a murderer. But she was there, she saw everything, she knew what happened." "What did happen, Claire?" "I already told the police and the judge, for God's sake. You were there." "I know. But tell me again, go back over what you remember." "I heard the car come back, which didn't make sense. They came in through the front door and Gilles turned the electricity back on. That's when he saw me with the piece of paper in my hand. The drawer was open, I must have looked... well, he understood straightaway. The hate in his eyes. Unimaginable hate. I'd seen him fifteen minutes earlier with eyes full of tenderness. It was this inexplicable turnaround that terrified me more than anything else: the devil. He threw himself at me, tried to snatch the letter from me, I backed away, wanting to put it down on the desk, I was really scared, the letter slipped, Gilles grabbed me by the throat, and my hand alighted on the rock that Alice had given me when she was a little girl, a big stone with a fossilized lizard on it, I picked it up and hit Gilles's head with it, I don't know how many times, I was beside myself. Then I felt blood trickling, Gilles fell, and I ran out into the garden. I don't remember anything after that or how long I sat there on the stump of the old mimosa before the police came." "Where was Mrs. Rossi while all this was going on?" "She was at the end of the corridor, four or five meters away." "And she didn't intervene? She didn't say anything?" "She may have screamed, I don't know. Then the police arrived." "It wasn't you who called them; it was Mrs. Rossi, whose own husband is a police officer. Did you not think of calling them?" "I didn't think of anything. I kept remembering his eyes." "The police questioned you at the scene. Did you mention the letter to them at that point?" "No. I was in shock, I was covered in blood. The ambulance took us all to the hospital. I never went back to the house." "Mrs. Rossi said in her first statement that you were waiting for them, lying in ambush, when she and Mr. Fabian came into the house and that you threw yourself at him, screaming as soon as the light came on." "In ambush? But for the umpteenth time I didn't know they were coming back!" "According to her, you did: When the three of you were in the car before you were dropped at the bus stop, she says she asked Mr. Fabian if she could go back to the house for five minutes to take some more measurements to help her reach a more accurate valuation. He apparently agreed so they must have left you at the bus stop and driven back to the agency for a tape measure before returning to the house as planned." "That's not true! It's a lie! They came back to make love, thinking I'd left. Make love, what am I saying? What sort of word choice is that? Suddenly it's all so clear, so obscenely clear. He took Viagra because he knew he was going to fuck her. Fuck her just like he fucked me, in every sense of the word. They're lovers, they're accomplices. It's monstrous! She realized that the letter could be incriminating, or maybe he had time to ask her to destroy it. There's no other explanation. Mrs. Niepce, I'm begging you, help me, I'm losing my mind."

II

◆

"Mr. Simmons, you are the literary agent of the novelist Claire Lancel, whose trial for premeditated attempted murder begins in a few days. The pandemic has considerably slowed judicial proceedings and turned attention to other things, but everyone remembers the facts, which date back nearly three years. The victim, the well-known theater director Gilles Fabian, Claire Lancel's former partner, is no longer in a coma. However, our sources tell us he will suffer significant long-term consequences, including partial amnesia. Can you tell us what frame of mind the author is in as her trial approaches? Does she have any regrets? Will she explain her actions? She's shut herself away at home: Is she writing a new book?"

I dispatched the journalist as best I could, like all the others, although I had time to register that Gilles Fabian was now "well-known" while Claire was no longer a "famous novelist." I hope she won't see this video, I'm sure she would notice that. Fabian has gotten what he wanted, in a way. "I'm sorry," I told the journalist, "I have another meeting."

Miles McLawrence arrived a few minutes later, as punctual as an American who lives in France can still be. I was glad to see him again. I admire his films, and he knows that, but I said so again. He's already made excellent adaptations of books by two of my authors, and when I heard that he was interested in Claire's story, I saw it as a sign. I like the Bergmanian depth his movies have, the way he gets right inside a soul; and the fact that he's a godless Protestant is a good fit with Claire. I asked him how she felt about it: She was happy; she didn't want to meet him before the trial but had given me permission to pass on to him everything that she'd given me since it all started. There wasn't strictly speaking a book yet, perhaps there never would be, it was all in such a jumble and everything depended on what happened to her next, but she definitely wanted to share her story—her puzzle. So a screenplay, why not. "So long as he doesn't betray me," she'd said. "If you trust him, I do too," she added. I was moved to hear her still use the word *trust*.

Miles had worked on the project like the pro that he was. He was excited about the whole story and the legal-proceedings angle, but he didn't envision turning it into a thriller or a courtroom drama so much as a portrait of a woman. A portrait of a woman writer. To get closer to the enigma of how creativity relates to life. I approved: Portraits of women writers are so few and far between, on-screen or anywhere. So he wanted to know everything about Claire, particularly the things no one knew, things that the newspapers hadn't said. "You have to go through events in the correct order," I said. "Are you recording?" He nodded yes. I poured both of us a coffee and we started.

"When Claire first came out of prison I was worried about her. I was even scared her life was in danger. This woman who'd been so strong, so resilient—and fragile too, but her fragility was armed—now she was nothing but pain and dejection. Her attorney hadn't hidden the truth from her and Claire had distorted it to the point of going crazy. Nothing spoke in her favor, the whole world was against her, she kept saying over and over that she would get the maximum sentence. At first, I hoped the adversity would act like a spur: She hates a fight but she never admits defeat. Then I could tell she was nose-diving. She stayed at home, listless, seeing no one, taking fewer and fewer calls from her friends. Her depression was borderline paranoia, even if the media campaign against her was very real, with the Hyères incident only adding to the Laetitia Valy business. If it weren't for her daughter, I think we would have lost her. The first lockdown just reinforced her voluntary seclusion. I tried everything to get her writing again, her podcast, an article, a blog, but it was impossible. 'I can't, Rob,' she kept saying. 'I just can't do it.' She read a little—I'm not even sure of that. She watched absolute shit on TV, that much I do know. Initially, I thought she couldn't write because Fabian was in a coma. How can you focus on a book when you're dreading someone dying, and to make matters worse you feel responsible? She seemed to open up okay with the judge and her attorney, just after the event, she needed to explain what had happened, she wanted to establish the truth, and words have the power to do that. She even talked a lot with her cellmate, Agnès—they had a calming influence on each other, loosening the grip of each other's pain. But talking isn't writing, it's not the same language, its source is not the same, nor its destination, nor the person it's destined for. When, over the course of the investigation, she started to get a clearer idea of what to expect, particularly when the charge of premeditation was brought against her, that's when she went under. Her temporary freedom didn't change anything, she was still locked away in her head. I thought that her silence was dependent on Gilles's but when he came out of the coma, although Claire's attorney was delighted, nothing had changed for Claire herself. Being amnesiac, he couldn't say what had happened, so he couldn't lie, but he also couldn't tell the truth—unless amnesia is his ultimate pretense, and there are a few of us who think it is. Either way, there'll be no communication between them—ever, Claire has made that clear. This hypothetical truth was fading. If and when I did manage to get her to talk a little in my attempt to rekindle her appetite for writing, she said she had no words left, that words had forgotten about her. She was in the same state of distress as after her son died:

Everything had forsaken her, including the words to express the fact. She felt dispossessed by her voice, abandoned by herself. And worse still, she'd interiorized what Gilles had told her at the end: 'Everything you write is shit.' She adopted it herself as a statement of fact. I really despaired seeing what a hold that bastard still had over her. He'd robbed her of what constituted who she was, she could no longer write 'I,' she couldn't assert her voice. I realized that the day she emailed me two sentences from *Adolphe*, a book she kept by her bedside. There was no commentary, just this from when Ellénore dies, abandoned: 'She wanted to weep, there were no more tears. She wanted to speak, there were no more words.' The demise of that pronoun transliterates the demise of the individual who's been absorbed into an impersonal state. It's sublime.

"I remembered that citation when she sent me her first poem a few weeks later. I was surprised because she'd never written any poetry but just so happy to see the process of writing set in motion again. It was logical for her to come back to it through poetry. Poetry responds to an impulse in the moment, it doesn't need to be structured like a novel, over time. But what really struck me was her use of the pronoun 'she.' Claire made her return to language with this objectifying device because she was no longer a person.

"From then on, I encouraged her. The tiniest sign of life from her was reassuring, the disjointed snippets of text she sometimes sent me, nothing much, mostly snatches of dialogue, as if she were writing for the theater, using an oral tradition to blow the cobwebs away, and she never asked me what I thought.

"I don't really know what happened then. There was a terrific kind of acceleration—although it felt to me that time was going very slowly. Or maybe, if I'm honest, I do know. I'd sent her a link to Cukor's film *Gaslight*, something for her to watch during the second lockdown—but also out of intuition, you can guess why. I hoped we'd talk about it afterward. She watched it and bingo... like a miracle. An apparition. Or rather a vision. She saw the truth—she didn't understand it or hear it or feel it, nope: She saw it. A snippet of truth, like the end of a piece of string and now all she needed to do was pull on it. And the thing she mentioned first wasn't the storyline or the dialogue, but the actor's eyes, his face. Charles Boyer, such great casting for a criminal husband, I'm sure you agree, a lethal manipulator who, under his honeyed exterior, has killed before and wants to kill again. Well, Claire could see the truth in the lie on his face, and in the deceit in his eyes. And she told me that, as she watched, she'd remembered the look on Gilles's face at specific times in the past: It was the same, exactly the same! The switch from warmth to ice in his pupils, the duplicity... like a madman! She was screaming into the phone with... gleeful terror, if you see what I mean.

The sheer joy of knowing is independent of what it is we know. It doesn't really matter if the truth itself is hideous when we see it, it's the truth.

"After that, things happened quickly. She tugged on the end of that string and the whole ball came tumbling down. I don't have any chronology for the journey she went on. She must have surfed the Internet with some keywords, and she started watching other films; she wanted to see that look in other actors' eyes, in different stories, so that—or this is what I think—she could build up an Identi-Kit picture. You could ask her. I definitely remember the day she came across Tim Burton's *Big Eyes*. You know the one? Not really your thing, I imagine, but it's interesting because the woman in the film's an artist and her husband takes her place by appropriating her paintings and her success. When he's exposed, he tries to burn her and her daughter alive. It goes that far: total destruction. 'Rob, I can see myself there,' Claire said. She was communicating again, that was the first sign.

"From then on, thank the Lord, another part of Claire woke up: Claire the insight machine. When I read her books, I often think that elucidation is their absolute backbone. A hunger to know is what propels her books. But something different happened this time. It was as if she needed to reconstruct not just the story but the chaos, too. She'd thought she knew the dictionary of love by heart, but it had been ransacked, it was illegible, with pages missing or torn out. She needed to restore some shape and meaning to that incoherence. To comprehend the incomprehensible. To extract the truth from oblivion and denial—his *and* hers. It was hard for her. The darkness was probably deeper than she thought, and the light hurts when you come out of darkness. She had—"

"I'm sorry to interrupt, Rob, but aren't you overdoing this a little? It's not like she watched a couple of films and overnight uncovered the terrible secret lurking beneath the illusion of love! She knew this man, this Gilles Fabian, she'd seen him operating in real life, she'd even had her revenge—yes, I know we mustn't use that word. But still, by striking him, she settled the score, in her own way, when the scales had fallen from her eyes. What she came to understand later, over the last three years, just confirms what she already knew, right? Were there really other secrets in that drawer?" "That's just it, there were. That's what I'm talking about, Miles. Before she embarked on her investigation, naturally she thought about what she'd experienced, but—" "Her investigation?" "Yes. Her investigation. Up to that point she'd thought things over, of course she had, but all the thought processes she could manage were filtered through her personal pain, in other words with a very narrow perspective. Heartache is short-sighted, it stays glued to details. Huddled on its little scrap of land, pain thinks that it's unique and specific. Those films showed her that it wasn't. that other people had experienced it. Some had depicted it on-screen. Others had studied it, deciphered it, formalized it, and explained it. And she realized that beneath her own memories, however painful they may be, there was a whole unknown world of experiences. The truth was this palimpsest. And that's when Gilles became a character in a story. It didn't all happen overnight, it took months; pain evolved into thought and life into words."

"What did her investigation constitute in practical terms?" "I don't have precise details, she didn't always let me into her workshop—or should I say laboratory? There's a clinical dimension to Claire's research, you can see it in her books, a cold, poised, methodical eye—she would have made a good doctor. She's like an X-ray when she puts her mind to it. Or it's a dissection—it all depends on whether the subject is dead or alive. Once she's started, she sets love out on the lab bench and scrutinizes it unflinchingly, probing the heart and the loins. There are so many investigative tools these days. Her knowledge must have started with books—with psychoanalysis and philosophy but not just them. In the same way that in her novels she can quote from Proust and a Joe Dassin song in quick succession, she must have browsed haphazardly between YouTube and TikTok videos, sites about people's personal experiences, some more inane than others, online articles, and specialist papers. The Internet makes things easier: One word leads to another, a footnote takes you off in a new direction, you hop from link to link—the definition of intelligence, basically. I can see how she did it. She went from one discovery to the next, interrogating all the knowledge at her disposal, following every lead, just about managing to distinguish knowledge from opinion and theory from experience, and never sparing her suffering. So it was when she was doing some Facebook stalking that she came across Marina's profile, that's Gilles's mistress in Toronto. She recognized her own house in Marina's photos from the summer of 2019. The garden with Marina posing in a bikini, wearing one of Claire's hats. The stump of the mimosa tree where Marina had taken selfies cuddling up to Gilles, like a statue on a plinth. When Gilles said he was renting the house, he was really spending vacations there with her and sending Claire her 'share' in her pitiful studio—three or four hundred euros, and even then she had to ask for the money. It was a hell of a shock, I remember her voice cracking as she told me on the phone. Then she picked herself up again. There's a perverse pleasure in realizing just how ignorant we are. She rewatched a recording of a *Don Juan* that Gilles had directed a while back. She started to suspect that his lying and betrayals were not, as she'd originally thought, impromptu lapses but constituted a system, an established structure. Fragmentary details that she hadn't noticed came out of the shadows and slotted together. Here's an example: Claire once told Gilles about a girlfriend of hers who was a pop singer and had had a brief fling with George Clooney years ago. Gilles had been unusually inquisitive, and she'd put this down to his weakness for celebrities. Well, she found out that Gilles had contacted her singer friend on Messenger that same evening—the friend showed her: 'I think I saw you on rue Daguerre this afternoon. I didn't dare approach you and now wish I had. Maybe we can rectify that, I'm one of your most loyal fans.' When Claire checked the date with her diary, she realized that not only was he with her in Hyères at the time but he'd also been in a relationship with Marina in Toronto for three months. The fact is he never stopped looking. Or lying. After that, how could she *not* suspect that everything to date had been smoke and mirrors? She tore all her own memories to shreds, mercilessly ransacked her own relationship. When she worked her way back through it, all her time with Gilles seemed to have sprung up out of a blind spot. Anyone would have thought she would fall apart, particularly as that's when she heard that Agnès had taken her own life in her cell. The day before she'd told Claire on the phone: 'Mom is so mean, she never comes to see me.' But Claire toughed it out, she was stronger than the truth. I'll admit there were days when she went off the rails—when I say she's methodical . . . that's not always true. She sent me texts along the lines of, wait, I'll find them. Here . . . December 20, 2020: 'Other people don't exist for Gilles. He lives in a world of objects. There are no faces for him. Just mirrors in the labyrinth, just pawns on the chessboard.' January 6, 2021: 'No dialogue possible. All conversation is a sham.' Or this one from January 15, 2021: 'The Nazis didn't allow the Jews who worked on communal graves to use the words *dead* or *victims*, they had to say *figüren*—puppets.' Her friend Émilie admitted that she had to bring Claire down several times from out-of-control ravings in which Gilles became a total monster whose every word and every move were deliberate and intended to destroy her. The Internet can have that effect, she says, altering the way people describe their own lives, with a proliferation of paranoid interpretations. Émilie managed to bring Claire back to a more humanist outlook. But as well as her reading, she must still have been grilling Georges, calling people over and over, and coming up with hypotheses. The one thing that her attorney and I dreaded was her getting back in touch with the woman from the real estate agency!

"Well anyway, she raked over everything she could. Detectives will follow up the most unlikely stuff, there's no such thing as a bad clue, even if they are false leads. And there was a similar sense of trial and error in her writing. After the poems, came the fragments of scenes, at one point I received what seemed to be the beginning of a sci-fi novel—a sort of dystopian fable practically unrelated to the source of inspiration, I'll show you, and with an epigraph that says a lot: "The death of human empathy is one of the earliest and most telling signs of a culture on the verge of descending into barbarism.'"

> At the turn of the 2030s, a significant number of people were seen to have developed a distinctive affliction whose key symptom, before delving into its complex ramifications, was a complete absence of empathy. Individuals with the condition felt no consideration for other people, did not recognize the emotions of those close to them, even in distressing situations, and if they did recognize them, generally displayed no concern. Sufferers felt only indifference for anyone but themselves and therefore treated other people like objects to which they ascribed no inner life, meaning that they could harm them, subject them to pain, or even kill them without feeling any more remorse than if they had knocked over a chair or thrown it on a fire. They manipulated other people like puppets, pulling them apart before abandoning them.
>
> This absence of empathy and, by extension, of ethical principles, as science defines it, spread in various forms, and the different strains were classified by a Franco-American research team in issue 347 of *The Lancet* in June 2025. Their scientific article described a hyperdevelopment of the ego and a dwindling of emotions such as forgiveness, tenderness, and love in favor of rivalry,

resentment, intolerance, and hatred. The conclusion was supported by a table. In type I, known as sunny, the subject presented a self-assured and self-centered extrovert personality that openly exerted dominance. Type II, referred to as dark or hidden, was more difficult to detect and therefore more dangerous. Subjects affected a modest, even humble, exterior. It was therefore in type II that the more serious and calculating pathology was found: All variants, out of indifference or unawareness, displayed complete disregard for the harm they caused other people, but only type II individuals derived essential and unlimited pleasure from that harm.

All new discoveries must be given a name, so this rapidly spreading pathology was named Nark's disease. Researchers were amused by the coincidence between the core of the problem—narcissism—and the name of the American psychiatrist, Professor Nark, who ran the research project in his Paris laboratory. It seemed inevitable, even more so than with Alzheimer or Charcot, that the condition should be given the name of its discoverer. In some instances, a decision is made to name conditions after the first known sufferer, which explains why Charcot's disease came to be known as Lou Gehrig's disease in the United States after the famous baseball player who died of it in 1941. The difference with Nark's disease was that, although there were numerous victims, they were affected indirectly: Those who died of it did not themselves have the condition but were close to someone who did and suffered the consequences of that person's symptoms. When Narks were type II, with the hidden and malign variant, they were not easy to identify, and therefore neither were their victims who, according to scientific findings, died of depression or sickness, or by suicide. In the early 2030s, people started to say someone "has Nark's" just as readily as they would say someone "has Alzheimer's." In both cases, this condition affecting cerebral function was not identified by patients themselves for the simple reason that patients, other than in very rare exceptions, were unaware that they had it. The words "I have Nark's" were therefore a linguistic aberration as unexpected as, for example, "I'm dead" or "my son is my grandmother." However, the song "I Have Nark's," released in 2031, was a hit and people danced to it all through that summer (lyrics in endnotes).

It was of course not accurate to say that Professor Nark had discovered this pathology. He had simply, over several years, put together an overview of many observations and convergent symptoms. Narcissism was not a recent discovery and, in any event, did not in itself constitute a disease: Since Freud and Melanie Klein, it was acknowledged that there were good and bad forms of narcissism—a narcissism of life and a narcissism of death as André Green suggested in his book *Narcissisme de vie, narcissisme de mort*. Having robust self-esteem tended to augur well for a happy life based on a confident childhood, and individuals should strive for this objective, overcoming the neurosis associated with failure. But for more than a century, observation had already shown evidence of the devastation that could be caused by an incorrect dosage of ego attributed either to permissive parenting of spoiled children or, more frequently, to a childhood trauma that had often gone unnoticed. Art and literature represented narcissism in a great variety of forms. Professor Nark himself devoted a seminar to Orson Welles's film *Citizen Kane*, where the tyrannical life of a man incapable of love is explained at the very end by a childhood upheaval. Hitler had himself been physically abused as a child, Nark reminded his listeners, sparking a lively debate about excessive psychoanalytical interpretation in history. However, it was in political spheres, where this pathology was overrepresented, that its ravages were at their most spectacular because victims of Nark's despotic manipulation were not mere individuals but whole nations. As George Orwell's prophetic novel *1984* demonstrated, enslavement affected humanity by discrediting language and the truth. Professor Nark had referred to this as early as 2017 in a comment about contemporary America when Donald Trump was confronted with his own self-aggrandizing lie claiming that the sun had shone on the day of his inauguration when it had in fact rained all day, and responded through a White House spokesperson to say that "Sometimes we can disagree with the facts." Recognizing no limits, feeling all-powerful, denial of other people, adhering indiscriminately to lies and the truth: Trump, Putin, Kim Jong Un, to name only the most recent, all presented the characteristics of Nark's disease. The more controversial case of France's President Macron was under investigation by the National Center for Scientific Research in Paris.

"If I'm honest, I'm not sure that the plot would have held up for two hundred pages but still, what a relief! This was proof that Claire was starting to write again, and even reconnecting with her humor. She might end up following leads that just silted up frustratingly, but she'd gotten herself going again, she'd started looking."

"What was she looking for? What *is* she looking for?" "What detectives look for: the truth. And what writers look for: a form in which to couch it. In fact, on reflection, I think she must have used a real detective. You'll see for yourself; there are some things she couldn't have found out on her own. Precise details about events when she wasn't there, scenes involving people she's never met in real life." "Well, she just invented. Writers invent stuff, don't they?" "Yes. Maybe. Maybe I'm losing it. Either way, if you put it all together—her findings, her reading material, her analyses, and her musings—it's aiming to achieve a complete reconstruction, as the justice system says. Claire is carrying out her own investigation. In her mind, the true crime scene isn't the house but the past, and that guy's brain! She delves into every nook and cranny, searches through memories, and probes the foundations. And she's paying a hell of a price! She's more interested in the truth than in happiness. That's the heart of your film, if you want it to be a portrait of her." "Hmm... that's not at all what comes across in the sources I've managed to read. She was happy and just didn't want to know, the opposite in fact. She was convinced that she knew the truth. No hint of anything else going on in the background. A clear case of psychological blindness, which is very surprising in a writer. She says it herself, the thing she said more than anything else was 'I totally trust you.' She even claims she never searched through his phone or doubted his word. Do you know many women like that, Rob?" "Hah, now you're asking, Miles... this won't go beyond these walls! In theory you're right. It's contradictory. I think that, so long as she loves and feels loved, Claire makes it a point of honor to respect her partner's... mystery, to put it bluntly. Trust and restraint as a moral code for a woman in love. A lack of transparency as a condition of durability: not knowing everything about a partner in order to endlessly rekindle desire for him. And stay tolerant of his differences. But the moment love fails, there's no valid moral code and no limit to the inquisition. The writer reappears. She takes the story and completely pulls it to pieces; she takes the guy and strips him naked. Why do you think Gilles made her promise not to write about him? The only difference from a pure and hard radical attitude is that she has doubts, including about herself. When she destroys, she still desires. As she has her revenge, she still loves. She's like Attila the Hun burning everything and hoping the grass will grow again.

"Anyway, I received these pages by mail the day before yesterday. With a title and several epigraphs—she's feeling her way with this too. Scenes that have resurfaced or that she's rewritten—with you in mind, I think, a movie. I know she's sent them to her attorney, in the hope that their revelations about Gilles's incredible violence might provide arguments for her defense speech. The scenes build up the kernel of a meticulous portrait of him—I would even parody Perec and say 'an attempt to completely consume a man,' as if Claire stationed herself in a corner of the past to watch him, to consume him with her eyes. She goes over the top in here, there's fury and an almost disillusioned coldness, and no attempt to be appealing, as if she's given up hope of being believed. But then again, and this is weird, she talks *to* him when she talks about him, she summons him: Instead of saying 'I,' she says 'you,' making this a sort of, how can I put this, not so much autofiction as yourtofiction, which is probably what we do with all the stories we tell ourselves about other people, in love more than anywhere else; but the net result is that Gilles talks to himself. She gives him eyes to see himself. She forces him to have the clarity he doesn't have, the memories he can't hold on to. And as she writes, she forces herself to as well, because writing is a dual process of reminiscence and disenchantment. Here, look, this is what I've called this file." "Elat y Riaf. Sorry, Rob, my Arabic's not very good." "No, it's my dumb joke. It's 'fairy tale' backward, because the idyll here is in reverse: It reveals its evil underside, prince charming is a toad, Pinocchio stays a lying puppet and never turns into a good little boy, and the princess ends up as Cinderella, trying to rekindle the embers in the hearth.

"So, there it is. Now all we can do is cross our fingers. We'll see each other at the trial, anyway."

IDENTI-KIT PICTURE

♦

Literature has the same impact as a match lit in the middle of a field in the middle of the night. The match illuminates relatively little, but it enables us to see how much darkness surrounds it.

—WILLIAM FAULKNER

Man is just an incomprehensible monster.

—BLAISE PASCAL

Your name is Gilles Fabian. You're in Lille for three days, invited by the Catholic University to talk about Good and Evil in puppet theater, and you've taken Dr. Jekyll and Mr. Hyde as your example; more subtle than Bras-de-Fer and Guignol or Punch and Judy. The students looked rapt, but they all left as soon as the talk was over, even the girl who was undressing you with her eyes, even the professor, so you've ended on your own, which you hadn't planned for. You feel pointless, hollowed out. In the next lecture hall, there's a "Meet the Author" with Claire Lancel. You haven't read any of her books but she's Violetta's favorite writer; Violetta read some passages to you the other day to show you what was wrong with your relationship, if that word still means anything—you just pretended, you weren't listening. Even so, the general tone seemed to be cruel toward men—these women novelists never explore their own shortcomings.

You go in, she's reading an extract, you sit down at the back. You're not a fan of these stories about dead children, hard to avoid pathos. People think their little lives are interesting. You're dangerously bored. But still, you like her voice, she doesn't lay it on too thick, she seems gentle, not at all as you would have imagined her. When it's over, you're trying to make up your mind to leave—to go where?—when you see a man go up to her, eager to compliment her. You take on the challenge, come on, decision made, you move closer, eyes downcast, guessing—you know women—that she doesn't need praise but emotion. She smiles at you. You invite her for a drink. She isn't free. Tomorrow, then? You agree to meet in the hotel lobby—you're staying at the same hotel, the one the university always uses. You spend the rest of the evening on Tinder, which your son downloaded for you recently. You don't like one-night stands but you'd rather sit looking at one possible face after another than time passing one second after another.

Claire comes down the stairs. She looks a mess—dressed like the ace of spades, your mother used to say back in the day, that was her expression—she isn't even wearing lipstick. You're thrown. It does take the basics of attractiveness to get you interested. Unless she doesn't find *you* attractive . . . you'd be surprised. She does, you can see it in her eyes—catlike eyes that look right into you, it's almost embarrassing, a sort of metaphysical strip search. She wants to know who you are, that's her charm, but you don't risk anything, you're good at being impenetrable. She asks questions, what you do, where you live, whether you have children—they all do it, they want to know whether you're with someone. You're evasive. And anyway, you're not with someone, you're with her. You live in the present and don't owe anything to anyone.

You very quickly turn the tables, you put questions to her. You listen, holding back: Women have had enough of men who always think they're the main character, you've read about that. Claire opens up very easily, it must be normal for her. Her father's just died, well, a month ago, but the pain is raw. "Tell me, Claire—can I call you Claire?—were you very close?" you ask, tilting and nodding your head, looking just between her eyes, it's less intrusive. She sighs. Without her bushy eyebrows, she'd have a graceful face, she should get some tweezers—beauticians know about this, the line of a person's eyebrows is the architect of the whole face. She's wearing the sort of chunky sweater you'd expect on a trucker, she's about as sexy as a coffee percolator. Her father's death was a shock, she says, but not as bad as the meeting with the executor after the funeral, when she discovered that her father had disinherited her and her sister, leaving them only the minimum required by law, favoring instead his second wife. "To think it was my grandfather, my mother's father, who gave him the funds to set up as a dentist in Rouen—Dad was from a poor family, he had nothing. Whenever my father thanked him, my grandfather always gave the same reply, we were told this a hundred times, he would say, 'I'm doing it for my grandchildren, all this will be for them.' It was a sort of tacit contract, which is what people did in those days. My father broke it—my grandfather was dead so...It feels like a betrayal to me. I spent my whole childhood, and beyond, showing my father how much I loved him. He always looked glum—he and my mother fought a lot—and I worked hard to put a smile on his face, I wanted to make him happy. I wrote him little notes and slipped them under his pillow, I was always in a good mood, I worked hard at school. For him, to please him. It didn't change anything. I put his silence down to his personality, his past. I still thought he loved me, though. But he didn't. I didn't count. I've had a really tough time these last few years, bringing up my daughter alone, he knew that, he could have wanted to help me, to leave something for her. Nothing. I've said too much, I'm sorry for oversharing like that, we don't even know each other. I just wanted to explain why I'm sad: I'm grieving the father I thought I had."

You listen. You usually get bored quickly, you're never interested in other people for long, particularly when they talk about themselves, unless you want something from them. But you got lucky this time, you're passionate about the subject. You have a thing about fathers. Women and their fathers, you're happy to dig deeper on that. Their husbands, too, occasionally. The men who were there before you, in fact. You want to know what went wrong, what women find wanting in other men. The nature of their disillusion. First, it's so you can do better, and then, you'll do worse. You identify where it hurts, and while they're admitting to the wound, you're registering both what might soothe it and what would infect it. You isolate this place that needs healing, and when the time comes, that's where you'll strike the fatal blow. Savior then executioner: your flight plan, whatever the weather.

Do you know this? Is *plan* the right word? That's the big question, the dizzying question because the answer has a chokehold on all the wonderful memories. When you listen to Claire—your eyes full of the compassion that you wish you felt—you're not being cynical, no, not at this point. You want her to like you, to make her forget her grief. "I'm desperately sorry," you say, and if you dared, if she'd put on a pretty dress, you would take her hand. You file her story in the hodgepodge of stuff you already know—wooden dolls with cracked bodies and faded cheeks: Women are afraid of being abandoned. They want to be loved. So do you. But *you* know how to avoid loving and being abandoned. Too risky. As for being loved... You smile.

You offer her another drink, she orders chamomile tea. She couldn't have been any clearer. She pays her share. Feminist—fine. You leave together and the gratitude in her eyes makes you feel good. The trust she's put in you is your victory. You don't need another, you don't want her, not really—desire has never come in a rush for you. Anything that's out of your control makes you anxious. Although it's beyond your scope to formulate it like this,

Claire has helped you get through the evening. You were at a loose end, unhappy, not that you admitted it to yourself (whatever you do, don't apply the word *unhappiness* to anything), threatened by a familiar empty feeling that she helped you ward off. You've filled yourself with her gratitude, and you see yourself in that light.

In the corridor outside your respective rooms, you exchange contact details. You're pleased. The connection's been established without too much intimacy, you're not committed to anything, it's perfect. Your life is peppered with these low-ranking but vital characters who make your anonymity bearable, its walls are lined with these temporary mirrors—their eyes—which stave off your loneliness and in which you look valiant. Afraid that you might run out of the reflections they provide (it's a huge danger), you generate them here and there, in different cities, countries, circumstances, neighborhoods—which is why you avoid the countryside, Sundays, and deserted places. You establish contact, make a connection, then leave these bit-part players in the background of your life, no, on the horizon is more accurate, keeping them hovering between the present and the future, maintaining a distinctive relationship with all of them for rainier days, each of them believing this relationship is unique—and in a way it is because you adapt to every one of them. In that guessing game "If I were an animal" you'd be a chameleon. In the long tracking shot of time, some will end up on the cutting-room floor or fired with no warning, others will be kept waiting for their scene, understudies, plan Bs if the word *plan* hasn't been vetoed, some will eventually be called or recalled to the set—lovers, friends, it doesn't really matter, even if love is so much better at putting fire in a person's eyes. There are also the figures in the shadows—the former trainee who still writes to you, the woman who runs the restaurant downstairs from your apartment, the girl at the greengrocer's who gets in a flap when you smile at her, the housekeeper in your building who sometimes gives you coffee at her place, neighbors, salesgirls, a tour guide, a Realtor—all of them in thrall. This small crowd is in position, playing useful roles in your day-to-day life—a whole system of instant reassurances, a wink, the bat of an eyelid, a look in which your charm has its effect and serves you. That's what the puppets do. Because, if we look closely, this is more like a puppet theater than an animated film. Puppets with eyes. You know how to move them without being moved yourself, manipulation is your job, your vocation even, and you've used it pretty successfully so far, but boredom also has strings to its bow—boredom, tyrannical boredom that relentlessly pursues novelty in the hearts of strangers. So you have to fight hard, constantly finding new dolls to dress up, more ciphers in which to be reflected. It's never-ending. You're fighting for your life. Saving your skin in other people's eyes. "See you soon, then," you smile at Claire with your key card in your hand. You tell yourself you'll contact her again: She likes you and you don't want her to forget you.

It is December 31, 2013. You reluctantly come to this party at Nathalie and Christian's place. You've been promised that Laetitia Valy, the famous author, will be there, and you'd like to see her, to get her interested in a project of yours, and maybe more. Last time you met, she cut you dead, but you haven't given up hope, you get the feeling that she finds you attractive. Which is why you decided to accept the invitation, even though you're worried that at some point in the evening people will put on music and start prancing around like gangling puppets, relegating you to the edge of the room, glass in hand, a passive observer condemned to smiling. But you don't feel like watching other people, still less like smiling at them. You need someone to pay attention to you, especially today. You've had another fight with Violetta, your partner, if that word still makes any sense, she bombarded you with what she'd allegedly learned from your last couples therapy session, that you're a narcissist who's incapable of loving anyone, starting with yourself. That therapist woman is ignorant as well as ugly: In the myth, Narcissus loves himself, that's just the point, he falls in love with his own image. Besides, if she did give this diagnosis, it can only have been about Violetta herself, who's a liar and so pretentious. You've had enough of therapy, anyway, you started it as a token of your good faith but you never believed in it. All that blathering never gets anywhere: Violetta is crazy and always will be. End of story. She's always crying when you don't understand why and then wants to make up when you're not trying to work out how to. You can't see anything in her eyes anymore except for the inadequacies she pins on you—which are in fact hers. You feel exhausted and angry when you think of everything you've done for her, of the adoring love that you've given her in vain. To no avail. To end up here. And on top of that, being insulted by a shrink with a face like a frog. You've had it with her kid cluttering up the living room with his console, twice now he's left the thing on the piano along with his glass of Coke, the little asshole. The only advantage of your last fight is that she wanted to stay at her place with her children. So now you have your evening to yourself.

You come through the door, turn your head, and scan the room. At first glance, Ms. Valy is not here, you would have spotted her scrolled chignon immediately. In the group on the right-hand side of the living room you recognize Carole something-or-other, an influential arts journalist, she has great breasts but she's a hard-line feminist, a former student of the prestigious École Normale Supérieure—you're wary of *normaliennes*, girls who went there, they think they're the best and insist on being right about everything. You want to show yourself off, not measure yourself up to someone. Next to her is, what's her name now, Claire, yes, that's it, Claire Lancel, smiling at you. The author. Or, sorry, should that be authoress—definitely need to watch your step, militant territory. She smiles at you, but not just any smile, it's radiant, her eyes single you out in a beam of light. You remember what Flaubert says when Frédéric meets Madame Arnoux for the first time: "It was like an apparition," except that in this instance you are the apparition, even though you've met before. She looks at you in a way you've never been looked at before, or not that you remember. Yes, women find you attractive—and so do men, as it happens—you know that; you don't find it hard to seduce them. But this is different—or do you just need it to be, you need something to happen, to change your life? No, you're sure of it, you can see it: She's singling you out from the rest of the world, she's choosing you, and—finding yourself caught up in the ardor in her eyes when you go over to her—she charms you. A completely enveloping sensation! You feel chosen. Of course, you're worthy of it but even so, this stuff doesn't happen every day. You thought you looked handsome in the mirror earlier, before you left, this blue suits you, and Claire's eyes confirm that. One little snag, though, one flat note: You don't like the sloppy way she's dressed. It was the same the first time—where was that? In Bordeaux? Or maybe Lille?—but boots and a turtleneck on New Year's Eve, that's really something. It's a bad sign, a sign that she thinks she's a diva who doesn't care about social codes: The great novelist Claire Lancel, of course! You're suddenly impressed, whatever you may want to feel. You read somewhere that Isabelle Huppert bought the rights to her last book to make a film adaptation. And yet she's looking at you, you have a future in her eyes. What if this was your opportunity—your lifeline? You usually get the feeling you were born under a lucky star: At the worst points in your life you've always been able to bounce back. You can move on to something else the way other people move from one room to another: You open a door and out you go. You couldn't give a damn if someone's still knocking at the door. Maybe that moment has come. But you're not sure of yourself—and certainly not of her. She finds you attractive, fine, you find her attractive, sure, but there's nothing to prove that it will stay the course. Still, a bird in the hand is worth two in the bush: Who knows what those two wild birds would do to you, while this little chick's eating out of your hand. You've never been on your own, not one day without someone who mattered. That's why you're still with Violetta, despite the clashes, and even though her popularity has crashed so dramatically that you're now a little ashamed of your relationship—you've lost track of *you* in it, the mirror is empty.

How to seduce Claire? How to make her love you? That's what's going to occupy you, the way a city can be occupied. You will be occupied by her, invaded by her, her image, her enigma, a need to leave the other men she may have loved way behind you. And all through the months that you'll devote to surrounding her, deciphering her, learning about every aspect of her, all through those months you'll feel powerful. Anxious but determined. In the end, she'll love you because you'll be the best. Unless she loves you already, for no reason, like in the movies. That would be just her style. Having said that, in your experience, if you want to be loved you need to make yourself lovable. You'll find a way. You've had a lot of practice.

In the meantime, here you are sitting on her red sofa in her apartment. There are so many colors, such quantities of useless things, and the photo of a good-looking man (her husband?) in a metal frame is unsettling and irritating (she could have put it away when she knew you were coming), you wonder whether this is too much for you, too much life to filter, too much data to process. And too big a role to take on. All this yellow, all this red... You're not a college kid. But then neither is she. She's still beautiful, which is something feminists don't like you to say, and the conquest doesn't look difficult. Don't all women want the same thing? In any event, you advance cautiously, particularly as Violetta is also still in the frame. You hate the thought of separating from her forever, and most of all you're scared she'll leave first, therapy will make her slam the door. Then you'd be all alone. So, softly, softly you're setting up the next incumbent, as much as you can, although proceeding softly doesn't come naturally to you—but you've learned it from women, you know how to play the part. For a while now you've been prospecting candidates to succeed Violetta, without actually making a move. Laetitia Valy, number 1; Zoé, a gallery manager you met on Tinder—you're keeping her on standby, sensing she has issues. You even thought of reaching out to Louise again, but she called you every name under the sun when you dumped her overnight for Violetta—shame, you feel nostalgic about the sex parties that you went to together. Plus Claire Lancel, then. You fantasize about it. You can just imagine Violetta's face when you tell her that you're with this novelist! That exhilarating prospect adds to Claire's charm.

In this conquest that's been occupying you since January 1st, several circumstances are working in your favor. First of all, Claire is very quick to open up, you already noticed this in conversation; but there are also her books: a fount of information! Reading them spares you the long and tiresome discussions usually needed to get to know someone, even if, like all women, Claire likes to talk. You learn more about her from her books than you want to know! So much revelation of her inner character makes you think twice. Her sexuality, her desires, her fantasies; her past, her childhood, her disappointments, her sorrows; her likes, her dislikes, her taboos; her successes, her fallings-out, her failures;

her living and her dead. In a few months, you've read them all, without telling her; you've scanned her personality. Her life, her work: You know it all.

Which is why you couldn't bear it if she ever accused you of not having loved her. You were the one who was so interested in her, so attentive to the tiniest details, so eager to shower her with affection! It's easy to claim that your curiosity was ill-intentioned, that you were looking for her fault lines from the start, the places where you could attach the strings to make her your puppet. Why couldn't it be love? You were bewitched by Claire's qualities, her feelings, her passions, you recognized yourself in her as if in a mirror: You were both exceptional and you had met. You were intoxicated by the way destiny was bringing you together. At last, your ideal had materialized, leaving behind all the failures of the past. What luck! What a miracle! Didn't this occur to her too? Of course it did. You believed in it just as much as she did, and you won't let anyone say otherwise. Love is when you believe in it. Only time creates obstacles; some petty offense gets into the works and it's all over. Nothing withstands the passage of time; lucky charms are just cardboard cutouts. Love is for as long as you believe in it.

It's in Claire's novels, then, that you discover her world. Nothing new there: You're used to learning everything from books—novels, stage plays. That's your main mode of understanding life, along with the movies. They have mostly taught you the basics worth knowing about love—the signs and words. In fact, the apprenticeship never ends. Right now, for example, you're reading François Mitterrand's letters to Anne Pingeot, and you can't get over such passion from a man who was so outwardly austere, you gorge on it, it fills the void you feel, a physical deficiency, a pit in your chest. A character in a play once said: "Love is a sensation that we pass off as a feeling." But to you it's neither: You feel nothing. You were blown away the day that Claire impetuously quoted Benjamin Constant to you, the sentence seemed to have been written for you, you could have said it of her: "I knew that I loved her, but I couldn't feel it." No better way to express it: You recognize love, but you don't experience it. The knowledge never travels from your mind to your heart, or even your body—you're not so stupid as to confuse pleasure with love, even though you always murmur "I love you" when you come, precisely as a way of connecting sensation and sentiment, and also to reassure your partner. "I love you" is an infallible artifice, no one's ever come up with anything better, even in the most beautiful books.

So, literature was your first access route to this sensitive tissue that you don't know by touch. You mined her books for what you can't identify in life. You perused ardor, joy, passion, pain; you studied their every manifestation—words, gestures, mimicry. And you invariably swelled with emotions like a sponge before gradually shrinking in the glare of the sun. You visited Good and Evil without the patience to explore their complexities; after all, your puppets simplify Shakespeare and Dostoyevsky—surely goodies and baddies are enough to summarize morality? And opera taught you the fascinating beauty of betrayal.

More recently, you turned your attention to movies, and most of all to TV series that incarnate humanity using scenes from everyday life: There you found norms, role models that were easy to decipher and copy. Literature may have taught you to recognize love, to remember the words it uses, to identify signs of it and reproduce them, but nothing compares to images. Watching Netflix, you did and still do harvest and hoard loving looks, gestures, and behaviors. You soak it all up for copycat performances. Every woman is different, of course, situations vary, but so little when it comes down to it. Aren't they often interchangeable? Surprising her with a ring, just because; holding her little foot when she's lying on the sofa reading with her legs on your thighs; giving her flowers; looking deep into her eyes, etc. You don't feel the emotion, but you excel at emoting it.

This is how you give Claire all the outward signs of passion, in the same way that you give her gifts. You want to be loved by her. You want her to love you to distraction, as she's never loved before. You want to check the box for every heading on the lover's form. For her daughter, Alice, too. Being the ideal father that she's lost or never had—and being that for Claire herself, deep down; she was so let down by her own father. To get them both to love you, you must incarnate the dream man, a man who listens and understands and rescues. It requires a gargantuan effort on your part. One day, Claire arranged a lunch for you and her daughter to meet. You emerged a conqueror but were as exhausted as an actor after many hours of filming. As luck would have it, you'd remembered tips on playing the role of a stepfather from an excellent American series about a blended family, and you'd already used them on Jules: quiet strength, being prepared to listen to any difficulties, and tenderness but not too much.

Playing a part is draining, though. Because even if the range of expectations and feelings isn't all that broad, you must adapt to each new female protagonist. Sometimes you need to figure it out for yourself, improvise by guesswork like a blind man feeling his way: What does she want? What should you give her? And what should you take from her, when it comes to that? The problem is you really struggle to take an interest in other people. A great cloak of boredom bears down on you whenever someone confides in you or insists on having a conversation. "We need to talk" was your worst ordeal with Violetta and you value Claire's capacity for silence, although you also often see it as a lack of interest in you—when she's reading or writing, she gets away from you. Because, although you grow increasingly indifferent when someone tries to steer you into an unfamiliar psyche or even into a way of life that differs from your own, you yourself need to be noticed, to be taken into consideration; and you were quick to grasp that the mechanism—that's just the word that came to you—the mechanism presupposes reciprocity: You must give in order to receive. But you have nothing to give, nothing genuine, nothing spontaneous—there's no real life in a false life. You're a stranger to other people's emotions, except for anger, desire, and fear, which you've known since, oh, forever. You're impervious to both their sorrows and their worries, their likes and their joys; you're empty of all curiosity about them, you lack the compassion necessary for confidence. You're alone in your soul, if soul there is, and nothing that you feel can be shared.

And yet you want to be surrounded by other people. You need their respect, their admiration, their devotion. All that is contained within love. So then you must be loved. But because, inside yourself, you don't feel anything that you want to give, there's no alternative: You must fake it. Not with everyone, thank goodness—an impossible and futile challenge. No. Just the people whose eyes will give you a lovable heft. You scan their expressions to work out how to be. If you don't find admiration in their eyes, then there's nobody there. You derive an impression of living from the impression that you give. Appearances put the finishing touches on your existence and put their signatures on it; you can't feel the face beneath the mask.

Meanwhile, other people express themselves, lay themselves open, even, thinking—the pretentious fools—that they're gaining something from being known so well. A few also want to know you, they ask you questions and watch you. Claire, for example. At the restaurant with Alice, while you're free diving into your own depths to haul up an emotion stuck on the seabed and bring it back to the surface, Claire is pale, breathless, and you catch her: She's studying you. It's as if she's wondering who you really are. You don't want her to know, you don't want to know yourself—anything but that. You just want to pass yourself off as a good guy—an irreplaceable lover, a model father, a great character, perfection made man. Besides, "who you are" doesn't mean anything. No one *is* anything. I am, I am, I am . . . it's just iambic nonsense.

You can see, though, that in intimate situations rather than social ones, not all emotions are simulated. With you, some women, and men too, have allowed themselves to trust, succumbed to giving confidences, they've admitted their weaknesses, discussed their sources of pain or their hopes. Their honesty frustrates you. You envy this gift in other people just as much as you despise it, even if there is always an element of duplicity—you've read the moralists. It sometimes enrages you that they're able to abandon themselves when you can't. But you won't try. Lifting the mask is far too dangerous. It makes you fragile and vulnerable, the slightest thing could hurt you. It could even kill you: Oh, *that* you remember. At least that knowledge is inscribed in you. You're afraid of and you're trying to avoid something that's already happened.

You don't want any pain.

You can't afford it.

Is that really the right wording? Wouldn't the correct statement actually be: You don't feel any pain.

You wish you could, in fact. It would be proof that you're alive. When someone's downcast, then they must have been upright before. But you can't be cast down. All that's left of you is a dead stump.

One evening, Claire invites Émilie over with her new fiancé. You like the way Émilie looks at you, how she listens to you—you'll tell Claire about it after dinner, to make her suspect her friend of coming on to you. You mentally assimilate the way Émilie rests her chin on her hands, tilting her face toward you to demonstrate her attentiveness. On the other hand, the fiancé's unbearable, the kind of guy who takes the credit for everything. The conversation jogs along about puppets and automatons, then Émilie talks about her research into artificial intelligence—"I prefer natural ignorance," says the little know-it-all, and she throws her head back to laugh. Will AI replace humans? That's the question. Émilie explains that AI is a huge entity feeding off the entirety of human knowledge, but it still can't truly feel anything—at least not yet. It has remarkable cognitive intelligence, she summarizes, but no emotional intelligence. You and Claire exchange a look at this point, and you get the feeling she's thinking what you're thinking: That you too could be described like that. Claire's prescience has already scared you several times, like when she burrowed her nose into your armpit and said she couldn't smell anything, there was nobody there. "There's nobody there!" she giggled in amazement, lying naked and sweaty next to you. You experienced that statement as an arrow loosed with murderous precision. She could laugh all she liked, you found her insistence aggressive. "Okay, then, if that's the deal with AI, I'll just keep playing dumb," the other guy quips, and yet again you envy his ability to make the women laugh. Even though Claire is very much in love with you, you're scared that someday she'll open the door onto the emptiness inside you, that she'll peer into it, as if leaning out of a window, to gauge how deep it is. She sometimes does it fleetingly; she looks at you oddly, her eyes study you savagely, like a probe, then it's over. But you're sure that she'll see it one day, she'll write about it, and your destitute nakedness will be laid bare, she will present a stripped-back portrait of you—you've read her work, you know what she's capable of. You were astonished, for example, to find a sentence in one of her novels that she attributes to her ex-husband but that you could formulate about yourself without ever daring to pronounce it—and if her husband really did say it, then respect: "I'm a dead man who can come." You have to admit: You feel a kinship. Let's hope Claire never finds out, given that she's always citing you as a counterexample... The words you've said to her most often after "I love you" are "I'm not like your husband," and that's precisely because you are. "We're the same," is what you think to yourself. In the early days, Julien was your rival, then he became your model—in either case, the aim will be to outdo him. Claire will love you more and you'll make her suffer more. Too bad for her if she always falls for the same man. On the other hand, what you really need to avoid is her realizing this. The very thought persecutes you. You're only interested in meeting useful people, people who will serve some purpose or other for you. What if you miscalculated with Claire? What if she proves detrimental? You're afraid of her obstinacy, her tenacious need to understand—she sometimes jots things down in a notebook, her eyes hazy, lost in thought, or looking at you. You see her do it.

That's why you need to find a guardrail, literally: The truth would bring you crashing down, not the truth, no, but its revelation—truth published, in other words made public. You must protect yourself from her breaches, you can tell that this is an urgent necessity. The two of you are about to spend ten days in a house that your cousin has loaned you in Menton. You'll find a way.

You've been in the South of France for two days, in June 2014—the year of big love for the two of you. You've known each other six months, but this is your first opportunity to spend so much time together. On the first evening, you're happy—yes, you were happy. Claire belongs to you, she lives with you. She dances and twirls, marveling at a palm tree, a flower, a smell, everything is so gorgeous and it's thanks to you, her eyes love you. That night is powerful and sensuous. You like her abandon, the pleasure she derives from submission. The next day, after you've been to the market, she settles into a deck chair on the terrace and reads. Every now and then she closes her eyes, enjoying the sunshine. You ask her what she'd like for lunch, she hardly looks at you, "A salad, don't you think? We have tomatoes." She seems totally absorbed in her book. After you've eaten, she goes back to it, reading and underlining passages. You can't get over it. You call her from the bedroom, "My love…" You suggest a siesta and she joins you.

You're lying naked, drunk on pleasure, exhausted. The shutters are closed, it's already very hot. "I was wondering…What do you least like about me physically?" She puts her arms around you, sniffs at the crook of your neck, mumbles: "Nothing. I love everything." You wait for her to say, "What about you?" and because she doesn't, you launch off with, "The thing that bothered me, the first time, was that you're not waxed. Here," you specify, putting a hand on her pubis. "Really?" She sits up, a hint of alarm in her voice. "Why didn't you say anything?" "I'm saying something now. But it doesn't matter, my love. It's just so . . . old-fashioned. It doesn't make you any younger, that's all." "You're wrong about that: Body hair's making a big comeback in women. Think of all the photos of actresses with hairy armpits. It's actually super-fashionable." "Myeah. Well, I can tell you that on the other side of the Atlantic, all the American women are completely waxed." "Oh really! So you know all of them?"

You go quiet for a moment. Her sarcasm throws you. That's the perverse thing with Claire, this woman who amazes you, irritates you, and provokes you all at the same time: She never takes anything personally, criticism never seems to get to her. You'd happily explain this away as exacerbated narcissism, even though she's no longer in the first flush of youth. Either way, you're unsettled because that's exactly what you're trying to achieve: to spark a fight, at least some feelings of doubt, by attacking a weakness—which in women is usually a physical detail: It's impressively effective. When you were seeing a couples therapist, she pointed out that your constant digs hurt Violetta, the woman urged you to acknowledge this nasty impulse of yours and to fight it when it reared its head—unsuccessfully, according to Violetta. And to think that when you first met, Violetta had called your hemangioma a port-wine stain, deliberately, to remind you of your father's alcoholism, and did anyone talk about that? Hell no, there was no comparison. Of course. So you learned to follow up criticism with refutations—"It doesn't matter," "I shouldn't have said that," "You misunderstood me." The shrink said you had a need to make your partner feel insecure so you could then reassure her. To make her feel ugly or dumb, and therefore vulnerable, so that you could comfort her and she would always be under your control. She would be nothing without you. The root of all this was your lack of self-confidence, your fear of abandonment, and therefore of being hurt, which is why you exported all these threats to someone else. And blah-blah-blah. The therapist's smug Boy Scout smile, what a punishment that was—good God, spare me this flannel. "And anyway," Claire picks up the subject again, "an obsession with hairless vulvas comes straight from porn. And that raises a question: Women look like prepubescent girls when they're hairless. Enough to make anyone wonder what it is you all find so attractive about it."

Okay fine. So now you're a pedophile. "I've never watched porn in my life," you say indignantly (it's not true, you even watched one on mute earlier when she was reading). "And women are free to choose, right? If they get waxed, it's because they think it's better like that." "Pfft," Claire snorts, getting out of bed. "It's because *you* like it. Do you really think it's fun having your hair ripped out? It takes time, it hurts like hell, and you need to keep doing it! Women go to a lot of trouble to please you men, that's all."

The feminist's constant refrain. What about her, why isn't she going to a lot of trouble to please you? You don't admit defeat. "All I can say is looking at you now, as you are" (she has her back to you as she takes a towel from the closet), "I'm in no danger of confusing you with a prepubescent girl..." Claire laughs out loud: "Are you telling me that I'm fat?" and she throws the towel in your face. "And anyway," you soldier on while she comes back to bed, "when you wax, you get rid of the gray hairs. Because you can't disagree, a graying bush is anything but sexy." "I do have a few," she says in a slightly different voice and slips quickly under the sheets. "Oh really?" you lie. "I hadn't noticed."

You're not sure of the result of this afternoon's match. But the next day, Claire shows off a completely bare, clearly defined pubis. For a moment you're overcome, you hug her to you. Oh! If you loved her, how you would love her!

On this trip, and on others, you'll take photos of her and selfies of the two of you. One day, in several years, she'll look through all the emails you sent her, all the texts and photos. She'll notice that in the selfies, you're both gorgeous and smiling, but in the photos of her alone, dozens of them, images you always scrupulously forwarded to her, she never looks her best—to say the least. Posing like this in a one-piece swimsuit with her shoulders forward, she looks like an East German competitive swimmer; here she has her mouth wide open biting into a cupcake; in this one you can see the fillings in her teeth, her wrinkles picked out by the light, her vacuous expression. What's this constant payback for?

The fact is you can't stand Claire's happiness unless you're its unadulterated source. Which is why you'll never withdraw sexual pleasure from her because you're the master of it. So long as you can make her orgasm, or allow her to hope that you will, you have the upper hand (it's never occurred to you that she might sometimes fake it). You'll always play the piano for her because she admires you then and doesn't know anyone else who plays like you. But in this house in Menton there is no piano. And yet Claire thinks everything's wonderful. She's blossoming before your eyes. She's so carefree it rankles you. You hate it when she reads, when she writes, when she calls someone, when she dances in the living room, when she laughs with the delivery guy. You hate her small pleasures, her chirpiness, her plans, you hate the confidence you give her, the love that's growing. It's as if she's depriving you of it. You're going to take it all back. You want to live at her expense.

After two days in the house you're climbing the walls. Of course, you also brought books. You listen to music on your headphones, you watch videos on your laptop, you send emails to Zoé asking how she is, you post hearts on her posts. Nothing very stimulating. Meanwhile, Claire's so happy she forgets about you. You end up on your own when the two of you are together—you couldn't make it up! Surely the point of a partner is some partnership? She thinks her happiness is assured, and that's where she's wrong. You're going to make her pay. She believes that just existing is enough and she doesn't need to do anything to be loved. Who does she think she is?

In the meantime, seeing she won't deign to take an interest in you, you need to get out and see some people—being shut away like this is driving you crazy, and so is the silence. You suggest a trip to Saint-Tropez. You're on the road for a long time. The traffic jams don't bother you because they annoy her. Walking around the marina where yachts are moored you feel better, you're already tanned, you notice some appreciative glances. The people here reassure you, you're like them, rich and powerful; and better than them, intelligent. Claire looks pretty in the dress you bought her, and there's so much trust in her eyes, no one can fail to see that you're loved. You still need to make sure you have power over her, though. This is about her paying off her debt.

You invite her for dinner in an expensive restaurant. You've been there before, with Violetta—the way you remember it, she seemed more enthusiastic than Claire, even if the wind coming off the sea made her voice hoarse and she had to cancel several recitals. Claire seems to be trying hard, as if she doesn't really feel at home here or now. You know this for one simple reason: Neither do you. You never feel at home anywhere, starting with yourself. You're usually happy to fake these airs and graces, directing operations from the outside like the good illusionist that you are. The sea, love, making plans together. The whole rom-com. But you can feel some resistance this time. Claire isn't falling into the trap. She too has stayed on the outside, like you but in a different way. It's imperceptible, you may even be wrong, but your slight irritation acts as a barometer. You're sitting facing each other across a white tablecloth, chatting and eating your food. And yet neither of you is there: You're up in the theater's fly loft pulling the strings; she's in the wings watching. Hands manipulate, eyes watch. The puppeteer and the writer. Eyes register everything, hers will eventually spot the hands, unless they've blinded her. And if they can't stop Claire from seeing, then they must at least keep her quiet, gag her. "My love. What if... what if we made a promise to each other," you say.

The picture's clear to see now. Claire Lancel and Gilles Fabian. The autobiographer promises never to write about her lover; the Pinocchio specialist promises never to betray his. The end of the story is in its beginning, the promise holds within it the lie. Who they are, what makes them tick, what they will become: They will never come closer to the truth than this evening, surrounded by the fragrance of mimosa over extinguished candles.

And yet you're wrong to worry that you've been unmasked at this point. It's too soon. To see something, a person needs to believe it's possible. For now, all of Claire's imagination is projecting an aura of kindliness onto you. Harm is beyond the scope of her mental depictions, too far removed from the image she has built up of you, that she has built up because of you. So, when you ask her for the rental money at the end of your stay, she saddles your cousin with her obscure feeling of reproach, without saying so out loud, she doesn't want to criticize your family. It's only years later that she sees the look in your eyes at the exact moment you asked her for the money. She sees it again in a film, on a face that isn't yours, in response to different circumstances. But the same expression as in your eyes. It must have been filed somewhere in the half shadows of her memory. Your fake expression, and the words you said. You gave too many explanations, like a bad liar—she remembers that: why your cousin prefers cash to a bank transfer (yes, cash, you used the English word), how she asked you to leave it in the drawer of the nightstand in the other bedroom, you know, at the end of the corridor, she'll come pick it up later, she needs money right now for her eldest son's college fees.

Claire withdraws six hundred euros from the ATM next to the pizzeria and hands the money to you. You put it discreetly into your pocket and keep it for yourself. You feel a furtive discomfort that doesn't extend to shame and dissipates when you think what she owes you: the sun, the sea, a dress, two dinners in fancy restaurants, and lots of love, so much pleasure.

There's another occasion when you have that look in your eye, the look from the film. There must have been other times that she's forgotten. It comes later in the story when you're at the house in Hyères. Claire has delivered the manuscript for her novel, she's working on her podcast and writing texts for a dance show on which she's agreed to collaborate. She also talks, a lot, with you, discussing the book you're writing about your life and about puppets. You confide in her; it's so harmonious. One day you come home from the market, and she hasn't even noticed you were out. You call her to come and help you put the shopping away in the fridge. She gets up and finds that you're not in the kitchen so she starts emptying the shopping baskets without you. She suddenly hears you howl, oh no, noooooooo, and she races into the study where she'd been working. You stand there frozen, next to the desk, which is now streaming with water. The look comes at that exact moment, she registers it but has other things to do. A vase has tipped over onto her laptop and smashed, and mimosa flowers are dripping onto her keyboard. "I'm desperately sorry," you say, not moving a muscle while she lunges for the laptop. She tears it from its cable, which is plugged into the wall—odd, she already charged it this morning. She hurries to the bathroom to get towels, you follow her, apologizing flatly as if it were nothing to do with you, then you justify what you were doing, you wanted to make her happy by buying some mimosa for her, that's why you put the vase on her desk—even though it's tiny—rather than in the living room, so that she could enjoy it, the vase just shattered for no reason, it must have been cracked. Like the excessive explanations about your cousin's rent, the profusion of excuses would appear suspect to Claire if the initial intention hadn't been so kind: She really does miss her mimosa tree! She is a little annoyed with you, though, for not doing something immediately in a situation where every second counts. What exactly were you doing in the time it took her to get there from the kitchen after you yelled? Passively studying the disaster with your arms hanging limply by your sides. "I was paralyzed," you add to your explanations. In any event, the laptop doesn't fire up again, it's dead.

There are two things that Claire doesn't think to herself at the time, even if you get the feeling that she has a fleeting suspicion. The first is that you wanted to stop her from writing. The promise isn't enough for you, writing is now an intransitive verb.

Nothing will ever be enough, in fact, the debt will always be outstanding. You think that you can appropriate all the things that you're trying to take from her: her vital energy, her urge to write. Why shouldn't the principle of communicating vases (yes, vases) apply to people? The more uncertain she is, the happier you are. The more she fades, the better you feel. The less she lives, the more you can breathe.

On the subject of life, there's a second thing that Claire doesn't think about—and this is just as well for you. It's that you'd like her to die. The idea did occur to her once in fact. You were in Toronto, she was crying on the phone, overwhelmed by personal attacks online and in the media, you commiserated monosyllabically or reassured her with a lazy "I'm here." At one point, she mentioned how alone she was, how frightened. She said, "At night I can picture myself jumping out of the window." You observed a long silence—none of the usual things that come to mind at times like this, the automatic rescuing words, "Don't say that," "Hang in there," "Do you want me there with you?," no, not even the "I'm here" that you said a few minutes earlier. Nothing. A dense, motionless silence like anticipation, filled with promise like a state of hope, your lips sealed on a death wish transmitted by satellite in a static hiss of loathing. Claire didn't complain at all, but you'd identified an unhoped-for hopelessness in her. Nevertheless, somewhere in a work of fiction that she won't write, you personify the character of the grieving widower whose devastating posthumous homage to his beloved denounces the despicable indifference of the world that robbed him of her. You play the part so well.

You came up with the idea of the vase without knowing how it would turn out. You saw a movie once—you don't remember what it was called, or maybe it was a crime novel?—in which a character throws a working hair dryer into the bathtub, killing his wife without dirtying his hands. Accidental death by electrocution, no one turns a hair. The Claude François method. No guarantees it will work with flower water, but you had nothing to lose from trying, and everything to gain. Claire's debt to you is growing: Her debt is her life. When she lunged to grab her laptop without thinking, you felt you were on the frontiers of untold pleasure. It sent a shiver down your spine, it engulfed you. The failure was both a disappointment and a relief for you. Mostly a disappointment: You wish she were dead, you want her silenced. Just shut her up forever! Her annihilation would send a geyser of life surging up in you, even if only for a moment, and you have a right to that. She's the price you have to pay so that you can live a little.

From that point on you will intensify the lethal bombardment, the attack on the things that define Claire's connection with you: her trust, her need to communicate, her wanting to give life some meaning and harmony. And you will do this while also binding her to you with the things she wants from you. You cultivate lies, obfuscating waffle, destructive strategies, icy indifference. You caress her and compliment her and say, "I want you." As a stranger to all the little things that melt a heart, you perform them by rote. You drive home the nail of malicious intent, denigrating her, undermining her self-confidence, her confidence in you. You pretend to listen to her, you smile at her. You know only cunning, flight and attack—the laws of the jungle. You don't know how to have a conversation or to soothe. You don't want to make reparations or give reassurances. You invite her out and give her gifts and read her poems. You humiliate her and impoverish her and throw her to the dogs. You say, "I respect you." You want her physically dead, socially dead, just dead. You say, "My love." You want her to be nothing without you, nothing with you—you want her to be nothing. You say, "I admire you." You take her in your arms. She's suffocating you and you don't want to be without her. You're trying to achieve a funereal dynamic that combines the most fervid cruelty with the most fervent attachment.

You love her.

And here's the proof: You hate her.

◆

There's still one question, Gilles, and it torments me, it's the question that clatters against my sanity like a branch against a shutter, relentlessly. What we don't have is any proof. All I can do is endlessly study it in the secret drawer of my memory and in Charles Boyer's guilty expression in *Gaslight*, 1944. But *you* know. You don't need any proof. You've forgotten for now—unless your amnesia is the ultimate performance. Let's give you the benefit of the doubt. But while these events were actually happening, you, Gilles, know what you did, don't you? I don't mean your feelings, I'm well aware of how hard they can be to untangle. I'm not asking if you were lying when you said "I love you" to one or the other of us, to me; whether your words were genuine, here or anywhere else. I mean the facts. The actions, the acts. Whether you deliberately flooded the laptop, whether you plugged it in first: You know these things. You had to be quick about it, grabbing the charging cable, putting the plug into the socket, hitting the vase hard enough for it to break, stepping back, calling out. Did you do all of that? Your body must hold the memory of it now. Whether you unfairly kept six hundred euros, whether you deliberately answered my call on Valentine's Day, whether you weaponized my podcast to take your revenge on Laetitia Valy who'd rejected your advances: You must know all this. Whether, on the very day that the controversy blew up, you sent her a message of support, making it clear that the whole business was nothing to do with you, and that we—you and I—were no longer even together: You must know that.

And that's not to mention events from further in the past. When you invited your eldest son's girlfriend to a swingers' evening with you in Paris while your son was abroad, when you denied it so vehemently that he had no choice but to run away to Australia with her. When, coupling together two lies, you told your other son that Violetta didn't want him in the apartment anymore and told Violetta that he wouldn't be coming over anymore because he couldn't stand her. When you invented that Violetta was slapping your daughter, but only to people who couldn't corroborate your claims or report them to Violetta. When you told Mark, who'd asked for my contact details to set up the writing workshop in Toronto, that I'd changed my mind and thought Canada was a backwater, while telling me that my podcast had shocked him and had put him off inviting me, even though he didn't know anything about that podcast. When you scrolled through Tinder while I was asleep in your arms, when you hermetically compartmentalize your lies, when you misinform, when you insinuate, when you insist on untruths: You know all this.

You know. That sentence means the same thing in all those different contexts: You know you're doing the wrong thing. You know you're a liar, you're cruel, despicable, godless, and lawless. You know you make people suffer, you make them cry, you hurt and damage and destroy. "This is a place of tears," Scarpia sings in your favorite opera. It's your aria—the traitor's aria. You know because you're moved by it.

So this is my question: Why do you deny it all, even when confronted with proof, witnesses, text messages? Why don't you apologize, if only for the sake of convention? Why aren't you *genuinely* sorry when you say you're "desperately sorry," and why do you so rarely say it, even though you provoke such despair? Why do you never express regret, remorse, the possibility of wrongdoing? Why do you never ask for leniency, for forgiveness?

You say nothing, you're just there with your arms hanging limply, suddenly looking like a dope—that must be a first. You could be mistaken for Watteau's *Gilles*. Did you know that Watteau died of poisoning from the white lead paint that he used on that Pierrot costume? Immaculateness is dangerous, too much feigned innocence is toxic. You can die from white as white as snow. Never mind that. You decided to be perfect. Beyond reproach. You painted yourself white, with no shadows in the picture. Why should you apologize? What wrongdoings do you need to admit? You are virginal.

It's very hard to understand from the outside. Denial of reality on that scale messes with a rational mind. Is this a case of dissociation? Of dual personality? By definition, you won't be able to explain the problem, because you don't acknowledge that there is one. You may claim otherwise, but you stopped seeing your therapist the minute she brought a mirror up to you and you didn't want to see yourself. The anguish could have destroyed you, I mean, didn't the damn woman know that? But literature comes to your rescue yet again. Oh, you owe so much to literature—you must write about that someday, Gilles, or perform it onstage. It allows you to stay on the brink of madness without sinking into it; it gave you the keys so you don't have to stay, like Artaud, permanently at the very door to life.

That first evening in Lille, you avoided my trick questions by talking about the workshop you were running at the university. You and your students were analyzing the different representations of Good and Evil in puppet theater—the goodies and baddies, to put it simply. The story of Dr. Jekyll and Mr. Hyde provided useful food for thought. Yes, because there were two solutions: Either they were both represented by a single puppet, a double-sided Janus that could be pivoted to show the kindly Dr. Jekyll one minute and Mr. Hyde with his thunderous eyebrows the next—this was technically easier with a glove puppet or rod puppet. Or two different puppets depicted the separate characters whose respective decent and malicious identities never merged—in which instance string puppets were more appropriate. Dr. Jekyll, dressed entirely in white, was universally liked and respected, while Mr. Hyde, his exact opposite in a different body, incarnated crime and horror. The paradigm of evil is to shift the blame onto someone else.

You didn't tell the students this, of course, you remained scrupulously pedagogical, but in your own case you chose the second option both in life and—bizarrely—in your relationships: Dr. Jekyll was you. Mr. Hyde, your partner. The formula also works with *The Picture of Dorian Gray*: You are Dorian, perennially young and handsome, while the other figure, the one in the painting, is blighted by your rages, your envious belligerence, and your lies, growing ever more repulsive—a moral dumping ground, a trash can for your soul.

Except, that's not how it works in life, Gilles. There's just one person in the real world. A single body for good and evil, the beautiful and the ugly, the strong and the weak. A single heart for love and hate, shame and dignity, tenderness and anger. A single being who may be imperfect but can still be loved, and was loved. In my dreams I would have been the *other* imperfect being whose union with you would have been something "sacred and sublime," as Musset puts it so well. I dreamed of love and indulgence. It's over now. I've woken up.

At the very last moment, when you were about to be unmasked, you succeeded in making me your Mr. Hyde: I'm the one who's been accused of wanting to kill you. In the eyes of the public and in court, you will be as white as the blank page of everything that's been forgotten, and I will be as black as your soul. The jealousy, violence, and manipulation will be hung from my shoulders like a garment tailor-made for you. You will gloat to see my gaunt, lusterless, old-looking body brought before the prosecution; and, ever the accomplished puppeteer, your final delight will be to affix your mother's head to that body.

Evil is busy at work in the very depths of infinity. I will lose this case, almost certainly. I'm expecting that. But you don't win, Gilles. You disappear into your nonlife, pacing up and down the stony wastelands where the only blooms are funeral wreaths and artificial flowers. Your past has eaten away your future: One day there's humiliation and that day goes on forever. The people there are just things, and you're an inflated balloon dressed up as a person, a betrayed child empty of joy in a house built with bricks of hatred, a well of despair, a void, a stifled terror, a miserable executioner endlessly reappointed to the job, and there's nothing you can do about it. It's not your fault, no: The world is teeming with innocent monsters.

She's there
She said it
she promised
she believed in it
And yet
everything exists

to result
in a book
She takes the flesh
that made her
heart melt
and turns it into
papier-
mâché
The hands
that held
the strings
of her desire
are now
sentences
And nothing
to do with caressing her
She's there
She wants to understand
wants to hold the meaning
She remembers
the chronology
And the words they said to each other
she's not deaf
As for the joy and heartache
that she felt
she's an old hand at that stuff
Humor
She wishes there had been some
Struck by a word
the horror of it all

The blind spot comes back again
watching cautiously
She has whittled away
her soul
But another person's soul
the opposite
unassuaged soul
the black night of their soul
she's just chasing the wind
She might as well hold the ocean
in a glass
Life is
ineffable
That's the sad thing
about beginning
a book
She's not fooled
as she is at the beginning
of love
She knows
she'll never manage that.

III

◆

"Mrs. Niepce, I must stop you there for a second time. For several long minutes you've been regaling us with a novel—you've taken inspiration from your client! Outlandish stories of theft dressed up as something else, a computer willfully disabled with criminal intent, endless bullying and verbal humiliation, and Machiavellian behavior intended, the court has surmised, to depict Mr. Fabian as a dangerous sociopath. And yet you provide no proof—not one instance of proof, I stress the point—of the material and psychological abuse you describe. The investigation has not produced any indications, however small, to support your theory, quite the opposite. The document you refer to has never been found either at the house or anywhere else. The investigators have fruitlessly contacted every establishment likely to have delivered it, and the only one that has folded, a company called Coubard, left no archives. You allege that hidden narcissistic sociopaths operate in the shadows like this, leaving no trace or witnesses—that's too easy, given that Mr. Fabian can't answer to your gratuitous conjecture because he has lost much of his memory, and we all know how. Lastly, need I remind you that it is your client who is on trial here today, Mrs. Niepce? Mr. Fabian is the victim."

"My learned friend, narcissistic sociopaths do exist, it's a recognized pathology, as Dr. Schnerb explained in detail earlier. The fact that they're not easy to expose and often pass themselves off as victims is, I'm afraid, part of the thorny problem highlighted by this case."

"Come now, Mrs. Niepce, this is ludicrous. Mr. Fabian spent several months in a coma! Isn't that enough for you to recognize his status as the victim?"

"Yes. But before that he himself had an invisible victim. There is also such a thing as psychological murder. My client simply defended herself in a momentary violent stupor."

"We will grant you the word *violent*, Mrs. Niepce. As to the motives that drove Mrs. Lancel to strike her former partner, the jury will retain only the material facts and not fashionable hypotheses or fantasy diagnoses. Mr. Fabian, and there's nothing unusual about this, wanted to start a new life with someone else and therefore to sell the shared house, inspiring lethal jealousy in Mrs. Lancel. Everything else is literature, if I may say so. I strongly advise you, Mrs. Niepce, that from now on you focus your defense speech on the question of premeditation. It will be more productive."

Gilles was sitting at the front, in a wheelchair, his head tilted slightly to one side, like the first time he came to my apartment—he had this way of beguiling with sadness, stripping himself of all violence, reduced to pure affability. The perfect victim, worthy of the utmost compassion.

We saw a procession of witnesses: colleagues, relations, and friends who came to say how lovable, kind, and obliging he was—with a short fuse, occasionally, hotheaded, you could say, but it was soon over. Ambitious, yes, even pushy, one of them had mentioned briefly, but he admired other people's success. Charming, of course, he liked to be found attractive, but not a womanizer. Respectful of women. A feminist even. His mother described what a wonderful son he'd always been. None of his previous partners had been called as witnesses, and with good reason, they would have done a disservice to the plaintiff, but not one of them had wanted to testify to my advantage either, despite my attorney's urging. Élisabeth, the ex-wife who'd been depressed since the divorce, had argued that, despite all her grievances, she didn't want to disadvantage the father of her children; Violetta blamed me in part for her difficult breakup with Gilles; as for Louise, she never wanted to hear about him again. The highlight of the plaintiff's case was a video recorded by Marina Nikitine in Dubai, where she now lived. On the wall behind her was a brightly colored poster advertising a cartoon. She spoke in English, her voice emotional. Someone who'd been sworn in simultaneously translated her words in a voice-over, and the tape was also subtitled in French.

"My name is Marina Nikitine, I'm thirty years old, I'm an American of Russian descent, my parents fled the communist regime in 1980. I met Gilles in the elevator in Toronto in 2018. I clearly remember that first time. From the lobby of the building, I'd seen him put a tall dark-haired woman into a taxi with some luggage—he told me later it was Claire Lancel. We rode up together and he asked me if I lived around there. He had this amazing smile and a to-die-for French accent, I liked him right away. But he was the same age as my dad and he was with someone. I was twenty-six at the time, with a one-year-old boy, Sacha—I've had a little girl since then. I was separated from Sacha's dad, it was hard. Gilles lived on the floor above, looking over the street, I looked out on the park. One time he came to ask me for some salt, another time I asked if he could translate a document from a French bank—I worked for HSBC. Basically, we hit it off. We had coffee together, we told each other our life stories.

"Right at the start he told me he wasn't happy in his relationship—he could at least pat himself on the back for never giving in to her longing to marry. She was a social butterfly, an ambitious social climber, they were totally mismatched intellectually—he told me, I remember this, that she showed absolutely no curiosity about anything except for herself, on vacation she never wanted to visit any sights, she wasn't interested in other people. She was a typical French writer, petty-minded and self-centered, a million miles from Canada's vast expanses and America's literary geniuses, Faulkner, Hemingway, Kerouac—well, anyway, that's not exactly my department. Oh yes, and another thing, she constantly humiliated him, she even prick-teased the workmen on the construction site opposite his apartment—some kind of nymphomaniac. He stayed with her because he didn't want to hurt her, and also because he was fond of her daughter, Alice, I think. I used to tell him about Sacha's father, it wasn't any prettier. Gilles was always happy to help me out—he would watch Sacha when my babysitter was sick, he took me to the movies, I introduced him to rap music, he loved it. He wanted to have the same tattoo as I have! Honestly, he was so easygoing, he was tender and gentle, but also very knowledgeable, what with the theater, the piano, UNESCO, all that stuff—Personally, apart from numbers, I just don't know anything. And he didn't overstay his welcome like a lot of older guys.

"And then one day, not long after one of his trips to France, it must have been in November 2018, we bumped into each other in the elevator, he asked if he could come to my place, he looked very shook up. He said he'd split up with Claire, he couldn't take any more, she not only made everything about her, she was also making it impossible for him to be himself. She was threatening his career, she wanted to destroy him. And then he took my hand and said he needed something more real between us, and that was that. I fell head over heels for him. We practically lived together, sometimes at my place, sometimes at his—he gave me a key straightaway. He gave me so many presents, he pampered me, life was easy again and all because of him. And plus Sacha adored him. Such a great guy! A classic French lover, in other words! We even got engaged on Valentine's Day, he gave me the most gorgeous ring! Every now and then he would tell me that Claire was harassing him, she wouldn't accept the breakup. Sometimes he even seemed to miss her, but I could tell he was doing that to scare me. He told me that she was a great writer and I was uncultivated, I wouldn't understand. Like I would be jealous of some broad the same age as my mom! We did so much together, vacations, bungee jumping, crazy stuff. We went for a vacation at his place in the South of France. A really cool house. When we came home to Toronto he told me that he wanted to have a baby with me, and I could leave Sacha with his dad if I wanted. Well, I wanted both, so I thought it was better to wait. That was a good decision, looking back, I'd have ended up on my own with two kids! We also had plans for an apartment, where we would really live together, I'd looked into selling mine. In the end, he went off to France in November to direct a show, I was meant to join him so we could spend New Year's together, and that was it: He never came back. He doesn't even remember me, it's the saddest thing. I called I don't know how many times, I remember being totally out of my mind because he didn't reply, and eventually the police picked up. I didn't go see him, he was in a coma, anyway, and so far away, it wasn't workable. But one day I just wanted to let myself into his place with my key to check that everything was okay in his apartment, and this stranger greeted me at the door: the owner, he said, Mark. I didn't know Gilles was renting the place, he didn't tell me that.

"So that's it, it was my most wonderful relationship. Well, I shouldn't say that now that I'm married and have a little girl. But Gilles, if you can hear me, I still think you're fab. You're the best, sweetheart!"

Standing in the dock, I took the hit—it wasn't a huge surprise, but it still really hurt despite the dose of tranquilizers I'd taken. All through the video, I'd surreptitiously watched Gilles's reactions, the look in his eyes, his shudders and grimaces. He remembered everything, I was sure of it. The doctor had told the bench that he could reach no conclusions, and post-traumatic amnesia was technically possible after such a shock. But I personally could confirm Gilles was about as amnesiac as I was the pope. Putting on an act was in his DNA. His only aim was to keep up his performance as the perfect guy thanks to his Etch-A-Sketch mind. Amnesia erased everything in one go: his lies, his mistakes, his relationships, his shame. Let's make a clean break with the past. Total liquidation, all previous stock dispensed with. The most important thing is not feeling any pain. And I was constantly brought back to these convulsive questions: What did he think in his shadowy depths? Did Dr. Jekyll really not have a single flaw? These questions drove me crazy, more so than fears for my fate.

There was another question, one that no one would ask.

Was what we'd experienced love? What could I still cherish from my memories—what had been real?

The psychiatric expert called by Mrs. Niepce had answered these questions in his own way. He'd set out sociopathic mechanisms for the court, walking everyone through our relationship as if it were a how-to manual. "The process is always the same," he'd explained, and everything that makes love unique had evaporated with those words. Three stages: 1) love-bombing, seduction, and idealization; 2) denigration and belittling; 3) destroying. Seduction, reduction, destruction. The personalities of these deviant subjects are shaped by human failings. Emotional anesthesia, fear of all interpersonal relationships, horror of the intimacy that they pretend to establish, loathing of individuality, total absence of empathetic identification with other people, ignorance of other people's suffering and needs, relentless destruction of relationships, no moral scruples whatsoever. Abuse often suffered in childhood makes them abusers for whom other people are interchangeable objects that they debilitate and despise once they've evaluated their weaknesses. There's no true meeting of minds, just a toxic connection based on control, domination, manipulation, instrumentalization, a hatred of love, and a love of hatred.

So yes, the expert had concluded, the behavior described by my attorney presented aspects of the sociopathic dynamic and could drive a woman under its influence to homicide, even if suicide was exponentially more common, he'd added with a hint of reproach aimed at me. The public prosecutor had stepped in to state ironically that the three stages described seemed to apply more to me than to Gilles Fabian.

Charlotte Rossi, the Realtor, was sitting in the front row next to a little man with a mustache and in police uniform—her husband. Over the successive witness statements, she seemed to slump more and more on the bench. She'd watched Marina's video attentively without managing to hide her pained astonishment. An unknown aspect of Gilles's life had just struck a body blow to the story she'd concocted in her mind. When she herself was questioned shortly afterward, she was "no longer so sure" whether Mrs. Lancel had been there when she'd said that she and Mr. Fabian would go back to the house to take some more measurements. "Please be precise, Mrs. Rossi," the public prosecutor had reprimanded her, "the suspicion of premeditation rests on your testimony alone. It is therefore of vital importance." She didn't dare look at me. No, come to think of it, she may have said it afterward, in the car but once Mrs. Lancel had been dropped at the bus stop. "In any event," Mrs. Niepce had rejoindered, "when you plan to kill someone, you don't do it in the presence of a third party using an improvised weapon. Everything speaks in favor of an impulsive act, it's utterly self-evident." Luckily for Charlotte Rossi, of the two strips of medication found in the secret drawer, although one was indeed Viagra under a generic name, the other was an everyday analgesic, which reassured her police officer husband who was still perplexed by the chronology of events: Gilles Fabian taking Viagra and then returning to the house with Charlotte—that was odd. But now, no: The two things were completely unrelated. As for the missing document, the Realtor could add nothing to what she'd said from the start: There was no piece of paper. I wanted to jump out of the dock and scream at her, "Did you throw it down the toilet?" But what was the point? She too was a victim, in her own way. I had another plan.

Gilles had also been questioned but he'd said very little. He had no memory of the assault or of what had happened in the days leading up to it, he couldn't be of any help. When asked about his health, he'd said that he was still very weak—he'd gestured at his wheelchair—but he'd courageously returned to his creative work. His anterior memory was returning in snatches; he remembered Claire, for example, he recognized her when he saw her and even had a few flashes of happy times with her. He'd directed an insufferable smile toward me. Then, because he needed medical attention, he'd asked—via his attorney—for damages and interest totaling a sum, according to their estimation, that tallies peculiarly neatly with what he owed me to buy me out of the house.

Article in *Midi Libre*, Thursday, October 13, 2022

There was a dramatic turn of events at the law courts in Draguignan this afternoon, where novelist Claire Lancel has been on trial for the premeditated attempted murder of her former partner, Gilles Fabian, a theater performer. Fabian is no longer in a coma but still suffers memory loss three years after the event. Following turbulent exchanges in which the public prosecutor repeatedly criticized the defense for trying to influence the jury with unfounded allegations, the presiding judge allowed the defendant to be the last to speak, as is customary. "Do you have anything to add?" he asked. Claire Lancel, wearing a white dress and as pale as a ghost herself, stood and said, "Yes, Your Honor." Without looking at her attorney Mrs. Niepce, who seemed unprepared for this, she turned toward Gilles Fabian in his wheelchair and made the following declaration (verbatim):

Gilles, I'm so sorry to have weakened and debilitated you in this way and I sincerely ask your forgiveness for the harm I've done you. Because of me you've lost your memory, or at least the doctors can only give credence to the confusion you describe. Amnesia must be an appalling feeling. Not knowing what you've done, how you've felt, not being able to accept responsibility for your own existence—it must be terrible. You do recognize me, though, you said so, and I'm glad of that. So I'd like to describe for you forty-eight hours of your past life. This account probably won't help you, but it will help me.

On February 24, 2017, you came with me to the César Awards ceremony at the Salle Pleyel in Paris. I'd been invited by the producers of a film in competition, *Farewell*, adapted from one of my novels and starring Isabelle Huppert. You'd bought a tuxedo for the occasion, and I'd rented an evening gown. As we skirted around the photo-call on our way into the auditorium, the director spotted me and called me over, he wanted a photo of the whole team. I shook my head but he insisted. So I handed you my shawl and purse. "I'm sorry," I said, smiling, "I'll only be a minute." You didn't wait for me; when I came back you'd already taken your seat in the auditorium, your face expressionless and my things on the seat next to you. "I'm sorry," I said again. "That's when I realized the size of her ego," you later admitted to Georges—who was your friend at the time, if you remember. "How did that make me look, left on the sidelines with her little purse? She deliberately humiliated me in front of everybody who's anybody in Paris. Isabelle Huppert's sarcastic glance—don't make me go there. But I could also tell she was hot for me, it was obvious."

We'd been planning to go to the house in Hyères together the next day, but I'd had some interview requests after the film had won a César Award, so you went alone and I joined you two days later.

You arrived in Hyères at the end of a terrible storm. The lighting and wind had been very destructive. There were fallen trees, missing roof tiles, collapsed verandas, and ruined gardens. In our garden, though, there didn't seem to be too much damage, a few upturned containers, a couple of branches hanging from the mimosa tree, which was in bloom. Nevertheless, you called a company named Coubard who'd helped us previously with the hedge. Coubard Junior examined the mimosa and immediately reassured you, clearly relieved himself: The tree was unharmed. Even so, you asked him to cut it down. He didn't understand. You told him he wasn't paid to understand. He stammered that he couldn't do it, cut down a healthy tree, such a beautiful tree. "You don't need the money, then?" you asked. He called his father, came back to talk to you again. He agreed, he would do it, but he wanted you to sign a disclaimer. He came back that afternoon with a typed letter and a carbon copy; you signed, he kept one copy and gave you the other. You put it into the secret drawer in the desk your mother gave you. You made him promise not to discuss the matter with anyone, and he cut down the tree while you strolled around the neighborhood lamenting the irreversible damage caused by the storm. The next day, you held me by the waist when I broke down in tears at the sight of that raw stump.

At this point, Claire Lancel looked at the presiding judge and the members of the jury, slowly, one by one, then she turned her attention back to the plaintiff and said:

That was a crime, Gilles, yes, a crime, an act of hatred, and nothing, not forgetfulness or denial, not amnesia or lying or everyone else's incredulity can alter the fact that you committed it. It's the truth, it's real. And I need things to be real—do you remember that?

After two hours of deliberations, the jury found Claire Lancel not guilty of premeditation. For involuntary battery, she was sentenced to two years in prison with eighteen months suspended as credit for pretrial detention. She therefore walked free from the Draguignan law courts. The plaintiff was awarded damages and interest for the physical and psychological harm he has suffered, and the sum will be determined at a later date.

I'd asked to slip out through a hidden door, leaving Mrs. Niepce to take the credit for the verdict in front of the journalists' mics. I felt... free. I joined Rob in a bistro a couple of streets over, he'd ordered champagne. He introduced me to Miles McLawrence who congratulated me enthusiastically, what a fantastic outcome! He wanted to make a film about the story, he wasn't sure yet what angle he would take: either about me or about the investigation and the trial. I told him with a laugh, although I meant it very seriously, that if he put the trial in his film, I wanted a Hollywood ending after the suspense of a thriller. First of all, he, Gilles, or his character to be more precise, would have to die, it would be more clear-cut. "He doesn't serve any purpose, anyway, amnesia won't breathe anything new into him, not even explanations. He's not answerable for anything. Irresponsible. But that's what she's missing, and she'll never get it: an expression of regret. So she strikes him and he dies. Exit. With him dead, she risks a heftier sentence and has no proof in her defense, she can't even talk to him anymore. The audience is convinced that the jury's going to slaughter her. And just before they withdraw to deliberate, there's the sound of a door being thrown open, a hubbub in the public gallery, people turn around, there's whispering: A young man walks along the aisle up to the bench and asks to speak. Okay, I don't think this would be possible in real life—or maybe in the States? There are sometimes scenes like this in movies, the eleventh-hour witness. Anyway, he's allowed to speak. And he tells the story—it's Coubard Junior, you guessed—he tells the story of his mimosa tree. Saying that even when he was a little kid he would make a detour on his way home from school in winter to see it; sometimes he'd pilfered sprigs from it for his mother, and later his girlfriends; he often took photos of it, and even has one in his living room at home; he didn't want to cut it down, no, he really didn't: He knows it was wrong. And he weeps.

"Do you see, Miles, that way everyone realizes this isn't just a private issue, it's a question of morality, of ontology even: Everyone must protect beauty, peace, their own joy and other people's joy, and love. Our very humanity is at stake."

And then I stop. What the hell—I'm basically giving Miles McLawrence a lesson in filmmaking! But Miles agrees, he smiles—and what a smile!

Epilogue

♦

It felt strange being back there, in that huge glass-and-metal construction where, years earlier, I'd laid eyes on Julien for the last time. We'd come out of the room in which we'd just torn each other to shreds over Alice under the seasoned eyes of the magistrate and her court clerk, "I refuse to pay child support that will just finance her mother's facelifts—and bad ones at that," Julien had told them. I was so wounded that I deliberately headed away from the elevators, with my face down, wanting never to see him again, and definitely not to look him in the eye, putting a good distance between myself and twenty years of marriage torpedoed by spinelessness and lies. And yet still ringing in my ears now was something that had never faded, the distress in his voice, his pleading hesitation, his hoarse anguish as he'd whispered after me in the maze of the law courts, "Wait, where are you going?," then he'd shouted as I almost started to run, "Hey, come back! Where are you going? Just come back! We'll lose each other!" I'd reached the end of a walkway that didn't lead anywhere and, rather than turning back to him, the husband, lover, and father, I'd locked myself in the restroom. There was silence for a minute or two, and into that pause came one of those moments of raw truth that we'd so sorely lacked in the past. With a barely audible sob he said it again, "We're going to lose each other." Then the film camera that followed him everywhere came back, I heard it, it had tracked all the way along the corridor to save him from collapse—the absurdity of the situation had probably occurred to him as he stood there by himself outside the ladies' restroom, and then, turning his face to the great judge who constantly promoted him in the Actors Studio of his life, he said solemnly and with emphatic finality, "That's it, then. Farewell." "Farewell, Julien," I said through the door.

So there I was again, I could hardly believe it. It wasn't all that surprising, though: Gilles was just the same, he too couldn't stop pointing his finger at the perennial guilty woman and demanding reparations from her. The very day my novel came out, my editor and I both received an emergency injunction requesting to ban the book and withdraw it from bookshops, on the grounds that it violated his privacy.

The brand-new building had already aged a lot and when you stood in the entrance hall and looked up through the floors and their walkways, you were reminded of the people who'd thrown themselves over the railings—a disastrous divorce, a residence permit refused, a bankruptcy. The architect hadn't thought of the law courts as a place of injustice. The summons named the site of the meeting as the office of Judge Ménard in the seventeenth magistrate's court of the Paris courthouse, the one that specializes in matters concerning the press and publishing. "Ménard? That's bad luck," said Carole. "He's an A-grade sexist, I even wonder if he's been transferred here because he was making too many waves in family affairs—a total masculinist who always understands his own kind." Fine.

Inside the courtroom, I spotted my attorney in conversation with my agent. Rob came over to meet me, he must have been keeping an eye out for me. I could see he was keen to put me at ease. "I was thinking, Claire, once this little thing is settled, you should go back to your novel about the Narks. That dystopia of yours is already a reality." This was June 12, 2024, three days after Emmanuel Macron had dissolved the French parliament. "In fact," Rob continued as if what he was saying was obvious, "it's the same pitch as the book that brought us here, but on a national level: an immature, narcissistic man, who's having a crisis aggravated by his massive denial about his own failings as a leader, uses the whole country as an emotional punching bag and, on an insane impulse, manages to destroy everything he's pretended to love. Malfunctioning egos, it's the new zeitgeisty issue—no, seriously, it's *the* hot topic."

Carole was there, my loyal friend, to the left of the dais, in a bright yellow sweater. As I went over to join her, I noticed Gilles in the opposite corner.

"Boy, has he aged," Carole said, guessing that—like her—I thought he looked handsome. He'd chosen a midnight blue shirt and a subtly aggrieved expression. On the lapel of his jacket was a showy drop of blood—the Legion of Honor. "He was slender and so fine...that legionnaire of mine...showing the tattoo on his neck he said, 'no trace, no case,' showing the one on his heart, 'nobody here.'" I could sing now. Inside my chest the tolling bell beat out the end of love too loudly—indifference is so slow to come—but seeing his hands no longer had an effect on me. His hairline had receded. The marine depths of his eyes were no longer somewhere to bask. Someday soon, and it will pain me in spite of everything, they'll just be as green as leeks.

The hearing began. The judge informed us of the complaint and Gilles's attorney stood up. In a moment he would justify the requested ban on this toxic (*toxic*) book, but first he wanted to make a statement: Above and beyond the materiality of the facts, what most affected his client was the writer's lack of honor. She had made him a promise and had not kept it. She had betrayed him. Now, Gilles Fabian saw ethics and a respect for other people as crucial virtues, establishing a stark contrast with his former partner—and this, incidentally, had already been brought to light by a previous trial. Gilles was sitting bolt upright in his chair. Pressured by my staring, his automaton face turned toward me, I could see the word *partner* sinking like a stone in the cold waters of his eyes. His attorney was now back to the criminal book and its points of reference that were numerous and clearly abusive, as he intended to demonstrate before my attorney pulled them apart one by one, not without offering sarcastic congratulations to the plaintiff for regaining sufficient memory to distinguish between truth and fabrication, and to be in such good health when, in the book, he was dead.

My attorney was appealing to anyone quick to laugh, getting them on his side. I personally would have preferred a different defense strategy, but he didn't want that, arguing that we needed to avoid anything that likened my book to an autobiography. He was bound to be right. And yet . . . what I wanted to say was that it wasn't a novel about Gilles. It was a novel about me, about the tragic reiteration of failure in my life. I failed and I failed again—did I get any better at failing? The jury's out. My father, my husband, Gilles, not to mention the ones that didn't matter (Arnaud, too, laid to rest somewhere between the pages of a book). Every time, the illusion of love had been painfully ripped apart and had left me there, witless, wondering what had happened, what I'd done wrong; and why, despite all my efforts, it hadn't worked. I'd been a disappointing daughter, an unsatisfactory lover, an inadequate wife, and even a deficient mother to a dead son. I'd never succeeded in giving them everything they wanted or simply satisfying them with my loving presence. I hadn't made them happy. At least that was the image of me that they reflected back to me, the feeling I was left with at the end. Or perhaps I'd chosen, singled out, and loved only men who couldn't be happy, never in their lives, as if it were my job to confirm for them over and over again that love was powerless, flawed, absent, or impossible? So many hopes and so many books to arrive at this pitiful constant: Whatever they say, whatever they do, people always pick the same type and it all starts again, their heartache takes another ride on the merry-go-round, and as they sail around reaching out a pole to unhook a prize, they always bag the same one, feeling triumphant when all they've done is secure more misery. The subconscious as the only dating site. OurTime is over. When they can, they turn it into a book, but they don't want to, that's what I want to tell you, Gilles: I didn't want to write this book. I wanted to keep my promise and fill your joy with mine.

I'd thought of using a Philip Roth quote as an epigraph for the book and even considered calling it *The Story of Life* because that sounded like some universal law with personal experience blended into it: "The fact remains that getting people right is not what living is all about anyway. It's getting them wrong that is living, getting them wrong and wrong and wrong and then, on careful reconsideration, getting them wrong again." I gave up on the idea in the end: The epigraph would give away too much of the flavor. And I wanted readers to get it wrong along with me, to get it just as wrong as I did, in all its breadth, in the early days. They don't know they're being told stories. They believe, they're like me. The famous definition of what a novel requires—consenting suspension of disbelief—also applies to love. In order to read a book and in order to love someone, you need to be fooled.

So I'd called my book *Tosca's Kiss*. In the opera, Tosca, hounded by the police chief Scarpia, promises to give herself to him if he spares the life of the man she loves, a painter who's due to be executed. Scarpia gives his word, while secretly sending orders for the execution to go ahead. When he takes her in his arms to claim his right, she stabs him, crying, "That is Tosca's kiss." In other words, neither of them keeps their promise. But then are their betrayals the same? Isn't Tosca's perjury more valid than her tormentor's?

Perjury, personal revenge, these were exactly what Gilles's attorney was in the process of condemning with furious vigor. "A despicable settling of scores," he hollered as if there were a thousand people in the room. I was tired of this unoriginal refrain, this small-minded and hackneyed metaphor. But come to think of it, yes, a settling of scores, why not? If writers aren't here to point out what it costs to be alive, then what is their fight? Debts, thefts, write-offs, unearned profits, scams, bankruptcies. If art doesn't keep the accounts and false accounts, then who will? When words don't show us the slate, when novels don't make people pay up, then a writer is just another fraudster.

Our attorneys reeled off their arguments, but the content was lost in a muted hubbub. I couldn't help looking at Gilles—this would most likely be the last time, as with Julien in this same place in the past. Perhaps he was right, after all: Perhaps we should just hold on to the best of life, the memories, filed back there, the wonderful memories. I took off my glasses—did I still want him to find me attractive? From that distance, with the help of my shortsightedness, with all the shadows erased by the room's harsh fluorescent lighting, Gilles now looked like a photo of himself at age seven, on the beach in Marseille with his mother, one of the only pictures of him as a child with her, their last vacation together. I'd seen it at her home, hanging in the hallway, then I'd stolen it from her album. Why? I don't know. Perhaps because in that photo he was the age at which his mother left him to go off with another man. I also had photos of my father at the same age, but none of him with his mother—she'd been cut out of all of them with scissors. Gilles has one knee bent and his other leg touching his mother's leg. He's sifting sand through his hand. He's a little boy with a gentle, sensitive, slightly timid expression, and the recognizable red birthmark shaped like a mouth—a kiss? a bite?—and that smile with the dazzling teeth; anyone would want a child like him, a child with him. I also have photos of his grandparents, hard-line communists whom I never met; they don't look very accommodating, but I like them. I retrieved them from the wastepaper basket by the desk, where Gilles had thrown them. I even have a photo of Violetta, he said bad things about her, but she looks kind, on paper. When I love a man, I'm moved by his whole life. I store his memories in my mind, alongside my own. That's how we secretly stay together in a place before everything that love is.

"This novel is the story of life," my attorney was declaiming portentously, "not the story of a particular man or woman." He was following our line of defense to the letter. And yet it *is* us, I thought to myself for the pleasure of inhabiting that decommissioned pronoun one last time. We were the same, you and I, two children who'd always been afraid of abandonment and had been forced to compromise in order to stay alive with this terror of death. We'd created roles for ourselves and had performed them to perfection. When we come across charming people, do we kick them out of the door to life? Starting from this shared threshold, our paths had diverged. We played our roles with other people, you to master them, me to be loved by them; you to make their unhappiness the condition for your vital energy, me to make their happiness the condition for mine. Your hate spread to all women, my hope to all men. We both failed. Our paths crossed again, briefly, around a tree trunk. On the bark you carved the words "Nobody Here" inside a heart. Mine bore our initials. Both were shot through with an arrow. It was over now. The fiction was still writing itself, but you were pretending in real life while I was pretending in a book. And that was a major difference.

Sometimes, though, it happened, the exhausting demands released us: in your case the need to give nothing in order to keep the pain at bay, in mine the need to give what I hoped in vain to receive in return. And so we abandoned each other, naked as newborns, weary, happy, helpless, it happened, I mean it really happened, not in the pantomime invented by our childhood terrors, it did happen, didn't it? In the delicious luxury of idleness, when doing nothing isn't nothing, and living isn't vacuous. And then we knew that—by uniting our vibrant strengths, admitting our weaknesses in a mood of trust and faith, ensuring we shrugged off the shame of having betrayed and disappointed—we knew that we would lose our fear of suffering and dying and being alone; and the anguish became less burdensome with the words that expressed it. So everything is full of promise, but it's a waste of time believing in promises? It doesn't matter. We believed in each other. Promises are never held. So what? We held each other in our arms.

"She left when I was seven." Your voice rises into the silence in the bedroom. It's nighttime. We've made love fervently, such oblivion, and you've nestled into the crook of my shoulder and taken my hand to settle it on your head. You smell of vetiver. "I have no memories of her from before. I mean no happy memories, or any idea whether she was gentle or tender or kind or brutal. Nothing. My first memories are of disappointment. I was terrible at schoolwork, always last in my class. I remember my teacher asked to see my parents at the end of the year and told them I didn't understand anything, I could hardly read despite all her work, and I was never really there. Sweet boy, sure, smiley, a nice smile, but not bright, a little backward even. A long way back, retarded, basically. I didn't understand what they wanted from me. I was in my bubble. But I could see their shame when they stood up without asking any questions, keeping their heads down, apologizing to the teacher for the inconvenience I was to her.

"My mother must have thought I took after my father, a dockworker who wasn't badly paid but was no more than a manual laborer in her eyes—she could do better. She ran a beauty salon that he'd bought for her but that she'd built up. After four years she already had three employees and was earning more than him. She's always had a head for business, and that commercially motivated phony friendliness—well, you know her."

She must have met her lover at the salon. "He was just the type to have tanning sessions or a chest wax. A pretty boy. I despised him." Your parents were always arguing, your mother broke crockery, at night you'd sometimes hear her yelling, "You're not a man!" She'd started cheating on your father and had made you her accomplice. "She slept with her lover on Sundays and the evenings when my father was on the night shift, she made me watch for him at my window. From my bedroom I could see the parking lot where my father parked his Renault 4. She'd sworn me to secrecy. Back then I used to play with my finger puppets a lot, different characters made of fabric given to me by one of my aunts, Lucie's mother. I also had a Pinocchio made by my uncle who was a carpenter. I didn't have brothers and sisters, I was bored—I hated reading, that came later—so I got all those little guys talking, I made up stories with goodies and baddies, my father was a goody, my mother a baddy. When both of my parents came home late, I got a little scared all on my own in the dark apartment, but my puppets kept me company. One evening, Dad came home earlier, exhausted, his face sagging with sadness, and I said I would put on a show I'd invented just for him. He said, 'Okay, little guy,' and sat down on the sofa. I told him the whole story with my fingers, putting on different voices, the cuckold and his son had Marseille accents, the wife and her lover spoke in shrill voices like lying show-offs. I'd put the little-boy puppet on my thumb, he was in midnight blue felt, I remember, with green eyes and hair made of yellow wool, I wanted him to be separate from the other fingers, not mixed up in their scheming. 'Oh! My love, you have to leave,' the index finger said in a high-pitched voice, 'my husband will be home soon. And you,' she added, turning threateningly to the thumb, 'zip it.'"

I take your hand and kiss your fingers one by one. "My love," you whisper. "Keep going," I say.

"A few days later when I was staying the night at my aunt's house, my father came home unexpectedly and found them in the bedroom. Well, he can't have gone into the room, he heard them through the door, that was enough. They divorced. He'd have done better to have killed her, it would have settled the matter. It was my mother who paid the mortgage for the apartment, so my father moved out. He and I ended up in a one-bedroom apartment that he left empty—except for our two beds—for too long. Later he rented a piano for me." "You didn't stay with your mother?" "Pfft... Do you really think she wanted to be saddled with me? A dunce tied to her apron strings? Her new guy was a gynecologist, he wrote successful books about women's liberation, ha ha, your mother probably read them too... she was being offered a new life, money, the world. I didn't matter, I was just something from her past, a loser, like my dad." "You don't know for sure, Gilles. Mothers tried to be free back then. It was often men who stopped them. It doesn't mean she didn't love you. You never know, it could be like my grandmother: She fought for you but lost you. In those days, adulterous women..." "That's what she says. Yeah right...When my parents separated, I would spend weekends with her at our old apartment. The first time, I let myself in as usual, with my key, it was my home, after all. Well, the next Saturday I couldn't open the door. She'd changed the lock." "Oh, that's horrible! You must have been so sad! But you should try to...maybe not forgive her, at least to understand her. It would help you. And she's so happy to see you these days." "That's because I've succeeded in life. She can't get over seeing my name on posters. The dunce turned into somebody, and he still has further to go. Sure, now she's happy to be my mother. And my son this, and my son that. It's all an act, fake. She doesn't feel anything, nothing at all. She's cold. An ice puppet." I stroke your arm and say, "Feelings are always more ambiguous than that. I—" "Ambiguous? No. It's such a pain, Claire, the way you always want to airbrush everything. I've seen them, I've seen the papers. There's no ambiguity, I can tell you." "What papers?" "The divorce papers." I look at you questioningly. "There were two lines. 'By mutual agreement and consent, Mrs. Fabian will keep her business. Mr. Fabian will keep the child.'" "Gilles, darling..." "In those papers I was referred to like an item up for negotiation. I wished I couldn't read." "Gilles..." "My mother sold me. My father bought me. End of story. So when I saw him crying like a baby...my whole childhood boils down to my dad listening to Alain Barrière's dumb song 'You're Leaving.'" You sing quietly in a whiny voice, "*You're leaving me, I'm scared of winter so icy, I'm scared it's so empty, the absence of joy, I'm left here alone and lost, like my darkest days as a boy, I'm scared of you, I'm scared of me, I'm scared the silence will come to be.* I know it by heart from hearing it so often. And then two voices bleating *Don't leave me*. He cried, he drank like a fish, he used prostitutes in the Old Port and told me about it. Even after he remarried, he was still in pain because of that bitch. And I told myself, never that, never. I don't want any pain. I want to be happy." "It's impossible to go through a whole life without pain, you know."

You pull away from me and lie facing me. In the half-light your eyes gleam with a fury I can't grasp as you peer at me. You cling to your hate as though realizing that if you surrendered it, you would have to confront your pain. I take your hand and put it on my breast—somebody here. You relax, you come back and press yourself to me, your mouth to mine, your stomach to mine, our feet intertwined. "Well, I manage it very well." "Are you happy?" "Yes, I'm happy. I'm happy with you." "Well, *we're* happy then." You leave a moment's pause. I close my eyes.

"Yes, and the important thing is what we have is real."

We made love again, you really wanted to, even though I was tired—*you* were a man.

Our attorneys, the poor things, were still arguing about the nature of truth and the quality of fiction; they were weighing stories of a felled tree and physical resemblances—did Gilles look like George Clooney? Really? I put my glasses back on. Gilles hadn't moved a muscle, life seemed to have withdrawn from his face, leaving behind shadows, amnesia truly was consuming his face—had it really thrown everything into a black hole of memory lapse along with the first seven years of his life, his fears, his longings, his cruelty and failings? I looked at Carole and, sitting there in her yellow sweater, she smiled at me. One day, at the beginning I think, I told Gilles about my happiest childhood memory. My recollections of where we were are hazy but we were lying down on that occasion too, yes, we must have been—these stories always come after lovemaking.

"We never went on vacations with our parents—my sister and I—they left us with our grandparents, in summer and winter. Except for one time, and I don't know why, just one time the four of us went to Le Lavandou together, I've never forgotten that name, it's such a soft sound. One day we took the car and drove along the coast road for a while. My parents weren't saying anything, they were both smoking, each with one arm leaning on the car door. The weather was glorious, as it sometimes is in the South of France in February. Then the sea disappeared and we were on a smaller road. My father told me to lie down because I used to get carsick. After a few minutes we stopped and my father cut the engine. I sat back up and then, I can't describe it, it brings tears to my eyes every time I think about it: Dazzling! A field of mimosas, dozens and dozens of mimosas swaying gently in the breeze. All that yellow like a great splash of joy. My parents, my sister. It tore my heart in two. The sun had a fragrance. Happiness had a color. The preacher's Garden of Eden was right there.

"I ran from tree to tree and gathered a bunch of the flowers. My hands were dusted with light powder, the fluffy little pompoms were unlike any other flower, and they smelled totally unique too. Birds flitted across the sky of yellow and blue. Everything was different, magical. I couldn't believe my eyes. I was intoxicated.

"My mother and sister were walking along the path and my father was already heading back to the car. I went and joined him. He told me to put my bunch of flowers in the trunk, it would make a mess of the seats. He smoked as he studied the scene. 'It's beautiful, Daddy,' I said. He nodded but didn't reply. 'It's so beautiful.' Then I fell silent, I'd run out of words. When it was time to get back into the car, I blew a kiss to the light. 'We'll come back here, right, Daddy?' He mumbled something. 'Promise?' 'Of course we'll come back,' he said, glancing at my mother. I climbed into the back seat; he was already at the wheel and I put my arms around his neck. 'Is that a promise?' I asked again in his ear. He looked at me in the rearview mirror. 'Will you be a good girl?' he asked. 'You'll never upset your daddy?' 'Never!' I squealed. 'Never?' 'Never. I promise, I swear,' I said, patting his hair, which was starting to leave a clearing at the back of his head. He put the key in the ignition. 'So will we come back, Daddy? Do you promise?' 'Yes,' he said, 'I promise we will.'"

CREDITS AND ACKNOWLEDGMENTS

◆

The two Antonin Artaud texts cited on pages 270–272 are extracts, the first from a letter to Jacques Rivière (June 6, 1924) and the second from the live event at the Théâtre du Vieux Colombier (January 13, 1947).

Besides explicit references, this book contains quotes—some of them modified—from Adorno, Arendt, Baldwin, Baudelaire, Beckett, Brel, Constant, Duras, Lacan, La Rochefoucauld, Louise-Marie de France, Morand, Nietzsche, Rousseau, and Shakespeare.

I would like to thank my loved ones whose affection was with me as I wrote this novel; and particularly Stéphanie, who knows why.

ABOUT THE AUTHOR

Camille Laurens is an award-winning French novelist and essayist. She received the Prix Femina, one of France's most prestigious literary prizes, in 2000 for *Dans ces bras-là*, which was published in the United States as *In His Arms* in 2004. Her previous books include *Who You Think I Am* (Other Press, 2017), *Little Dancer Aged Fourteen* (Other Press, 2018), and *Girl* (Other Press, 2022). She lives in Paris.

ABOUT THE TRANSLATOR

Adriana Hunter studied French and Drama at the University of London. She has translated more than ninety books, including Marc Petitjean's *The Heart: Frida Kahlo in Paris* and Hervé Le Tellier's *The Anomaly* and *Eléctrico W*, winner of the French-American Foundation's 2013 Translation Prize in Fiction. She lives in Kent, England.